1.

Hope for Tomorrow

Judah Knight

 GreenTree Publishers

Hope for Tomorrow

Printed in the United States of America
ISBN-13: 978-1-944483-06-7
ISBN-10: 1-944483-06-3

Greentree Publishers
www.greentreepublishers.com

Dedication and
Special Thanks...

This book is dedicated to my wonderful children. Who could have known that being a parent would be so much fun? You have brought such joy to your parent's lives.

My books are always a product of a vast team of readers, proof readers, editors, and friends. It would take more than a page to list the names of everyone who contributed to this book. Thanks to all of you who made this one possible. I'm especially grateful to my copy editor, Edwina.

CONTENTS

A SPECIAL NOTE

Thank you for choosing the second book in *The Davenport Series*. If it's been a while since you read the first book, you may enjoy refreshing your memory by reading the final chapter of book one before beginning *Hope For Tomorrow*. You can find the last chapter of book one at the conclusion of this book beginning with page 303. We would also like to offer you a **free gift**. Turn to page 297 to learn how you can receive Judah Knight's novella, *A Girl Can Always Hope*, for free. We hope you enjoy Judah Knight's *Hope for Tomorrow*.

CHAPTER ONE

Sorting It Out

"This ranch is beautiful, and he is gorgeous," Ann said out of the corner of her mouth.

"Shut up," Meg answered quietly as she closed her car door. "Though you don't have a brain, he does have ears."

The trip to Jon's ranch had been uneventful, but Ann grilled Meg the whole way with more questions about her new beau.

"He's not my beau," Meg insisted several times on the ride out.

"Right," was all Ann could manage.

Meg had done her best to describe the beautiful scene that Ann would see at Jon's sprawling estate, but the proper words escaped her. She had never seen a more picturesque home in her life. The substantial, wood-plank home was encircled with a wide front porch set off by Tennessee field stone that went half-way up the over-sized columns. Small mountains surround the rolling pastures. The entire estate would be a fabulous cover photo for Southern Living. It was magnificent.

Meg dreaded telling Jon that she somehow managed to lose the car key to his Mercedes-Benz sports car when she accidentally dropped it from Ann's fourth floor balcony. When she borrowed his car the previous day, she knew it was a bad idea at the time. She just could not bring herself to say "no." She had been afraid that driving his car was insinuating that something romantic was going between the two of them. She lost his car key, and there was nothing she could do about it. There was no way to avoid facing the music. It would cost a lot for her to replace the key, but she was determined to do it. Maybe coming to Jon's ranch to help count the gold he found under the floorboard of his yacht was a bad idea too.

Meg raised her voice so Jon could hear her from the front porch. "Jon, this is my friend Ann. Ann, meet Jon Davenport."

"Hey, Jon," Ann said as she approached the porch. "It's great to meet you."

"Hello, Ann," Jon replied as Meg could tell he was taking in her tall, slim body and striking, auburn hair. "Thanks so much for helping us out while we were in Florida. I also appreciate you helping us with this project."

"It's not every day I get to count gold," Ann said with a smile. "I'm glad to help."

"Ann, this is Judy," Jon said as Judy stepped out the door onto the porch. "Judy is sort of my housekeeper, mother, fashion consultant and conscience all wrapped into one body."

Once formal introductions were over, the small group made their way across the yard toward the three-car garage. Meg explained what happened to Jon's car key, and he laughed. Knowing she had spent almost two hours on her hands and knees in the bushes looking for the missing key, she failed to see anything funny about it. Jon simply shook his head when she insisted on buying him a new key.

"I'm doing it anyway," Meg vowed. "I lost it, so I'll replace it."

"Yes ma'am," Jon said with a grin. "I learned a long time ago that sometimes it's just best to agree."

Meg would have replied, but she was moved to silence when Jon opened the door to the garage. Because the morning sun was so bright, the interior of the garage seemed quite dim in comparison. She squinted into the gloom and saw small, metal ammunition boxes lining the tables. Ann opened the lid to the first box and gasped as the gold glittered in the morning light.

"We have 100 of these," Jon explained to Ann. "Don brought the ammo boxes to us when we pulled into the marina on Marathon Key, and they were perfect for transporting the gold back to Georgia."

Ann raised an eyebrow. "Don?"

"Don Best," Meg offered. "He's Jon's pilot."

"Ohhh," Ann nodded with a smirk. "Jon's pilot. Right."

"It all happened so fast," Jon continued. "We found the coins under the floor of my boat and had to do something to get them all home safely. If Alvaro Lopez had not fired his pistol inside the galley, we never would have discovered the gold.

"Who is Lopez?" Ann quizzed.

"He was the leader of a drug ring, or maybe I should say pirate ring," Meg replied.

"You mean he tried to shoot you?" Ann gasped. "You didn't tell me that."

"Well, he started to, but Meg hit him with a scuba tank," Jon answered as he winked at Meg. "The gun went off, and we later realized there was a hole in the floor. When we pulled up the floorboard for inspection, we uncovered all of this gold."

"And jewelry, too," Meg added.

"When I called Don for help," Jon continued, "he somehow found these boxes. Now, we get to count it all."

"I've always dreamed of counting gold," Ann laughed, "except in my dream, the gold was mine."

Meg laughed uncomfortably, but Jon seemed to appreciate Ann's humor.

"First of all," Jon continued, "we'll have to sort out the coins as to type, and then we'll stack them according to date. I looked at some of them, and they appear to be old Mexican gold pesos. I know it's not all Mexican, however, because I recognized some Saint Gaudens as well. I had these tables delivered yesterday, and Roger and I turned the garage into an open work area. He thinks we're sorting through some things to give away. He's off today, so we don't have to worry about him knowing about the gold."

"Roger?" Ann and Meg questioned in unison.

"Roger helps us around the place," Judy replied.

"Well," Meg said. "We better get moving. This is going to take a while."

Jon and Meg paired up on one side of the garage, so Judy and Ann teamed up on the other side. Ann gave Meg knowing looks throughout the morning, which Meg took to be a signal that her friend assumed something was going on between her and the millionaire...*or billionaire is more like it.*

After three hours of sorting, the coins seemed to be divided into four main areas: the South African Krugerrand, Mexican gold, the more common Saint Gaudens gold, and a stack of miscellaneous coins. Most of the coins looked to be in mint condition, which Jon explained would help give them the highest value. Once everything was divided up, the group went into the house for a lunch break.

"There's a lot of gold out there," Ann said. "Shouldn't we be in the garage guarding it?"

Jon laughed and replied, "No one knows the gold is here. Besides, we have a security system around the main compound. If anyone comes near the house or the barn, we are warned. We're okay."

"Seeing those stacks of gold seems unreal," Meg said.

"Are you sure that's all real gold?" Judy asked.

"I'm sure it's real," Jon said. "I suppose it could be counterfeit, but if it is, it's good counterfeit. Once we get it all counted, I'll have some of it verified for authenticity."

An hour after their lunch break, Judy and Ann determined there were 3000 Saint Gaudens coins. Jon opened up his laptop and logged into his computer. A few seconds later, the other three heard him whistle.

"What?" Meg asked. "What is it?"

"The Saint Gaudens coins are worth anywhere from $1,700 to $1,850 per coin," Jon said.

Silence fell over the room as they all began to calculate in their minds what that meant.

Ann broke the silence and said, "Do you realize that means that right here on these three tables is over five million dollars?"

"That's unbelievable," Meg said. "I had no idea one gold coin was worth so much. If the Saint Gaudens are worth $1,700.00, how much would these South African coins be worth?"

After a few clicks on the keyboard, Jon replied, "They're about the same."

"We already know there are 1500 of those," Meg said. "We just haven't determined all the dates yet."

"That means there may be close to three million dollars' worth of the South African gold," Ann said with a fast calculation.

Judy sat down in stunned silence as the other three gathered over the Mexican gold.

"Let's count these together, and then we'll begin organizing all of the piles into categories based upon dates and condition," Jon said.

After another hour, the group determined there were two thousand Mexican coins, most from the early twentieth century. To Meg's amazement, the Mexican coins would total around four million dollars.

They put the coins back into containers and were careful to place layers of cloth in between each level in order to protect the gold. If their calculations were right, this meant all the coins totaled about twelve million dollars. Realizing its value had not even been considered, Meg thought about the jewelry they had found along with the gold. There was no telling what it was worth.

"I hate to leave all the excitement," Judy said, "but I better get back into the kitchen or we won't have anything ready for dinner. You can snack on something if you're hungry, but I'm thinking of putting together a big meal to celebrate."

Jon answered, "Okay, Judy. Thanks so much for helping us. We'll be in later."

Judy went back to the house, and Jon turned toward the other two women. "It's obvious we need to do something with all of this gold rather than store it in my garage. I met with my lawyer yesterday, and he said we should consider opening up an account in the Caymans. If we do that, we won't have to worry about government involvement at all. It's all legal. People do it all the time."

"I agree," Meg said as she rubbed her hand through her hair. "Let's get this put up as fast as we can. It makes me nervous having this much gold around."

"Well, you know part of it is yours, so you should think about what you want to do with it."

"Jon, this gold is all yours. It was under the floor of *your* boat."

"With all we went through together and the fact you helped me discover it, I think it's only fair that some of it belongs to you," Jon said as he winked at Meg. "I'm thinking you should take about two million of it, and then I'll use some of it to fund our next adventure, that is as long as you're willing to be a part of it."

"What adventure?" Ann asked.

"We talked about trying our hand at searching for sunken treasure," Meg said, "but I don't know if that's a good idea."

"Sunken treasure?" Ann questioned. "Are you serious? What in the world gave you that idea?"

"While we were in the Bahamas, we read an article about seventeenth century Spanish galleons that had sunk throughout the Caribbean and Bahamas. After diving a couple of times, we began to dream about what it would be like to find one of those ships."

Though Meg trusted Ann, she was not sure if Jon would appreciate her telling everything about their dive in the

Bahamas. She figured it was Jon's adventure, not hers, and he might want to keep it secret. *I suppose the gold coin I found on the reef is mine, but that's all. Jon can just mail that to me.*

"I can buy a boat and all of the equipment we need for around a million," Jon continued. "I could hire a couple of people to help us for another couple of hundred thousand. Let's just say one-and-a-half to two million of the gold will need to be cashed in for that project. Meg, if you get two million of it and the venture takes two million, I still end up with around eight million. I think I get the greatest end of the deal. I do think you should take the jewelry too. I would look funny wearing a diamond necklace."

Ann's mouth dropped in surprise. "What jewelry? Oh yeah. You said something about jewelry earlier."

Before Meg could speak, Judy stuck her head through the door and asked her and Ann for help in the kitchen. Meg was sure Judy didn't need any help but just wanted company. They closed up the garage and entered the house through the kitchen door. Judy returned to her work while the two younger women found aprons to wear. Meg watched Jon through the kitchen window as he strolled toward the barn. It was obvious he was exempt from kitchen duty.

When the two younger women looked around the kitchen, they were amazed at what Judy was "throwing together" for dinner. Judy admitted she had decided they should have a celebration for their discovery, but she wanted to celebrate the treasure of friendship.

"It would be easy for us to get our focus on gold and sunken treasure," Judy said. "I want to do something tonight that will help us to focus on the true treasure, which is friendship and love. I thought I would put together a special meal to help us think on what's important."

Meg thought that Judy was being a bit sappy and wondered what was really on her mind. She figured that Judy had been trying to get Jon married off for a while, so this *celebration of friendship* must have been her attempt at matchmaking. She was right about one thing. All of this gold could sure mess with one's mind.

"You are so right, Judy," Meg agreed. "Perspective is important. The truth is I don't know what to do. Jon is insisting some of the gold belongs to me, but it's his. I'm not sure that his perspective is right."

"Well, Meg, I think it is. What I think is that Jon is in love."

Meg blushed. "Judy. He's not in love. We're just friends."

"If I can be honest, Meg, I think you're in love too…but no, don't say anything. Let's just have an enjoyable meal together and all of this other stuff will sort itself out."

Meg was grateful she didn't have to continue that conversation. The trio went to work to create a feast fit for a king. After another hour or so in the kitchen, Meg set the dining room table with candles and a beautiful arrangement of flowers Judy had sitting on the hallway credenza.

"Judy," Ann declared after dinner preparations were completed. "Since we still have a little time, I would like to clean up a bit."

"My clothes are still here," Meg offered.

Ann looked at her with disbelief. "Really?"

"Yes. I stayed here two nights ago…in the guest bedroom. I left my things there. I'm sure I've got something clean you can wear. I'd like to clean up and change clothes too."

"How about telling me about this search for treasure while we get dressed?"

"Uh…sure."

CHAPTER TWO

A Night with a Few Friends

Meg walked into the guest bedroom wrapped in a towel as Ann was trying on another dress. Ann found three different dresses in the guestroom closet that would fit. Meg pulled out some clean gym shorts and a tee shirt and stepped into the bathroom to put them on.

As she returned to the bedroom, Ann said, "I don't think I fill out your clothes quite like you do. Sometimes it's just not fair."

"Ann, that's a dumb thing to say. You are the one with a perfect body."

"I've always thought my legs were too long, but I guess I'm fine with it."

"Yeah, too long like every gorgeous model I've ever seen," Meg laughed. "You're going to be a prize for some guy one of these days."

"Finding him is the real problem. Maybe I'm too picky, but I just can't settle for anything less than my ideal."

"I think you should have standards, Ann. You'll find him in time."

Ann said, "It sure looks like you've found yours. Jon's a real catch. He seems perfect in every way I can see. I guess you've…"

"Why do I feel like you and Judy are teaming up against me?" Meg interrupted. "I'm telling you there is nothing between us. We just had an enjoyable time and then helped each other through some tough experiences. That's what friends do."

"So, friends stand on the back of a yacht in the Bahamas in a lip lock and then just move on with their lives?" Ann simpered.

"I meant friends help each other," Meg replied with exasperation. "Okay, so I'm a little confused, but I'll work through it. I wish he would stop talking about me taking part of the gold."

"Changing the subject won't help, but I think you should take some of the gold. It is obvious he wants you to have it, and it's not any skin off of his back. The truth is, Meg, you don't even have a job."

"I don't know, Ann. I still have money from Steve's insurance. We'll see."

The two of them finished getting dressed in some of the clothes Meg had purchased in George Town. Meg was relieved that Ann never brought up the search for treasure. After putting on make-up, they went downstairs to the dining area just as Jon walked into the house.

"Good gracious," Jon said. "What's the special occasion?"

"Well," Meg surmised, "Judy says we are the occasion. Why don't you get dressed for dinner? We'll be ready in about ten or fifteen minutes."

Jon rubbed the stubble on his chin. "We are the occasion?"

Jon hurried upstairs to clean up while Meg and Ann stepped into the kitchen to make the last minute preparations. As Jon returned to the dining area, the three women began placing the food on the table. They sat down to a delicious meal of Baked Chicken ala Milanese served with lemon supreme sauce, almond green bean casserole, Italian stuffed mushrooms, and homemade dinner rolls. Judy topped the meal off with a delicious mocha pots de crème.

As Jon saw the incredible meal being placed before him, he said, "Okay, what's the occasion? I give up!"

Judy stood and said, "The occasion is…us. Tonight, we are celebrating the most important treasure in the entire world–friendship and life. I want us to be reminded tonight that life is not about gold, treasure, bank accounts, and nice cars. Life is about relationships, and what we all share together is very special."

There was an awkward silence around the table as each person tried to evaluate whether or not they shared a very special relationship. Meg and Jon knew one another pretty well, but Ann was quite new to the equation. Judy saw something about the group that tied them all together, whether they each saw it or not.

Jon broke the silence, "You are so right, Judy. May I propose a toast? Here's to friendship and adventure and to all the ingredients that make us…uh…family."

Family? Really? Had Meg heard him correctly?

Everyone picked up their glasses, held them in the air, and drank. The four of them dived into an amazing meal and talked and laughed together for a couple of hours. Jon began telling stories about Meg when she was a little girl. Ann almost fell out of her chair with laughter when Jon told of Meg trying to break the record for sitting on a trashcan.

"The funniest part was that I happened to walk around to her backyard about the time she and her friend, Marie, were discussing various options for relieving their bladders. They didn't know I was there until I started laughing at Marie's suggestion."

"That's hilarious," Ann said as tears streamed down her face. "How old were you, Meg?"

"I can't believe you're telling that story, Jon. I was eleven years old. It was just at the age when I can't think of anything worse than the boy I had a crush on walking around my house to hear me…talking about that subject."

"Well, it was pretty funny."

"Yeah, but we did break the record. I don't know if it was a Guinness Book of World Records record, but it was enough to get our picture in the paper. Those were great days."

"If you ladies are willing to be a part of the next adventure, we've got some more great days ahead of us," Jon said.

Meg leaned forward in her chair. *Ladies? Does Jon mean that he wants Ann to help us search for treasure?*

Jon continued, "One of those great days for me will be tomorrow as I fly to the Caymans. I contacted Don earlier, and he said he would be happy to fly me down tomorrow. He was home alone because his wife and kids are visiting her parents for the Labor Day holiday. I have to be at the airport at six in the morning, so I'm thinking of hitting the sack soon. Meg, I've separated enough Saint Gaudens coins to equal two million dollars, and I've put it, along with the jewelry, in my safe."

Meg tried to refuse the gold, but Judy interrupted her. "Sweetie, I've learned that when Jon has his mind made up, there is no changing it. Just take the gold and jewelry."

"Too bad tomorrow is Labor Day or you could get it in a bank around here," Jon continued. "I can help you with it on Tuesday, when I return from the Caymans."

Judy spoke up, "Meg, why don't you two spend the next two nights with me? I have a catering job tomorrow in town, and you could help me with it. I could use the help, and it would be a lot of fun."

"I guess that's fine with me," Meg said. "I haven't figured out what I'm doing. I live alone, so it's not like I have to go home. My mom has my cat."

"I'd love to," Ann said. "I don't have any plans for the day off, and doing a little cooking with a pro would be a lot of fun. I'm not sure about two nights though."

Meg said. "I can loan you some of my clothes, Ann."

"You've got to be kidding. I don't think I can fit my fat self into your clothes."

"Give me a break, Ann. You don't have an ounce of fat on your sexy, little body. You're just a bit taller than me. I've got something you can wear."

"Okay, as long as it's no trouble."

"It will be no trouble at all, Ann. You are welcome here any time," Jon said.

Judy slipped into the kitchen to begin cleaning up while Jon shared ideas about starting their salvage business. Though Meg told Ann some things about their dives in the Bahamas, she had not told her about finding the gold. As she and Jon gave Ann the details of their discovery, Meg felt badly for misleading Ann earlier when she told her that they had only read books about sunken treasure. Ann was a bit shocked that they had actually found some treasure. Once Ann got passed

Meg being a bit deceitful about them finding gold, she sat shocked in disbelief.

Jon said, "I was thinking we'll have to buy a boat and hire someone who knows what they are doing before we can start any kind of salvage attempt. We're also going to have to do some research."

Meg said. "I had already decided not to go along with your treasure hunting scheme."

"Why would you want to miss out on that?" Jon asked with obvious disappointment in his voice. "You've got to admit that the scuba diving part of the last couple of weeks has been amazing. This time, we could dive without having to worry about any hoodlums messing with us. It would be the time of your life."

"I don't know," Meg continued to waver.

"So what else do you have to do," Ann chimed in.

"Are you tag teaming against me?" Meg laughed. "I'm not sure I would even know where to begin, that is if I'm going to be a part of this venture. What do you do? Google *shipwrecks* or something? I doubt that would do us a lot of good."

"I have been thinking about another possibility," Jon answered. "You could go on an excursion to Seville, Spain."

"Spain? You've got to be kidding," Ann said in shock.

"Yes, Spain. The General Archive of the Indies is housed in the *Casa Lonja de Mercaderes*. It is home to the largest repository of ancient documents in the world regarding Spanish history. This repository houses some nine kilometers of shelving, thousands of volumes, and millions of pages of information about Spanish colonies in the new world. With a little help from someone who knows how to look through all of those ancient papers, you might be able to learn some valuable information that would be of great help to us in our search."

"How did you know about that?" Meg asked.

"This is not the first time I've thought about sunken treasure. I got interested in the idea many years ago when Mel Fisher found the *Atocha*. You know, his find was worth about 450 million dollars. Can you imagine finding something like that?"

"I kind of feel like we found the mother lode under the floor of your boat; I can't imagine $450 million," Meg said.

"I think for now, I need to get this gold to the Caymans, and you two beautiful women need to plan a trip to Spain. Ann, can you get off from work for a week?" Jon asked.

"That will be no problem. I still have two weeks of vacation I need to take before the year ends. I could stand spending a week in Spain."

"Okay; okay," Meg held her hands up. "You two are scheming against me. I'll at least think about it. I guess tonight can be like a slumber party. Maybe I can find the picture of a house we saw for sale on Great Exuma on the Internet. It was so beautiful."

"I haven't gone to a slumber party since I was about fourteen," Ann said. "This will be fun."

****

Jon went outside to the garage while the three women continued to talk around the table. He knew that he loved Judy like she was his mother, and he had to admit that he enjoyed having Meg around. Could he really love her? Did she love

him? He had a feeling that he could see Ann being a good
friend too.

He felt a little guilty for lying about the gold he left for
Meg. He had put all but one million dollars' worth of the Saint
Gaudens in the safe for Meg, but he decided it would be best
not to admit that to her at this time. He knew he could take her
coins to the Cayman Island bank later if she wanted him to, or
she could just do with them whatever she wanted. He had also
set aside another two million dollars' worth of gold to purchase
a salvage ship and fund the treasure hunting operation.

He backed the van up to the garage door and began the
monotonous chore of loading the containers of gold. When he
completed the job, he pulled the van into the garage and locked
the doors. He set the alarm and headed into the house. He told
the ladies goodnight and eased upstairs while listening to them
ooh and ahh over the pictures of the house in the Bahamas.

"Jon," Meg called from the bottom of the stairs as he was
closing the door to his bedroom.

Meg hurried up the stairs as Jon opened his door and
stepped into the hallway. He had already unbuttoned his shirt,
and thought that Meg appeared to be a little embarrassed at the
view of his bare chest.

"Jon," Meg said hesitantly. "I don't know how to say what
I'm thinking or feeling. First, you are too good to me…
and…well, I…"

Jon stepped in to rescue Meg from the growing, awkward
silence, "We've had a great time together, and I think we're
going to have an amazing experience with the salvage, if you
will do it with me. I think we need to talk when I get back from
the Caymans."

"Okay, Jon," Meg said, and she reached up and kissed him on the cheek.

Jon not only appreciated Meg's beauty, but he also loved her special aroma that always sent him over the top. It wasn't perfume or shampoo. It was just what he thought of as Meg. He lay awake for a long time thinking about the uncertainty of his future. What was his next step, and where did Meg fit in? After a while, he drifted off to a restless sleep filled with dreams about Meg Freeman.

CHAPTER THREE

The Flight

Jon reached across to the bedside table to silence the clock that sounded like a warning for a five-alarm fire. Trying to remember why his alarm clock was ringing at such an early hour, he lay in the stillness as the fog drifted from his brain. His first thought was of the gold. He shot straight up as he remembered that he was to meet Don this morning.

After dressing, he carefully opened his bedroom door, hoping to avoid the familiar squeak of the hinges. Though the squeak was there as normal, it seemed not to disturb anyone, so without a sound, he slipped into the hallway.

He stopped for a moment at the door to the guest bedroom and imagined Meg sleeping in the large, queen size bed. He even considered going in to kiss her goodbye, but then he remembered Ann was spending the night as well. While there were plenty of empty rooms in the house, he realized it was probable that Meg and Ann were sharing the bed together. He couldn't go in and kiss her anyway. Men married again after their wives died, but he just wasn't sure he could go into another relationship.

As Jon pulled up to the familiar hangar at the airport, he noticed a twin-engine plane sitting on the asphalt next to the building. Motioning for Jon to enter, Don opened the door to the tiny office on the north side of the building.

"I've got some coffee made, if you want some," Don said. "I would fix you a cup, but I'm not real sure how you like it."

"Thanks Don," Jon said. "I'm a simple guy. I just like it black and thick."

"My father was that way. He used to let coffee sit all day in his Mr. Coffee and then drink it as if it had just been perked. I thought it was the worst tasting stuff, but he loved it. We're going to have to take the Cessna 402 instead of the Gulf Stream. The jet is in the shop for routine maintenance. Though the Cessna has some age on her, she's a good plane. It may take us a little longer to get there, but she'll do fine. I've done all the pre-flight inspections, so I'm ready to take off whenever you're ready."

"Sounds good. Let me get some coffee, and then we need to get these containers aboard. It's going to take some time to get them all loaded. Too bad we don't have help."

Within about forty-five minutes, the two men had loaded the containers of gold into the plane. Once the tower cleared them, they were airborne and soaring toward the Caymans. Almost four hours later, Don landed the small plane at an airport on the north side of Key West for refueling, and the two men were back in the air within thirty minutes after touching down.

After another hour of flying, Don pointed to the land off in the distance and told Jon they were nearing Grand Cayman. Without warning, the engine coughed and sputtered.

"What's wrong?" Jon asked as he looked at Don's troubled face.

"I'm not sure, but both engines are losing power."

The engines coughed back to life again, but within another minute, the two men sat in an eerie silence as the plane began to drop. The experienced pilot fought the controls to keep the nose of the plane up in hopes he could somehow ease it into the water. Telling Jon to call for help over the radio, Don handed his headset to him. After twisting a few knobs, Jon decided the radio was dead. Suddenly, everything went black when Jon's head banged against the control board upon impact with the hard surface of the sea.

****

Judy, Meg, and Ann worked all morning in the kitchen as they put the finishing touches on the lunch they were to serve for the Kiwanis Club annual Labor Day picnic. The women were serving barbeque pork with a sauce Judy claimed as her own, secret recipe. Though the pork had been smoked all night in an outdoor smoker, Judy had boiled it first to make it tender and moist. Along with the barbeque, there were baked beans, Brunswick stew, and blackberry cobbler. They carried the food over to the park in Canton in an enclosed trailer that Judy pulled behind a huge Suburban.

The line of Kiwanians snaked around the pavilion, and Meg thought they would never quit coming. Her legs ached from the strain. When she served the last plate, she felt that if she had to smile and say you're welcome to one more person, her face would break. Judy warned her that while cooking and serving was tiring, cleaning up would be no fun either.

The catering had been a great success and Meg thought that she might enjoy helping Judy again sometime, though she needed to get a little more mentally ready for the physical challenge.

"I think I'm about to fall over," Judy said as they crawled into the Suburban.

"You and me both," Meg agreed. "If I had to put one more scoop of Brunswick stew in a bowl, I think my arm might fall off."

"I would like to treat the three of us to a massage," Judy offered. "I know just the place to go."

"Oh, Judy, that sounds like heaven," Ann said. "We must have served 200 people."

"I think it was close to that," Judy agreed. "Let's get a massage, and then I'm taking us out for Chinese food. If I have to even smell anything that resembles barbeque for a week, I might get sick."

Hoping to have heard from Jon, Meg checked her phone. *Why am I anxious to hear from Jon? I guess I'm just curious if he made it to the Caymans. There's nothing wrong with that.* She saw to her frustration that she had forgotten to charge her phone. She put her dead phone back in her purse and prepared herself to be pampered by what Judy called "a real professional."

After an incredible day together, the three ladies returned to the ranch exhausted but thrilled with the fun they had together. Ann hugged them both and got into her car to go home. Though Meg had urged her to stay the night, Ann reminded Meg that she still had a job to go to the next day.

Meg didn't want to go home, so she decided to stay at the ranch one more night. Judy asked Meg if she wouldn't mind feeding Jon's yellow lab before coming in, so Meg walked over to the garage where she remembered seeing the can containing the dog food. When Meg got to the guest bedroom, Judy had stripped the bed of linens.

Judy said, "Now that I've stripped the bed, I realize I don't have any clean sheets. I guess I'm falling down on the job. Why don't you just sleep in Jon's bed? He won't be home until tomorrow."

"Oh, Judy, I can't do that. That just wouldn't be right."

"He won't care. It's the best bed in the house. We won't even have to tell him you slept in his bed. Just enjoy it for tonight."

Knowing deep down that she wanted to sleep in Jon's bed, Meg looked into the master bedroom. She longed to smell the scent of this man, and against her better judgment, she agreed. Watching Judy amble down the hall, she stood in the doorway to the master bedroom without making a sound. The odd thing was that when Judy passed the linen closet, her fingers swept across the door. *Why did she just touch the closet door?*

Meg waited until the hallway was clear before tiptoeing down toward the linen closet. To her surprise, it was full of towels *and* sheets. *Did Judy just lie to me? Is she trying to force me to sleep in Jon's bed? I should show her. I could find sheets to my bed and not play her game. At the same time, I do want to...*

Meg didn't make a sound as she closed the door to the closet. She looked down the hall toward the guest room and then to the illumined doorway of Jon's room. A grin spread across her face as she slowly made her way back toward the master suite. She closed the door and imagined Jon lying down on his bed. After standing still for a moment, she decided that sleeping in Jon's bed wouldn't be a bad thing. He would never have to know.

She pulled off her clothes and stepped into the beautiful, tiled shower. The hot water massaged her tired body like the skillful hands of a master masseuse. *What a day it has been! I think I could sleep til noon tomorrow.*

As she got out of the shower, she realized she had left her clean clothes in her room, but instead of walking next door to get sleepwear, she decided to sleep in one of Jon's tee shirts again. She had to pull open three drawers before she found the right one. Meg saw a copy of a Jeff Shaara's Civil War novel on the bedside table and began leafing through it.

After about two chapters, Meg's eyelids began to close as the lack of sleep over the last few days was beginning to tell on her. Within a few minutes, she lay asleep on Jon's bed with his book by her side. Most nights, she slept under the covers in total darkness, but she drifted off to sleep with her bedside lamp still on.

****

While holding onto Jon for over three hours, Don was grateful that at least the seas were calm. He knew Jon had hit his head pretty hard. Even though Jon seemed to be somewhat aware of what was going on, he had a hard time holding onto the flotation device that had been under his seat. It had been a miracle that either one of them had survived the crash.

Although Don managed to keep the nose of the plane up as they crashed into the water, the jolt had knocked him almost senseless, and it was clear Jon had a concussion. Don looked at his watch and noted that it was now after 2:00 in the afternoon. He began wondering if anyone had noticed them fall off of the radar. It was fortunate that he had been able to grab the emergency bag in the cockpit before pulling Jon out the broken front window of the plane.

While the plane had filled with water, Don held onto Jon and pushed his way through the gushing water into the open sea. Inside the emergency bag, Don found two life jackets, a first-aid kit, flare gun, and a waterproof box that contained some crackers and water. He had also managed to throw out the Styrofoam floater from under the seat, so they at least had something to hold to. Because the plane sunk so fast to the bottom, he was unable to grab anything else from the cockpit.

Even though he didn't know their precise location, he knew there was a deep trench running through this region that would make recovering the plane impossible. He hoped someone would find them before dark, because he didn't think they could make it through a night in the ocean. Don had always heard stories about sharks eating downed pilots, and he had no desire to go through an experience like that.

Don heard a sound overhead and realized there must be a plane nearby. Knowing that he had just one shot, he pulled the flare gun out of the waterproof bag. He held the gun high out of the water and fired. The plane continued on its westward course, but within a few minutes, he saw the plane circle back around much closer to the water. With all of the energy he had, he waved frantically at the plane. The plane rocked its wings back and forth as a signal that the pilot had spotted them in the water. The plane began to fly wide circles around the spot where they were floating.

Within an hour, Don made out a Coastguard Cutter heading toward them. After over four hours of floating around in the Gulf, the two men were pulled aboard, and Jon was carried below to the sick bay. Don told the captain about their crash and discovered that the Coast Guard had already been notified of a missing plane. When Don stopped by to check on his employer, Jon was resting with an I.V. in his right arm. He was informed that within the hour, Jon would be air lifted to the Cayman Islands Hospital on Grand Cayman.

The pilot for the H-65 Dolphin that would take Jon to the hospital allowed Don to fly with them. By the time Jon was strapped in, he was lucid and talking. Don reassured him that everything was fine, though they lost their cargo.

Over an hour after being pulled from the ocean, the Coast Guard helicopter landed on the helipad of the hospital, and Jon was wheeled into a room. As they were getting him settled, Don asked for Meg's phone number. Jon quoted the number before insisting that Don tell her he was fine.

"Tell her that it's no big deal, and I'll be home in a day or so."

Don tried Meg's phone several times, but it went to voice mail.

"It sounds like her phone is either turned off or her battery is dead," Don acknowledged. "I'll try again in a few hours."

CHAPTER FOUR

Unexpected Company

Judy came into the kitchen to get a glass of milk and heard the alarm warning her that someone was coming up the driveway. She knew Jon had said he might come home tonight, and she thought for a moment of her mischief in placing Meg in his bed. Judy was confident that Jon would not sleep with Meg, but she thought it might nudge him forward a little in his relationship with the woman that Judy knew he loved.

She turned off the alarm to make his entrance easier. She picked up her glass of milk and padded back to her bedroom with a mischievous grin on her face.

****

In Meg's sleep stupor, she knew something didn't seem right when she felt the bed move as if someone sat down on the edge of the mattress. With her eyes still closed, Meg thought about the awkward moment she was about to experience. Jon must have come home sooner than he had expected. She opened her eyes and found she was looking into the smiling face of Philippe, one of the pirates and drug runners who had kidnapped her and Jon a few months earlier.

The last time she had seen him, he was lying on her cell floor in the pirate's lair, bleeding profusely. Jon and Meg had been enjoying the beauty of Conception Island and diving some of the incredible reefs in the area when Alvaro Lopez's thugs, Luis and Philippe, had kidnapped them. They were taken to Lopez's hideout and locked away in a cell. Meg knew that Philippe would have raped her and even killed her back then, but they had managed to escape the island. While imprisoned, they discovered that the pirates had joined forces with some terrorists and were going to release an airborne virus at the Republican National Convention. After she and Jon thwarted the terrorist's attempt to kill a lot of people at the Miami Convention Center, Meg thought Philippe had been captured and locked away in a Miami jail. The police must have arrested some other accomplice while Philippe remained free.

She let out a brief, blood-curdling scream before he covered her mouth. To her disgust, he sat on top of her as she wrestled against him. Meg knew with certainty she was about to be hurt, if not killed, as he placed a sharp knife against her neck. She stopped thrashing, and tears began to flow down her face.

"Well," Philippe said, "It's good to see you too. Why are you so surprised I've come for you? You should know that I have thought about you every night since our brief romance in the Bahamas, and I have been looking forward to our time together. We're going to have a little fun, and then you're going to show me the gold. If you are nice to me, I might let you live. Where is your jerk of a husband?"

"He's gone, but he'll be home any minute," Meg whimpered breathlessly under Philippe's hand.

"Well, you just better hope he doesn't come home while I'm here, or I'll slit his throat. He's caused me a lot of trouble."

Meg was desperate to think of some way to get Philippe off of her. He continued to hold the knife to her throat and told her she was dead if she made any noise. Meg knew with certainty that he would not hesitate to kill her.

Meg heard a horrible crack that sounded like a mix between something hitting a metal pole and a wooden baseball bat splitting in two. Drops of red blood splattered on her face as Philippe flew off of her to the floor beside the bed. She looked up in shock to see Judy standing beside her bed holding a frying pan. Meg jumped up from the bed and fell into Judy's arms. Tears flowed as if through a broken dam.

Judy held Meg and consoled her for a long while before speaking. "I need to call the police. Why don't you come with me downstairs?"

Meg could not speak through the terror she still felt deep inside. She nodded her head as if in a trance. Before leaving the room, Judy pulled a sheet off the bed and tied up Philippe's arms.

"He's still out cold and he's lost some blood, but I don't want to take any chances," Judy said.

Judy picked up Meg's cell phone from the dresser as she led Meg out into the hallway. She dialed 911 and spoke with the police dispatcher. After answering numerous questions and assuring the officer that they were both safe, she closed the phone.

"Deputies will be here in a few minutes. I'm sure they will also send paramedics, Meg. Will that be okay with you?"

Meg bowed her head and whispered, "Yes."

"Why don't you get dressed?" Judy suggested. "I'm sure the deputies will want to ask you questions, but they will have no reason to perform any kind of physical on you. I am right, aren't I? The creep did not have a chance to…hurt you did he?"

"No. I'm fine. Just shook up."

"Well, he won't be doing anything to anyone else ever again. The truth is he may not recover from the blow to the head I gave him. I'm sure I fractured his skull."

When the doorbell rang, Meg hurried into her room to get dressed while Judy answered the door. Meg pulled on some jeans and slipped into her sneakers. Hoping to get her cell phone, she eased back into Jon's room, but then she remembered that Judy had taken it. She felt as if there was no air in the room as her heart beat wildly in her chest.

She walked around the edge of the bed to make sure Philippe was still on the floor. He wasn't moving. *Is he dead? I've seen him like this before.* She was glad Judy had the foresight to tie the creep up with the sheet. Meg hurried from the room to find the deputies downstairs in the foyer.

One of the officers followed Meg and Judy into the kitchen and sat in a chair at the table while the other one went upstairs to make sure Philippe was secure.

"He's in the room just past the linen closet," Judy said. "I tied him up with the bed sheet."

Within another few minutes, an ambulance arrived with two medical personnel. It took some time, but the ambulance finally left with Philippe. After additional photos and questions, the officers and medical personnel left. Judy insisted Meg drink some chamomile tea that would help her get some much needed rest. After tossing and turning in Judy's bed for at least an hour, Meg drifted off in a fitful sleep.

****

Jon could hear the phone ringing over a thousand miles away as if he were calling Sarah, his assistant, from his office. It was 7:30 in the morning, but he was sure that Judy would be up.

"Hello."

"Hey Judy, you sound tired. Is everything okay?" Jon said.

"It is now. A man from the Bahamas broke in last night."

"What…Is Meg okay?" Jon blurted out as he sat bolt upright in bed. His head began to pound with the exertion. "Who broke in?"

"Meg's fine. She said the man's name is Philippe. I'll have to tell you about it when you get home. She's pretty torn up, though. I gave her some chamomile, and she's sound asleep right now. Where are you?"

"Well, that's another story. We crashed in the Gulf yesterday, and I'm in the hospital on Grand Cayman right now."

"You…what? Oh Jon. Are you okay? How is Don?"

"I'm going to be fine. Don saved my life. He's fine. I'll have to tell you my story later, too. I think they will release me today, and we'll fly home on a commercial flight. I'll call you back to let you know for sure when we're coming home. Get a pen so I can give you the number here. Have Meg call me when she wakes up."

Jon gave Judy the number before hanging up. He could not believe Luis or Philippe had tracked him and Meg to his house. That was way too close. He called the Cherokee County

Sheriff's office in Canton to get the details of what happened. After hanging up, Jon dozed off.

He lay motionless while the room seemed to be spinning around him. Someone was speaking on a phone, but he could not seem to bring himself fully awake. He had a severe headache, and his eyelids felt as heavy as sand bags. Though he fought to stay awake, sleep pulled him under for another couple of hours.

"Hello Meg," Jon heard Don saying a couple of hours later. "No, he's still sleeping, and I shouldn't wake him up… No…we're both fine. Well, Jon got a pretty nasty knock on his head, and we floated around in the ocean for a while, but we're doing okay."

"I am as awake as you," Jon grunted as he worked to sit up in bed. "Let me speak to her."

"Meg, Jon just woke up. He wants to speak to you."

"Hey, Meg. Are you okay?"

"I'm fine," Meg said as she began to cry into the phone. "What happened? Are you all right?"

"Just a concussion, but they said I can go home today. Don has seats for us on the 2:00 flight. We should land around 6:00. I need to know that you're all right. Judy told me it was Philippe."

Jon could hear more sobbing on the other end of the phone. "Yes, it was Philippe. I thought you killed him at The Fortress, or at least I thought he was picked up in Miami."

"Did he…"

"Hurt me?" Meg finished. "No. He was going to, but Judy got there just in time."

The floodgates opened, and Meg began to cry uncontrollably.

"I'm sorry," she sobbed. "It was a horrible ordeal, and then I learned this morning that you could have been…"

"Sweetheart, I'm fine. You can pick us up at the airport at 6:30, and you can tell me all about it."

"I'll be there," Meg said. "Jon, I'm so sorry."

"Sorry for what?"

"I'm just sorry. I guess we can talk about it when you get back. Are you sure you can travel okay?"

"I'm fine, Meg. I promise. I don't suggest you let me drive home from the airport, but I'm doing a lot better."

"Okay. I'll see you this evening. Be careful."

Jon thought for a moment that his being careful would not help him get home safe and sound. That would be up to the pilot. He heard some loud snorting and weeping coming over the phone before hearing Judy's voice.

"Oh, honey. Jon's going to be fine. Why don't you go take a shower and…"

"He called me sweetheart," Jon heard Meg say before the phone in Jon's hand went dead.

CHAPTER FIVE

Coming Home

Hours later, Meg parked the truck in the airport parking lot and hurried across the street to the terminal. She stood at the top of the escalators where she waited on the two men to come up from the train, but then, out of the corner of her eye, she saw someone being pushed in a wheelchair out of the elevator. It was Jon. As she ran toward him, he stood and held his arms out to her. She fell into his embrace crying into his shoulder.

"Oh Jon. You could have been killed. I would have lost you forever."

She looked up into his chocolate brown eyes noticing tears running down his face.

"I've been such a fool, Meg. I love you. I have loved you, and I always will love you. I'm sorry I almost let something horrible happen to you."

"What did you say?" Meg asked as the crowds milled around them.

With obvious confusion, Jon said, "Uh...I'm sorry I almost..."

"No. Before that."

Jon grinned and repeated, "I love you, Meg Freeman with all of my heart."

Meg pulled Jon's head down toward hers and pressed her lips hard against his as she melted into his body. Jon held her tightly as tears streamed down both of their faces.

"Why don't we take this reunion home," Don suggested with a laugh. "Meg, you go get the truck, and I'll push Jon out to the curb. He can walk, but it's better that he not overdo it with a long walk through the parking deck."

Meg pulled away from Jon but kept her hand against his cheek. "Okay. I'll see you at the curb as fast as I can get there."

After dropping Don off at the Cherokee County Airport where his car was parked, Meg drove Jon back to the ranch where they found Ann and Judy standing on the porch. Judy's apron was wrinkled and drawn where she had been twisting it tighter than a rope. Ann ran to Meg and wrapped her arms around her best friend. Though it now seemed like an eternity since the Philippe episode, Meg realized this was the first time she had seen Ann since the pervert's limp body had been carted off in an ambulance.

Jon insisted he was feeling fine, but if they wanted to pamper him, he would let them. As Meg helped him into the house, she inhaled the mouthwatering smells of meatloaf. She insisted that Jon take his dinner on the couch in the den, and she was going to serve him. Everyone else prepared their plates before they joined Jon in the relaxed atmosphere of pine and leather. During dinner, Jon shared his story about the plane crash followed by Meg and Judy sharing about their nightmare with Philippe.

"I am so sorry I was not here, but I sure am glad you were, Judy. It sounds like Philippe will do nothing more than drool all over himself and wait to be spoon fed for the rest of his life. Are you okay?"

"I'm still pretty shook up," Judy said. "I can't believe I hit the guy, but I would do it again in a heartbeat. He was just seconds away from really hurting Meg."

"I am so glad you were there," Jon said again. "How did you know he was here?"

"Well, to start with, I turned the alarm off when it warned me someone was coming up the driveway. I know that was a stupid thing to do, but I thought it was you. I went back to my room, but I noticed the alarm never beeped to tell me it was reset. You know I have a control panel in my apartment."

"I guess I've forgotten we put an extra panel in your room. I don't blame you for turning the alarm off. You had every reason to think I was coming home."

"I still shouldn't have turned it off," Judy continued, "but when it didn't beep, I thought that was odd. I've listened to you come in so many times that your habits are as much a part of you as the way your eyes twinkle when you smile. I always hear the alarm beep when you reset it."

"I didn't do anything at first, but the more I thought about it, the more it bothered me. I walked into the kitchen to reset it, and then figured I should make sure you remembered to lock the door. It was unlocked. I knew that wasn't like you at all."

"That's true," Jon interrupted. "I would have locked the door."

Judy nodded in agreement. "I went toward the family room to see if you may still be up when I heard Meg scream. I ran into the kitchen and grabbed the first thing I saw, the frying pan. When I saw that...that miscreant on top of Meg, I wanted to kill him. I've never been so angry in my life."

"Miscreant?" Ann laughed. "That wasn't the word on the tip of my tongue."

Meg chimed in, "As I lay there, I couldn't help but wonder what happened to the other guy; I think his name was Luis. I expected him to come in any minute and knock Philippe off of me. He never came in. Do you suppose he's around here somewhere?"

"My first thought is that Philippe was acting alone," Jon said. "Now, I'm wondering what happened to Luis. I guess you had to spend a lot of time with the sheriff today?"

"I did, and someone from Homeland Security wants to meet with me and you tomorrow."

"I knew you two were in the CIA or something," Ann said.

"Oh brother, Ann. It's not that big of a deal," Meg sighed as she brushed her off.

"I hate that we lost the gold," Jon confessed.

"Maybe we can find it," Meg suggested.

"Maybe, but we don't know for sure where we went down. Don didn't have time to look at the GPS as we were falling from the sky. All we know is that we could see land. We can try to find it, but odds are, it's gone. Don said that if we were in the location he thinks, the ocean is quite deep there."

"How deep?" Meg asked.

"Well, he thinks we were over the Cayman Trough, and the depth of the trough exceeds 25,000 feet. It's the deepest point of the Caribbean Sea."

"Wow, I didn't realize the ocean got that deep anywhere."

"At least we still have what I put in the safe for you plus some extra I set aside to purchase a salvage ship. I'm glad I decided you deserve more than what I first said."

"You also left the jewelry," Ann added.

"At least you're okay," Meg said with deep affection in her voice. "You didn't take all of the gold with you?"

Jon grinned as he shook his head.

"Well, I think that's my cue to go home," Ann said with a smile. "Some of us have to work tomorrow. Thanks for dinner Judy. It was wonderful."

"You're welcome, sweetie," Judy beamed. "Come back anytime."

Meg walked beside Jon as they climbed the steps to the bedrooms. Meg couldn't help but smile as she saw that Judy had not gotten around to putting clean sheets on her bed in the guest room. She knew she could do it herself. Jon took Meg into his arms. He lowered his head and pressed his lips tenderly against hers.

After a few moments, Jon said, "I love you so much, Meg. I'm sorry I had such a hard time expressing this. It shouldn't have taken two near disasters to bring me to my senses."

"Jon, I understand. Julie was such a wonderful person. She would want this. You know she would want this."

"I know. She loved me, and she loved you too. She would be so happy to know we have found one another."

They kissed again, and then Meg insisted she had better go to her bed and get some sleep.

"Good night, Jon Davenport. I'm so glad you're home safe."

"Good night, Meg Freeman. There's no one I'd rather come home to than you."

****

During the night, Jon was awakened by a blood-curdling scream coming from Meg's room. Grabbing his pistol from the bed stand, he leapt from his bed, ran into Meg's room. He recognized immediately that she was having a nightmare. After laying his pistol on the chair, he gently shook Meg's shoulders and called her name. Screaming, she rose up in the dark and punched Jon square in the face.

Jon grabbed her hands. "Meg, Meg. It's me, honey. It's okay. It's just me."

Meg fell into Jon's arms sobbing. "Oh, Jon. I'm sorry. I thought…I thought you were…I punched you didn't I?"

"I'm fine, sweetheart. Let's go back to sleep."

Meg laid her head back on the pillow while Jon pulled the blankets back over her body. He moved a stray strand of hair out of her face and kissed her. He stayed with her for another ten minutes before he eased back to his room.

The following morning, Jon slipped out of his bed and padded down the stairs, being careful not to make a noise that might awaken Meg.

"Good morning, Jon," Judy said. "Would you like some breakfast?" Her eyes widened when she saw Jon's face. "Good heavens. What happened to your eye?"

"Meg had a nightmare and thought I was Philippe. She's got quite a hook. I'll wait on Meg for breakfast, but I would like some coffee."

Jon took his coffee into the family room and opened up the morning newspaper. He still liked to hold a newspaper in his hands as opposed to just reading the news off the Internet. He saw where Governor Johnson was ahead in the polls, and Jon was thrilled to see that his father-in-law might very well be the next President. He wondered if Randall would still be considered his father-in-law if he and Meg got married. He couldn't believe the thought of getting married just entered his mind, but it felt very comfortable being there.

He remembered the fund-raiser dinner he was supposed to host on the twenty-fourth. All of the plans had been made by his assistant, Sarah, and she had told him before he flew out for the Bahamas that all he had to do was show up. He got out of his chair and walked back into the kitchen.

"Judy, has Sarah gotten with you on the plans for the dinner we're supposed to have here in a few weeks?"

"As a matter of fact, we spent some time last week planning some of the final details of the evening. I had one of your cows slaughtered plus we'll be slow-cooking a whole pig over a pit. We thought the backyard would provide the most scenic view for the evening; although, the front yard would be beautiful too. I think everything is set up. The greatest complication of the evening has more to do with security than with the dinner."

"That sounds perfect. I'm sure Randall's security team will have all of that handled. Maybe Meg and Ann could take their trip to Spain but plan to be back at least by the Friday before the dinner. That would give them some time away, not to mention they could make some headway on our next adventure."

"You still haven't told me all about your discovery, Jon. Are you going to keep that from me?"

"Judy, you know I can't keep secrets from you. What I'm about to tell you stays just between me, you, Meg, and Ann."

"Have I ever been prone to gossip in the years you've known me?"

"Of course not. You know that we mentioned to Ann an idea about searching for sunken treasure. We told Ann we had done some reading on Spanish galleons that sunk in the Bahamas."

"Yes, I remember that."

"Meg and I think we have discovered a sunken ship. Well…maybe. We didn't find the ship, but we found some gold and a jewel studded dagger from it. We plan to go back to dive the area. I'm going to purchase a dive boat that's more fitting for the project, and we'll see what we come up with. We just don't know for sure the name of the sunken ship or whether or not it's worth finding."

"That sounds incredible. It sounds exciting, but you know I'm too old to work on a treasure boat. Besides that, I already work for you."

"Well, I was thinking we would need help keeping our base of operations up and running. I've thought about making our base at a home just north of George Town on Great Exuma Island. There's a nice house there on a bluff overlooking a small bay."

"I'm going to guess that's the house that Meg was showing me and Ann the other night on the Internet."

"I would not be surprised," Jon agreed. "The shipwreck happened somewhere not too far offshore. It's possible we can stay onshore most nights while working the wreck site, assuming there is a wreck site. You could take care of us, prepare meals, and keep things running in your ever efficient manner."

"That would be most enjoyable," Judy said. "I suppose Roger can keep watch over the ranch while we're gone."

"Yes. Roger would have no problem with that. I'm sure."

Jon looked up as the top stair creaked. Meg looked like an angel standing there in her jeans and tee-shirt. He was positive angels could wear jeans.

CHAPTER SIX

A Morning Surprise

"Good morning, sunshine," Jon said. "How did you sleep?"

"I slept great, but I feel like I've been run over by a steam roller. Oh, Jon…your face. Did I do that?"

"It's no big deal, though it will make me think twice about getting in a fight with you."

Meg grimaced as she came down the stairs and touched Jon tenderly on the side of his face.

Jon took hold of Meg's hand and kissed her. "I'm sure the events of last night have nothing to do with you feeling rough this morning. I must say that while you may feel like you've been run over by a steam roller, you look like you just stepped off the front page of Cosmopolitan."

"Oh, brother. Give me a break. Flattery, however, might be a good move for you this morning."

"I didn't realize I was making a move."

"Hey, Judy," Meg said, ignoring Jon's faux pitiful look. "How are you feeling?"

"I feel fine. I was just about to go into the kitchen to put together some breakfast."

"That sounds good," Meg replied. "I'm starving. I need to go home at some point today. I can't just keep hanging out here like I'm on vacation or something."

"Why not?" Jon asked with a smile. "You're welcome to stay as long as you like."

"Maybe we should try to date like normal people do," Meg replied with a grin.

"Who wants to be normal?"

Meg knew the day would be busy for Jon, so after breakfast she grabbed her purse and headed toward the kitchen door. Jon followed her outside to her little Honda.

"I'm going to get your car back to you tonight," Meg sighed. "I'm so sorry I lost your key, but I will find it today."

"That's not necessary. I can get another key from the dealership."

"No. I insist on taking care of this myself."

"Yes, ma'am. I won't get in the way of a determined woman."

Meg looked up at Jon as her stomach felt like the butterfly house at Callaway Gardens. She seemed to be acting more like a middle schooler than a thirty-two year old widow. As Meg's heart beat madly in her chest, Jon leaned down and placed his soft lips on hers.

He stood up straight and looked into her eyes. "I'll see you tonight. You are coming back, aren't you?"

"I'll think about it," Meg answered coyly.

Almost an hour later, Meg was crawling around the shrubbery in front of Ann's apartment. The bushes were thick, and she knew that if she ever found the key, it would be a miracle.

After almost two hours of searching, Meg sat still in the dirt and leaned against the apartment building. The sun was hot by now as dirty sweat ran down her face. She picked up a small stick and threw it across the yard toward the parking area. Dropping this key had been one of the dumbest things she had ever done. *Well, maybe not the dumbest thing. I've done plenty of worse things.* Meg decided that a little break would help her gain a better perspective.

Meg had a key to Ann's apartment, so she went inside and helped herself to a drink from the refrigerator. Reviewing the events of the morning, she sat down at the kitchen table. During breakfast, Jon had said that he was going to go to his office for the first time in several months to see if he could actually work a while. Meg remembered seeing Judy smile. This was evidently a big step of progress for Jon.

He said that he also planned to stop by his friend's jewelry store to see if he could get Rita's opinion on some of the jewelry they had found under the floor of his boat. It irritated Meg that Jon insisted that the jewelry was hers. It was no more her jewelry than his Mercedes sports car was her car. She knew that she would somehow have to refuse the whole jewelry box.

She hated to return to the task at hand, but she was positive that the key was not in the apartment. With a wistful look, she pulled the apartment door behind her and headed back for the bushes.

****

As Jon stepped out of the truck in front of his house several hours later, Meg walked toward him with a triumphant smile. The key fob dangled from her outstretched hand.

"So you found it? You're amazing."

"When I set my mind to something, I'm pretty determined to see it through."

"I can tell. How long did you look for it?"

"I found it close to 3:00, so I must have spent about four hours looking for it."

"I could have bought a new one for $200. Was it worth spending your day crawling around in bushes?"

"Yes it was," Meg grinned. "I learned a lot about worms, ants, and spiders."

"As long as your day was profitable, that's all that matters" Jon chuckled.

Jon put his arm around Meg as they walked into the house for dinner. Judy welcomed them, and the three sat down to a wonderful meal. Meg couldn't help but feel like they were a little family. She also acknowledged to herself that she could get used to having someone like Judy prepare dinner for her every evening. After dinner and conversation, Jon convinced Meg to spend another night in the guest room. She still had clothes upstairs so there was no excuse she could think of to say no.

Long before sunrise the next morning, Meg was awakened by a light knock on the door.

"Just a minute," Meg called from the bed, still half asleep.

Jon said through the closed door, "I have a wonderful surprise for you today. Get dressed, and meet me downstairs."

"What is it?" Meg yawned as she came fully awake. She felt both excited and annoyed at the same time.

"Get dressed, and I'll show you. If I told you, it wouldn't be a surprise anymore."

"It's not even daylight," Meg protested.

"I know. That's part of the surprise," Jon laughed.

Meg groaned as she slid out of bed and tried to imagine what in the world Jon had on his mind. The single thing on her mind was more sleep. She rummaged through her clean clothes to find a pair of jeans. This was her last clean pair, so she was going to have to go home today to wash clothes. As Meg walked into the kitchen, Jon opened the door, and they strolled through the cool morning darkness. Jon's hand was large and warm, but Meg felt like his heart was even warmer.

The stars were bright and the moon was full. Meg had to admit that even though she had wanted to stay in bed, the cool morning air was refreshing. Everything was still and quiet. She couldn't even hear a single bird chirping. Because Meg lived in a busy little neighborhood in an Atlanta suburb, she wasn't used to such stillness.

Jon led Meg to the barn where Roger met them. It was apparent that Jon had made arrangements with Roger to prepare the horses for a morning ride because he had two horses saddled up and ready to go. She saw that Roger was a thin, wiry man of about fifty and had a nervous tick in his right eye.

"Meg, this is my good friend, Roger. He helps us out around here a lot. I don't know what I would do without him. Roger, this is Meg Freeman."

Meg reached out to shake Roger's hand. "It's a pleasure to meet you, Roger."

"The pleasure is all mine, ma'am."

"Have you ridden horses much?" Jon asked.

"No," Meg answered. "The truth is I'm scared of them."

"You won't be afraid of Angel. She's as sweet as they come," Roger said.

Jon helped Meg climb onto Angel's back before stepping into the saddle of his own mount.

"This is Midnight," Jon said. "I've had her since she was a filly, and she has grown into a wonderful horse. She may have more spunk than you would like, but I love her. I want to show you something enchanting."

"Enchanting? Won't these horses stumble around? There's no light for them to see."

"The horses don't need the light. These animals would know the trails around here with their eyes closed."

Jon led Meg out of the barn, and they rode across the pasture and up a trail on their horses. At first, she held tightly to the horn of the saddle because she felt like she would fall off of the horse. After a short time, she relaxed a bit and held the reins loosely in her hands. Angel was a gentle horse, which helped Meg to relax and enjoy the ride.

The trail climbed to the highest part of Jon's property and came out on a clearing that offered an impressive view of the valley below. Though this was a small mountain, Meg was sure the view would be breathtaking, especially at sunrise.

Jon helped Meg down from Angel as daylight started creeping across the sprawling ranch below. He held her in his arms as they watched the sun pop up over the distant mountains. As light flooded the valley below, the colors came to life, filling Meg with amazement and awe. It was more beautiful than a Fourth of July fireworks show. Over the next several minutes, the trees turned from a dark, indistinguishable mass to a brilliant green and red.

"This is so beautiful," Meg said.

"Yes, but you are more beautiful," Jon said as he leaned down to kiss her welcoming mouth. He knelt down on the ground, and held Meg's hands. "I love you, Meg Freeman, with all of my heart. I would be the happiest man in the world if you would agree to be my wife."

Meg stood speechless, unable to breathe. Looking down at this dear man kneeling before her, her eyes began to fill with tears. Shocked, she stood still with her mouth open.

Chapter Seven

Forever Is a Long Time

"Oh, yes, Jon! A thousand times, yes!"

Jon stood and pulled Meg into his arms. He kissed her before pulling back to wipe away a tear as it descended down her flushed cheeks. Jon slid a beautiful diamond ring onto her finger where her wedding band had once been.

"I want to marry you as soon as possible," Jon whispered.

"I can't wait," Meg said. "I'll be the happiest woman in the world as long as you are my husband."

They held one another for a long time as the sun crept above the distant mountains. Meg could hear Jon's heart beating and decided his heartbeat was the most peaceful sound in the world.

She held his face in her hands. "I've got to tell Judy and Ann. They'll be so happy!"

Jon helped Meg remount before he climbed on the back of Midnight. They plodded back down the mountain toward the barn, though Meg felt as if she was floating.

A doe and two fawns ran across the trail in front of the two horses and gave Meg such a start that she almost fell from the back of Angel. She regained her balance and saw that the forest was beginning to come alive with birds and wildlife. She thought about how she, too, had come to life through the love of Jon Davenport. She noticed for the first time the beautiful wild flowers growing along the trail, and the morning air was fragrant with the delightful smell of the forest.

As they returned to the barn, Roger took the reins from Meg as she dismounted. They walked toward the kitchen door arm in arm and found Judy in the kitchen where she toiled over breakfast.

Meg beamed before kissing Judy on her cheek. "Judy, we have some pretty incredible news."

Judy laid her dishtowel across the back of the chair with an expectant look. Meg held out her left hand so Judy could see the ring that glistened in the light of the morning sun coming through the window. Jon placed his arm around Meg's waist and pulled her against his body.

"Oh, Meg and Jon! I am so very happy for you. I was so hoping you two would finally realize you were meant for each other."

"I think we have loved each other for a long time," Meg acknowledged. "Now, I'll be the happiest woman in the world as Jon's wife."

"I'll be the happiest man," Jon replied. "Not only am I the happiest man, but I am also the hungriest man."

"Well," Judy laughed, "you have come to the right place. Sit down in the dining room so I can serve you both breakfast."

After eating, Jon leaned back in his chair with a cup of coffee. "I've got something else important to talk with you about. Why don't we refill our coffee cups and go into the family room?"

"My, that sounds scary," Meg said with half a smile.

"I guess it could be. It depends on how you like crowds."

That piqued Meg's interest and made her a bit nervous. She was not a real fan of crowds, but she had no idea what was on Jon's mind. The three of them refilled their cups from the kitchen, and Jon poured a little cream into Meg's cup. She smiled up at him, pleased that he remembered.

"Why don't we sit on the front porch swing instead?" Meg suggested. "It is such a beautiful morning."

"Sounds good to me," Jon replied.

"Do you need me for this conversation?" Judy asked.

"You already know all about it. I just need to fill Meg in on our dinner plans."

Judy set her coffee cup on the counter near the sink. "I think I'll start on dishes. Just let me know if there's anything new I need to consider."

After sitting down on the swing, Jon pushed with his foot to get the swing moving a little. He said, "There's something pretty important I forgot to tell you. The truth is I forgot about it myself until yesterday."

Meg leaned back in the swing and crossed her arms across her chest, being careful not to spill her coffee. "Now you are making me nervous."

"Well, I had a great idea on how to announce to the world that you are the love of my life and that we plan to get married."

"How is that Dr. Davenport?"

"I am hosting a fund-raiser dinner for my father-in-law on the twenty-fourth of this month. I would love for you to host it with me so we could announce to our guests at some point that we plan to be married."

"You've got to be kidding," Meg gasped. "How many people are going to be there? Are these like famous, rich important people?"

"Famous, maybe. Rich, yes. Important, some of them. I can't think of a more appropriate place to introduce the most beautiful woman in the world who will soon be my wife."

"What would I have to do?" Meg asked.

"Nothing but stand beside me and look beautiful."

"That might be a problem."

"So you have a problem with standing beside me?" Jon asked playfully.

"No, I have a problem looking beautiful."

"It is obvious that your mirror is broken. You will be amazing. We can greet our guests, and before I introduce Governor Johnson, I will introduce you. It will be a memorable night."

"I'm sure it will be memorable because everyone will see me die of fright."

"You will be just fine. I'll be right there holding onto you."

"If you say so. I'm getting nervous just thinking about it."

"You will be wonderful. My assistant, Sarah, and Judy are taking care of everything. They have some people who will be preparing the meal, setting up tents, and bringing in the chairs. We just have to show up to greet everyone."

"Okay," Meg mumbled. "I won't be able to eat all day without throwing up, but I'll be a good sport. I'm going to be out of my mind with nervousness until then."

"You'll be just fine," Jon encouraged. "I thought of a way to get your mind off of it between now and then. Why don't you and Ann go shopping for clothes for the dinner as soon as you can? I thought it would be nice for her to come to the event, if she would like. Then, maybe you could leave for Seville to The General Archive of the Indies on Saturday."

"That sounds wonderful," Meg exclaimed. "I am anxious to get started on our project, but I don't want to leave you."

"I don't know if I will be able to stand it either, but it will only be for a few days—a week at the most."

"It sounds like a wonderful trip."

"Okay. It's settled," Jon smiled.

"So, when do you want to get married?" Meg changed the subject.

"How about today?" Jon said seriously.

"We can't do that." Meg answered with surprise. "We need to make it special, and besides that, you have to announce it to all of the VIPs at the dinner. Remember? On top of that, I'm sure there are a few people who would like to attend our wedding. My mother would like to come. My sister and her family would want to be there as well."

"Okay," Jon said, looking at the calendar on his phone. "Today is September sixth. How about October twentieth? What do you think of that?"

"We can't get married that soon. That's not enough time to plan."

"Why not? What do you have to plan? It seems to me that as long as you have a dress and we have a place to get married, we're fine. Oh, I guess we need a minister to marry us too."

"Jon, that's crazy. That's less than two months."

"It just means you won't have as long to worry. It's not like we have this huge guest list. Let's take our family to some beautiful location and get married. We'll pay other people to do the worrying for us."

"Well," she hesitated for a moment before a smile covered her face. "Why not?"

"And you're still okay with going to Spain?"

"As long as we've got some of the details worked out for the wedding, we could go. I'm sure we'll still have plenty to do when we get back.

"You'll have time."

"I guess. I'll have no idea about what to do at the archives."

"I can have someone meet you there who can help you get started searching through the stacks of documents. You don't get a doctorate in history without developing a few contacts. The archives for that era are disorganized, not to mention they are written in what is almost code. It is Spanish, but sometimes it's hard to figure out. I read once that documents that old were housed in the basement in stacks that may or may not be in chronological order. It may take you a week or more just to get started."

"It sounds tedious, but I'm sure it will be exciting. I think Ann only has a week of vacation she can devote to it. She needs to leave some days for the wedding."

"A week should be adequate. If it's not, we can go back later. It's very important that no one know what you're doing. Why don't you call Ann to make sure she can go next week?"

"Okay. I'll call her right now. She's at work, but she might be free to talk to me. I can see if she can make arrangements to leave on Saturday."

Jon continued, "Make sure Ann knows that I insist on paying all of her expenses. Tell her that is my cost of doing business."

Meg leapt off the swing with such enthusiasm that a little coffee sloshed out of Jon's cup into his lap.

"Oh, I'm so sorry. I guess I need to be more careful with my excitement."

"I'm glad you're excited. I'm fine."

Meg hurried for her phone while Jon continued to enjoy the coolness of the morning. She spoke with Ann, who seemed to be real excited about the idea.

The screen door creaked as Meg stepped back onto the porch, followed by Judy. "I'm going to meet Ann this afternoon for an evening of shopping. I've got to buy some clothes to impress your famous friends. Judy, we're going to be eating out tonight."

"I think what's in the clothes will impress Jon's important friends," Judy said with a smile. "You two have fun. I'll take care of your man in the meantime."

Meg and Jon strolled hand in hand toward the garage before Meg stopped abruptly. "I didn't drive my car here. Remember? Your car was at Ann's apartment. I don't have a way to get home."

"That's not a problem," Jon smiled. "You can drive my car."

"Jon, I can't do that. It's...it's not right. You might..."

"Meg," Jon interrupted. "It is right. You can just drive it from now on. I know you're worried about what people will think, but I don't care what people think. I love you and you're going to be my wife."

"I love driving your car, Jon, but I think that it's best for me to drive my own car for now. This is all happening so fast."

"Whatever you want to do, sweetheart. I have a meeting this morning, so I'll get Roger to take you home. You know, you can be a stubborn woman."

Meg smiled up at Jon. "That's one of my finer traits."

Jon pulled out his cell phone and called Roger while they walked toward the garage. He opened the door of the work truck for Meg and pulled her into his arms. Jon kissed her with tenderness and enjoyed her sweet taste and the faint smell of her perfume. He held the door open so she could get in the truck. Roger opened the driver's side door and climbed behind the wheel.

Meg looked up at Jon. "I have no idea what time we'll be done."

"Why don't you give me a call to let me know when you're heading home?"

"I'll do that. You know, I should go back to my house tonight," Meg said. "People are going to start talking."

"People?" Jon challenged. "Who's worried about people? The truth is I knew you were going to say that. I've enjoyed you being in my house and wish you would stay."

"We'll be together forever soon," Meg maintained as she reached up to touch Jon's face.

"I'll call you tonight, Jon."

"Let's meet for dinner tomorrow night."

"Are you asking me out on a date?"

"Yes, ma'am, Mrs. Freeman."

"Then I accept. I don't know if I can stand being away from you until then."

"You don't have to stay away," Jon grinned devilishly.

"Absence makes the heart grow fonder," Meg said before the truck pulled away.

As Meg watched Roger steer down the winding driveway, she breathed a prayer of thanks for Jon Davenport.

CHAPTER EIGHT

Friends in Spain

"I can't believe we are headed for Spain," Ann exclaimed, giddy with excitement.

Meg reached behind her to find the seatbelt. "We better start by buckling our seatbelts. That flight attendant looks like Attila the Hun's sister. I don't think I want to mess with her."

"Give me a break, Meg. You're like a super hero."

Meg groaned as she buckled her own belt. "Yeah right. I'm more like Lucy Carmichael."

"Lucy Carmichael? Oh, you mean like *I Love Lucy*? The show?"

"Come on, Ann," Meg punched her arm, "everyone knows who Lucy Carmichael is."

"You're a lot older than me," Ann grinned. "I think that was before my time."

"I'm like…eight months older than you. It was before my time, too."

"Lucy Carmichael or not, let's just say that since you're like a CIA agent, I feel a lot safer being with you."

"Ann, I told you that I had nothing to do with the CIA. It was Homeland Security."

"Whatever. We're going to have such a blast. Isn't it amazing that one of Jon's former classmates is living in Seville with her husband? Didn't Jon say Cindy is like an expert on ancient Spanish documents?"

Meg reclined her seat a little. "She speaks at least five languages and has a PhD in something to do with ancient Spanish history. It's a good thing because I sure don't have a clue what to do."

The two women talked and laughed as their flight took off for Miami in the early Saturday morning hours. Though Meg had planned to read some on shipwrecks in the Caribbean, she and Ann spent the two-hour flight to Miami talking about her upcoming wedding.

Once the plane left from Miami, Ann leaned over toward Meg. "You do realize we are going to be wiped out by the time we get to Seville."

"True. We won't get to Seville until tomorrow morning, but they're six hours ahead of us."

Ann paused to request a cup of coffee from the airline attendant. "I doubt we'll be good for much research tomorrow. At least flying first class gives us a little more room to stretch out, but we're still going to be exhausted."

"You're right. We're not going to get there in time to search the archives anyway because it closes at 2:00 on Sundays. We can get some rest before meeting with Cindy for an early dinner. She'll go over the whole strategy with us so we can make the best use of our time there. Cindy says there's a pretty strong learning curve, but she can give us some pointers that will at least get us going on Monday. You're Spanish is pretty good isn't it?"

"Meg, you know I studied Spanish in high school and college. I also spent a summer in Mexico City after my junior year at Georgia."

"I remember. I was supposed to have gone with you, but I was too in love–or so I thought. My nanny taught me Spanish when I was a kid. She was from Guatemala. I also dated a guy from Columbia for almost a year during high school. We spoke Spanish together most of the time."

"Oh, yeah. I had forgotten about him. His name was…Domingo. Right?"

Meg pulled some books and notepads out of her tote bag. "You've got a great memory, Ann. Let's see how well it works on Spanish history. I brought books for us to read on 17th century Spanish galleons. I was amazed that I found something so specific."

"Yes, ma'am professor Meg. All kidding aside, you're right. We do need to get on task."

The two settled into their reading. Meg picked *The Spanish Treasure Fleets* for her book and was soon lost in the history of the ships of Spain. The plane was somewhere over the Atlantic by the time the two began discussing their books. While they learned a lot about Spanish ships, there was very little in the books about doing research. They would enter the archives as total novices, but each agreed to give it their best shot.

Almost twenty-four hours later, the two women dragged themselves off the Iberian airline exhausted and ready for a shower. Arriving at baggage claim, they were surprised to see a handsome man holding a bouquet of flowers with a sign that read "Meg Freeman."

Meg said to him, "I'm not sure who you are, but it's a little odd that you are holding a sign with my name on it."

The man's English was perfect with a mild Spanish accent that Meg knew Ann would find quite sexy. "Yes, ma'am. My name is Jose, and I will drive you to your hotel."

"How did you know we were coming?" Meg asked, though she was sure of the answer before it came from his lips.

"Senior Jon has made arrangements. He said I was to give these flowers to you."

"Is that a fact?" Meg grinned. "Did he say anything else?"

"Yes." Jose said with a big smile. "He said that if I kissed you, he would kill me."

Meg smiled as she took the beautiful bouquet of daisies, her favorite flower. Jose took the ladies' bags and headed to a black limousine parked at the curb. About thirty minutes later, the limo pulled up the tree-lined drive of the Gran Melia Colon.

"Excuse me, Jose. We have reservations at the Gran Hotel Lar close to Casa de la Memoria de Al-Andalus. This is beautiful, but way out of our price range."

"Senior Jon said that two beautiful women must stay in the beautiful Gran Melia Colon. Your reservations at the Gran Hotel Lar are canceled."

"I can't believe it," Ann said in awe as they pulled up to the front entrance. "I've never stayed in a hotel as nice as this in my life. I'm not sure I'll know how to act."

Jose stepped out of the driver's side of the car and popped open the trunk. An attendant was waiting with a cart for the luggage.

"Miss Meg, here is a cell phone that has been programmed for your use while you are here. My number is speed dial 1. When you need to go somewhere, you call me and I will pick you up. Enjoy your stay. Oh, yes, Mrs. Cindy is speed dial 2. Goodbye. Get some rest."

Meg and Ann were taken through the opulent lobby of the Gran Melia where they both stopped and gaped at the beauty of the paintings hanging on the wall.

"I feel like we're in an art gallery," Ann whispered. "Every one of these pictures go from the floor to the ceiling. They're beautiful."

Meg wanted to walk up the winding staircase, but the attendant took them to an elevator located in the corner of the lobby. Both women later agreed that they felt as if the attendant was more of a tour guide than a bellhop.

"Is this your first time to the Gran Melia Colon?" he asked in perfect English.

Meg figured their dumbfounded expressions should have made that clear, but she answered. "Yes, this is our first time. It is so beautiful."

"Thank you, ma'am," the attendant replied. "Our furniture comes from famous designers such as Philippe Starck and Marcel Wanders. We are very proud of them. The Gran Melia Colon is one of the most notable pieces of architecture in Seville, and many famous people stay here from all over the world. Just last week Clint Eastwood was here with his wife. You will be staying in a suite on the top floor that has been prepared just for you."

The two friends just looked at one another feeling like kids in a candy store. This was all like a fairy tale to Meg. The elevator doors opened to a long hallway lined with doors. It, too, looked like something in a magazine. Meg almost strained her neck as she allowed her eyes to follow the walls up to the tall ceilings. The crystal chandeliers sent tiny rainbows of light up and down the walls.

The attendant opened the door to their room, and Meg gasped at the beauty that was before her. The living area was impeccable–furnished with beautiful leather furniture. It offered every modern amenity imaginable. Meg tried to act dignified but was having a hard time containing her surprise. There were vases of roses all over the suite.

"Miss Meg, the roses are from Senior Jon. He sends his love. If you need anything, my name is Rodrigo, and I will be happy to serve you."

Meg reached in her purse to tip the man, but she had no idea how much she should give him.

"You need not tip me, ma'am," Rodrigo said. "That has been taken care of. If you need anything, just call the desk."

With that, Meg and Ann were left alone in the most elegant hotel room they had ever seen. They opened the doors to the balcony and were stunned by the incredible view of old Seville. On one side of the balcony was a whirlpool that seemed to call Meg's name, but she knew that responding to that call would have to wait until later.

"Look at this," Ann said as she read from a card on the coffee table. "They have a spa up on the roof, and we are invited to be their guests as often as we like. We are just to make an appointment ahead of time."

"This is unbelievable. Jon should not have done this. There is no telling what this costs, not to mention that walking out of a place like this puts a target on our backs. If I were a thief, I'd be camping out across the street from this place looking for some chick to knock off."

Ann nodded. "True, but Jose will be meeting us at the door every day, and I think he looks like he could handle anyone wanting to hurt us. I could tell by the way he carried himself that he must be ex-military. I thought he was kind of cute."

"Kind of?" Meg raised an eyebrow. "Remember we're here on business. I don't want to see you being swept off your feet by some Spanish commando taxi driver."

"A girl can have some fun, can't she?" Ann teased.

"Oh, brother," Meg responded. "You better go take a cold shower. I'll get my shower when you're done."

"Look at this," Ann said as she walked into the master bedroom. "You don't have to wait. You have your own private bathroom. It looks like your sweetie is spending all of his gold."

"This is over the top. He should not have done this."

"Oh, Meg. Enjoy it. It's his way of saying 'I love you' from thousands of miles away."

"It is sweet, and you better get your shower," Meg said as she shoved Ann toward her room. We have time for a little nap before meeting Cindy. Why don't we plan to leave at about 2:30? I could use some sleep."

"Yeah, me too," Ann agreed. "I'll see you in a bit."

When Ann closed the door to her room to shower, Meg picked up her cell phone to call Jon.

"Hey, sweetie," Meg said into the phone as soon as she heard Jon's voice. "What are you thinking? You're treating me like the Queen of England."

"You are my queen," Jon said, "and I love you so much. I wanted to pamper you."

"You are unbelievable," Meg answered. "I don't deserve being loved like this. I would have been fine at the Days Inn or even the local roach hotel."

"I don't know about that," Jon said with a smile in his voice. "It is obvious you've never seen Spanish roaches."

"Well, I just called to tell you we're here and that I love you. I miss you so much. I wish you could have come."

"It would have been fun," Jon agreed, "but this time with Ann will be special. Be safe and call me tomorrow after your experience at the Archives. If you call me at about 10 p.m. over there it will be 4:00 here. That will be perfect."

"Okay," Meg said. "I'll call you tomorrow. I love you, Jon. Thanks for everything."

Three hours later, Meg jerked awake not knowing where she was. She looked around the room before it all started coming back to her. She had to make sure Ann was up because they were to meet Cindy in less than an hour.

"Ann, get up. We're going to be late. We're supposed to meet Cindy at 3:00, and I don't even know how to get to the Restaurante Santa Cruz."

"You don't have to know how to get there," Ann groaned. "Senior Jose can get us there. Remember? He's like our chauffer, tour guide, and body guard all wrapped up in one. You've got to admit that he is a gorgeous body guard."

"He is indeed, but I didn't notice. I'm too enamored with Jon."

"Right. Too late. You've already said he's cute."

Meg and Ann hurried through the beautiful foyer to find their limousine parked just outside the front door. Jose waved before he opened the back door. They drove through the old town, and Meg noted how many one-way streets they had to maneuver. The two women rushed through the front door of the restaurant with three minutes to spare. As they walked in, they saw a short, but pretty forty-something year old woman waving to them from a nearby table.

"You must be Cindy," Meg said as they approached the table.

"And you must be Meg. It is a pleasure to meet you."

"This is my friend Ann. We've been through a lot together, and now we want to learn from you."

"I'm so thrilled you're here," Cindy said before lowering her voice a little. "It's best if we keep our talk general here in the restaurant because there are people around who are paid to be extra ears for news like that which I feel you must carry."

"What do you mean?" Ann asked.

"Discoveries like the one we will soon talk about create a lot of interest around certain places in town. There have even been people killed over such findings. We should keep our public conversations general and scholarly. We'll learn much that I'm sure will be most helpful for you. Does that make sense?"

"Yes, I understand," Ann said as she looked around the restaurant.

"You should begin now experimenting with Sevillian customs," Cindy told them. "You'll notice around the restaurant that a lot of the groups share a community dish. The locals refer to it as 'ir de tapeo,' which means 'bar hopping.' The idea is to eat small amounts from a lot of dishes. In our case, it means each of us should order a different dish, and we all share them. It's a fun way of being able to enjoy a lot of different tastes of Seville. You will see that when the waitress brings the dishes out, she'll give each of us clean plates. She'll assume we all want to share our meals"

"That sounds like a great idea," Meg said. "Could you help us with the menu? We both are pretty fluent in Spanish, but I don't recognize all of the dishes on this menu."

After studying the menu, the three ladies requested three different meals. Meg ordered gazpacho, while Ann stuck with the more familiar cod. Cindy's favorite was salmorejo, so she ordered a large bowl that could be shared among the three of them. True to form, the waitress brought out three clean plates and bowls. She placed the food in the middle of the table with large serving spoons in each dish.

"This is like eating family style back home," Meg noted. "I like it."

The three began enjoying their meal while getting to know one another. Half-way through the meal, Cindy was careful as she asked Meg a question with an obvious attempt to disguise her true interest.

"So you discovered some of the joys of the Caribbean during your recent visit?" Cindy asked.

"We had a wonderful time," Meg agreed. "It was in the Caribbean that Jon and I crossed paths again after five years. Needless to say, something very wonderful began happening between us. I think the circumstances helped move our relationship along a little faster than normal."

"Jon told me a little about that," Cindy said. "That must have been some frightening experience."

"You know, Cindy, looking back it is frightening, but as it all was happening, I wasn't that scared." Then Meg thought for a second before continuing. "The souvenirs we found around the reef drew our interest. We would love to know more about what we found. They're beautiful, especially one of them in particular."

"Did you bring them with you?" Cindy asked.

"No, but I have pictures of them on my iPhone," Meg answered. "I'll show you."

Pulling out her phone, Meg clicked on the photo app. Cindy looked casually at the pictures of the pieces of eight and the jewel studded dagger. Ann reached across to take the phone from Cindy.

"Oh my God," Ann said without thinking.

"It's obvious you haven't been to the beaches in the Caribbean," Meg shot back with a silencing stare.

Surely no one was listening in on their conversation, but if Cindy had concerns, then Meg knew they should be careful. Cindy took the phone back so she could take her time looking at each picture.

The ladies finished their meal before walking out together to the streets of Seville. Cindy confided that she had no doubt that the pictures on Meg's phone were indeed from the 17th century. Hopefully, they could discover something in the archives that would point them in the right direction.

"Are you familiar with the Jardines de las Reales Alcazares?" Cindy asked.

"The palace of the Kings?" Ann asked. "I can translate, but I have no idea what it is."

"It's just a few blocks south of here. Why don't we go see it? It has the largest late-medieval garden in Europe, and it is beautiful."

Ann placed her hand on her stomach. "That sounds like a great way to work off our lunch, or was that dinner?"

In her finest tour guide voice, Cindy said, "Peter the first ruled Spain from 1350 to 1369. His Alcazar garden was built upon Moorish remains and has typically eastern courtyards bounded by arcades that are sequestered behind high walls. I just read that in a tour guide."

"I was hoping you would speak to us in real English," Ann said with a grin.

Cindy smiled and continued. "The fact is that it is one of the most beautiful gardens in the world. In the sixteenth century, Charles the fifth renovated the gardens by applying some Renaissance features and creating a large labyrinth and a beautiful pavilion. My favorite time to come here is in the spring when the orange trees drop their fruit on the ground. It smells like marmalade. I think I gain weight every time I walk through the garden. A new garden was added in the twentieth century. It's all quite impressive."

"That sounds wonderful," Meg said. "I'd love to go."

After walking through the palace grounds for over an hour, Meg thought the gardens were amazing. It reminded her of Biltmore Gardens, back in North Carolina, on steroids. She invited Cindy back to the hotel so they could talk more freely in the privacy of their room. Once behind the closed door, Meg explained the whole story of their adventure in the Bahamas to Cindy and told her about the pieces of eight and the jewel studded dagger.

"We went back to the reef a second time and found the second piece of gold and the dagger. I'm thinking the dagger was the greatest find. I thought it might be the one thing we could trace."

"You're right, Meg. The dagger would be documented on any ship's manifest we might be able to find."

Ann had a quizzical look. "So if a ship went down and no one could find it, how would there be a manifest in the archive?"

"Well," Cindy answered, "Ships usually traveled in groups, and sometimes a copy of all the ships' manifests in an armada may have been carried on a different ship. If one ship of the armada sank, the other ships may have made the journey safely. The ships' manifests would all be collected together in a stack and filed away in the archives. We can hope that will be the case this time."

Meg yawned, covering her mouth at the last second. "I'm sorry. I'm exhausted."

"I suggest we get a good night's rest tonight because tomorrow is going to be quite long," Cindy said. "I'll meet you at the archives in the morning at 9:30. They open at 10:00."

"Okay, Cindy. We'll see you in the morning," Meg said.

CHAPTER NINE

Business Venture

After Meg and Ann left for Seville, Jon determined to work with his assistant, Sarah, to find a larger boat for their new treasure hunting business. Although he preferred using his yacht to get around the Bahamas, he knew that a larger vessel would be required for a real salvage operation.

He spent all morning searching Google for some clue as to what they would need in a salvage vessel. For one thing, this ship would need to be equipped with a crane as well as offer easy access in and out of the water for divers. Jon knew there would need to be room for the crew's quarters, and he wanted space for a lab.

Without giving thought to the fact that it was Saturday, Jon pulled out his cell phone to call Sarah. He was excited as he told her his idea of starting a salvage business in the Bahamas, but he was careful not to reveal anything about his discovery of gold.

"I've spent the morning looking at every research and recovery vessel you can imagine. I took a virtual tour of Jacques Cousteau's boat, and I've looked at every underwater salvage company's ship that was online–at least everyone I could find."

Jon heard one of Sarah's kids in the background. "Jon, I will be happy to help. I'm at Stone Mountain right now with Matt and the kids. As soon as I get home tonight, I'll get going on it."

"You can wait until Monday, Sarah. I was just so excited about it that I wasn't thinking about what day it is."

"I'm surprised you're spending your Saturday researching salvage businesses. I would have figured you would be spending the weekend with Meg. She seems like a sweet person. I'm so glad you brought her by the office."

"Thanks Sarah. She's gone out of town for a few days, so I was just killing a little time."

Sarah spent all day Monday doing research on salvage ships and what would be required for a successful venture. In doing so, she discovered a boat for sale that was a research vessel belonging to the National Underwater and Recovery Agency.

The thing that caught Sarah's attention about this ship was that it had been used in 1995 as a part of *The Sea Hunter* series to discover, remove, and conserve the *CSS H. L. Hunley*. The 171 foot salvage ship had been fitted with modern recovery equipment, including a special vacuum like the one Mel Fisher used in discovering the *Atocha*. Even though the ship was built in 1960, Russell had it overhauled in 1993.

Sarah also pointed out to Jon that the back of the ship was cleared and there was a good bit of flat space to be used for sorting through items brought up from the bottom. A two-man submarine came with the purchase and could also be stored on the foredeck.

Jon didn't make impulsive trips or spontaneous decisions, but Sarah informed him of this "golden opportunity" for a research vessel that just might work for his salvage expedition.

Jon instructed Sarah to make arrangements with Dr. Gerome Russell for him to tour the ship.

On Tuesday morning, after telling Don, his pilot, that he hoped to return in time to fly home before dinner, Jon walked from the jet and slid into the waiting rental car. Dr. Russell met him at the Miami Beach Marina where they climbed aboard a twenty-eight foot speedboat to head out to *The Discoverer*. Upon arrival, Russell guided Jon through the ship and explained in detail why he made the various choices about outfitting the vessel. He also reviewed some of the advantages of different pieces of equipment.

Jon was surprised at the amount of room in the ship. Below deck, there was approximately 150 feet of work space on one level that provided rooms and labs where artifacts could be processed. Several offices were also located on this level that could house as many as ten to fifteen employees of a small business. The lower level offered a living space for the crew. It even included an efficient, gourmet-like kitchen and dining area.

Jon especially liked the fact that a "master suite" was located on a level above the main deck that offered its occupants an open air view of the entire ship. There were two apartment type arrangements on this level, so Jon concluded the second one could be for the captain of the ship.

The main bridge was above the living quarters. The whole thing was quite impressive, and while it may not be the size of a small city, as some had said of aircraft carriers, he thought of it as the size of a country town.

Jon shared his dream with Dr. Russell about discovering Spanish galleons with the hope of not only recovering treasure, but also gaining historical knowledge about the men who sailed the ships. Russell asked Jon if he had any leads, and Jon acknowledged in confidence that he might at least know of a place to start.

After a great deal of conversation, Russell agreed to sell his ship with all the furnishings to Jon for his salvage project at a reduced price. The condition of the sale was that Jon had to allow NURA the opportunity to video the discovery with exclusive rights for a television and movie production. Jon agreed and pledged not only his current pursuit to Russell for NURA television opportunities, but also future discoveries as well.

Though Jon was ready to make the purchase, he asked Dr. Russell for a few days to think about the deal. He promised to have a decision within the week. He shook the scientist's hand and headed back to the airport to find Don.

****

Luis hung up the phone and turned to his new associate, Ricardo. "Okay, Ricardo. We need to do a little work. I know I heard the tall red-head say the word 'treasure.' Why would these two chicks be going to Spain?"

"Are you sure they were going to Spain?"

Luis cursed at being questioned. "Of course I'm sure. I watched them purchase tickets, and I got the agent to tell me where they were going."

"He told you where they were going?"

"Yeah. I told him I was the brunette's husband, and she was having an affair. I needed to catch the sleaze ball who was messing with my wife."

"I'm still amazed he told you."

"A one hundred dollar bill didn't hurt matters either."

"Give me some time to check out Seville," Ricardo said. "If their trip has something to do with treasure, I'll find out."

Luis thought about how fortunate he was to have run into Ricardo. It had been at least two years since they had worked together, but Luis knew the man was trustworthy. Not only was it good to have someone working with him, but Ricardo also had a dump of a house in the middle of Miami where Luis could hide out.

Ricardo was a large man with a round face who perspired continuously. Although he never made it past ninth grade, he had all the street smarts needed for survival in the jungle in which he lived. He had also become quite the computer whiz who was able to find anything on the Internet. He would be a good man to have on the team to help take down Davenport.

Luis walked back into the kitchen of the tiny rat hole he and Ricardo shared. At first, Luis had thought he should flee the country, but after more consideration, he realized the safest place to be was right under the noses of the authorities. After all, it was easy to get lost in a big city like Miami—especially if you were Cuban.

It had been sheer luck that Luis had spotted the hot, little American chica walking across the airport parking lot in Atlanta. He had thought the airport was the best place to steal a car so he could get away, and who do you suppose walked almost right in front of him?

Luis knew he should not have gone to Atlanta to join Philippe in the first place. Of course, Philippe had gotten impatient and decided to go out to the Davenports by himself, which resulted in disaster. After Luis discovered that Philippe had been caught, he hid out in the slums of downtown Atlanta for five days before deciding he needed to return to Miami.

He had to admit to himself that Philippe was right. This Meg woman provided quite the view. Maybe when all of this was over, he would at least have some one-on-one time with her before he killed her.

On a whim, Luis had followed the two women into the airport to see where they were going, and he discovered they were going to Seville. He had wondered why they would be going to Seville, and then he heard the word "treasure" as he stood near them, as inconspicuous as he could, in a coffee shop.

If Meg and her husband had discovered a sunken ship, all he would have to do would be to find out the exact location of the sunken ship. He could wait for the Davenports to bring up the treasure, and then he would kill them. The treasure would be all his. If this were a sunken Spanish galleon, he would have more money than his former boss, Alvaro Lopez, had ever even considered. Luis knew he had to be patient. Impatient people, like Philippe, make mistakes.

What a stupid fool Philippe was. He just couldn't let the girl go. It's a good thing he knows nothing about this pathetic joint. No one even knows I exist.

About an hour later, Ricardo walked into the kitchen holding several pages of printed type. "Your little chica may be onto something."

"She's not my chica, but what have you found?"

"If she has found treasure or if she is looking for treasure, I think she is in Seville to do research at the Archives of the Indies in *Casa Lonja de Mercaderes*. It seems that ancient documents about shipwrecks are stored in the Archives."

"Do we know anyone in Spain who could keep an eye on them?"

"I'm already on it. My cousin, Fernando, lives in Huelva. It's about an hour from Seville. I'll get him to follow the woman."

****

After some deliberation by phone with Dr. Russell, Jon agreed to accept the scientist's offer. The researcher also agreed to introduce Jon to a man who could captain his new ship, Captain David Buffington. Because *The Discoverer* needed to sail to Honduras to pick up a crane, Russell offered to pay for a trip to Honduras as a wedding gift to Jon and Meg on the condition they were willing to pick up the crane while they were there.

Jon had also decided to purchase the beautiful Bahamian home near Roker's Point on Great Exuma. He figured that it would make a great base of operations for their salvage company. The bay was deep enough for this new salvage ship, and there was plenty of room for expansion on the property surrounding the house.

"So, what now?" Sarah asked when Jon walked back through her office.

"I guess I just have to be patient and wait on Meg to get back. I'm not real good at being patient."

"I think the real Jon Davenport has returned," Sarah smiled. "Patience is a virtue. It's just not yours."

"I'm a patient man," Jon countered.

"You're patient about most things," Sarah admitted. "I'm just glad you're really back. I've missed the Dr. Jon Davenport we all love."

"Thanks, Sarah. It's good to be back. With this new idea, however, I may be gone a good bit."

"I'm excited for you. Just don't forget about us little people when you discover your gold."

"For starters, we're not sure if there's gold to be found. Secondly, you guys are my family. I could never forget you. I'm going to have to sign the paperwork when Meg gets back. I'm also going to close on the house near Roker's Point on Great Exuma."

"Why don't you meet Meg in Miami, take her to see her new house, and then give her the grand tour of your new ship?"

"Great idea. Do you think she'll kill me for buying the house without including her?"

"Well, let's see. You bought her a house that sits on a bluff overlooking the beautiful Bahamian waters that most people only dream about. If she's ticked with you for jumping the gun, I think she'll get over it."

CHAPTER TEN

Casa Lonja de Mercaderes

Meg and Ann arrived at the *Casa Lonja de Mercaderes* at 9:30 Monday morning. As expected, Cindy was there waiting on them. They went nearby to the Café de Indias for a cup of coffee and to wait on the archives to open.

Looking out the window of the coffee shop at the massive, square building, Meg was impressed with the size of the library that housed the historical documents. It took up more than a city block. At 10:00, they walked across the street to gain entrance to the Archives. Cindy didn't want to make it obvious that they were only interested in the basement, so she took her two friends on a tour of the place and concluded at the basement. It was fortunate that Cindy had full access to the Archives due to her professional affiliations. Most people could not just roam freely throughout the building.

Meg was shocked at the condition of the basement area containing these old documents. The newer documents upstairs were organized, but this basement area was damp and chaotic. Cindy explained that in many cases the stacks of material were in chronological order, but often times, people misplaced documents by putting them back in the wrong stacks. There was no clear system; therefore, finding a specific document was almost impossible.

"You just have to start reading through documents until you find the right one. You can assume the stacks to be in order, and thereby locate documents from a general area. Sometimes that will work, but a lot of times, it doesn't. Look at this paper, for example."

Meg and Ann looked over Cindy's shoulder. "It appears to be a historical description of some ship coming from Central America in 1648. You'll find all kinds of things in these stacks, and many of them will have no meaning for you. Sometimes, you can't even read the writing on the documents."

Meg felt overwhelmed. "How can we ever find anything of value?"

"We need to look for a ship's manifest containing pieces of eight and a jewel studded dagger. You will find plenty of pieces of eight listed on numerous manifests, but you might not find many, if any, daggers because the daggers may have been some sailor's personal treasure. We need to look for histories of ships that may have been lost around the western Caribbean. I know it seems impossible, but if it were easy, everyone would be doing it. Any questions?"

Meg and Ann just stood there shell shocked. This task seemed hopeless and Meg wondered what they had gotten themselves into.

Cindy seemed energized by the impossible task. "I suggest we each take different stacks. You can assume at first that it will all be chronological. If you seem to be stuck in an eighteenth century stack, move on to another one."

The three women began their tedious task. One by one they picked up pieces of paper and tried to make out the lettering on the document. Within an hour, Meg was exhausted and discouraged.

"How in the world do you do this all the time?" Meg wondered aloud. "If I had to do this every day, I think I would go insane."

"It can get pretty discouraging," Cindy admitted. "It's kind of like playing golf. You play twelve holes making three or four strokes above par on every hole. You decide you're going to quit and never play again, but on the thirteenth whole, you birdie the thing. In your excitement, you press on to finish the game."

Meg looked at Cindy in confusion. Because Meg didn't play golf, she was a little lost on the illustration. The word birdie was familiar, but she wasn't quite making the connection.

"After searching for hours," Cindy continued, "you will find a valuable nugget that will inspire you to stay the course. In your case, there could be millions of dollars riding on your discovery. It's worth the effort to continue."

Meg went back at it with renewed vigor hoping for a birdie, whatever that was. It didn't come until after their lunch break.

"Look at this," Ann said. "Here's what looks like a historical document about the Spanish Armada that attacked Sir Frances Drake off the coast of Panama. It seems that two of the ships later joined the *Terre Firma Armada* that carried gold from South America to Spain. One of the treasure ships, the *San Roque* was lost off the coast of Honduras."

"It carried the largest amount of treasure ever to be recorded on a Spanish galleon," Cindy reported. "I remember writing a paper on that ship when I was in graduate school. That treasure, or so the story goes, was rescued by slave divers and buried somewhere along the coast of Honduras. No one has ever found it."

"A second treasure ship of the armada, the *San Ambrosio*, was last seen somewhere east of the southern tip of Florida," Ann continued.

"None of the four ships containing the treasure ever made it back to Spain," Cindy said. "Let's make a note of *Terre Firma Armada* and do a little Internet research tonight. I'm thinking *San Ambrosio* was the smallest of the four ships, but it carried enough gold to total some 100 million dollars today. I wouldn't mind finding a scrawny little ship like that."

"I like the sound of that," Meg agreed. "Maybe the *San Ambrosio* is our ship."

"Don't get too excited," Ann warned. "There were numerous ships that went down, so it could be one of who knows how many. You know, an eighteenth century ship *could* have sunk carrying old gold from another time."

"Keep your eyes open for manifests," Cindy said. "If you found the manifest of *San Ambrosio*, and it included your dagger, then you might be onto something."

They spent the rest of the day reading barely decipherable Spanish scribbling. When the bell sounded at 3:55 indicating the archives would close in five minutes, the team felt they were no closer than when they had started that morning.

Meg continued to hold to the hope that it was the *San Ambrosio*, but she tried not to be too confident of that conclusion. Cindy invited her two friends to her home for dinner. She told them her husband was preparing a meal they would enjoy, and she made the suggestion that Ann invite Jose to join them. Ann jumped at the opportunity and pressed speed dial 1 on the cell phone. Meg was not surprised when Jose accepted the invitation. *Free meal. Beautiful woman. Why wouldn't he accept?*

During dinner, the three women were very careful to keep their discovery secret, but they did talk about the amazing beauty in Seville. While Jose seemed like a nice guy, they didn't know if they could trust him at this point. He shared some of his story that cleared up part of the mystery Meg and Ann had created from earlier conversations. He had once been a part of the Spanish navy and had served in what would be the equivalent of America's Navy Seals. Meg was quite impressed when she discovered he spoke five languages fluently.

Meg looked down at her watch and gasped at how late it was. She told everyone they needed to go. She was supposed to have called Jon an hour earlier and somehow the time had slipped right by. They hugged Cindy goodbye and thanked her husband for a wonderful meal.

When they were situated in the car, Meg sent Jon a text telling him she would call as soon as they returned to the hotel.

"So, you've been out clubbing I see," Jon later teased. "I was afraid the night life would pull you in."

"It is an amazing place, but it was Cindy's husband's cooking that pulled us in. We spent the evening at their house and got so engrossed in our conversation that time just flew by. Today was really something."

"Tell me about it. Did you have any success?"

"I don't know. It is a slow and tedious task. It will be a miracle if we get any leads. We found an interesting history about an armada carrying a lot of gold. All four of the treasure ships sank before getting back to Spain. One of them sank off the coast of Honduras. That was the one you and I read about in that book from the library at George Town. There was another ship in that armada called the *San Ambrosio*. Sources say it sank somewhere east of southern Florida. I'm not sure where the other two ships sank, but we know they never made it back to Spain. We are just getting started, but it was exciting to at least find a stack of documents that told of a ship sinking near our island."

"I think you're off to a great start. You're going to come back as a treasure ship expert."

The next two days went by with little fanfare. Cindy discovered a ship's manifest, but it appeared to be from the early 18th century, and the ship was never lost. She called her two friends over to study the manifest so they could at least see what one looked like.

Meg found additional histories that included more information about *San Ambrosio*. Although the *Ambrosio* was the smallest ship of the armada, it appeared she was loaded with gold. Meg seemed convinced that everything was pointing to the *San Ambrosio* as her ship.

****

Luis opened the door to Ricardo's bedroom. "Your cousin just called. He said he heard the tall redhead say something about the *Ambrosio*. He also said the two came out of the archives looking like they had just discovered something big. Could you do some research and let me know for sure if this is a sunken ship?"

A little while later, Ricardo came out of his room. "If it's the *Ambrosio*, they have discovered a seventeenth century Spanish treasure ship. It was the smallest ship in the *Terra Firme* armada, but even the smallest ship would have millions of dollars' worth of gold and silver."

"Millions?" Luis raised an eyebrow. "Now that gets my attention."

"There were seven ships in this armada, but only four of them were loaded with treasure: the *San Roque, Capitana;* the *Santo Domingo, Almiranta;* the *San Ambrosio;* and the *Nuestra Senora de Begona.* It seems the armada ran into a hurricane in 1606. One of the support ships made it back to Cartagena and two of them found shelter in Jamaica. The four treasure ships, however, were never seen again. Most historians think the *San Roque* sank near Honduras."

"Honduras?" Luis exclaimed in surprise. "That seems a little off course."

"It's said that the captain rescued the gold and silver from the sea, buried it, and sat on it for who knows how long while he waited to be rescued by another Spanish ship. Some people think he was rescued, and the gold from the *San Roque* was used to build *Basilica de la Virgen de los Desamparados* in Valencia. It is possible the *San Ambrosio,* made it to the waters just off the Exuma islands before sinking."

"Why do I feel like I'm sitting in a history class?"

"Well, boss. Something is going on. It will be worth keeping our eye on these women."

"I can think of a lot less pleasant things to keep my eyes on," Luis said with a sly smile. "Once we capture the treasure and kill the man, Meg will be mine. All mine! That is, she will be mine for as long as I want her. You can have the redhead."

"I like redheads," Ricardo said. "But if you are giving her to me, she must look like a dog."

"No, she is quite beautiful. She has a body any man would want and a pretty face. She will be a nice catch for you. I just want Meg. You might say we have a history together."

"Okay," Ricardo agreed. "Let's try to keep our minds on the treasure for now. We can think about women later."

Luis said, "If they are about to go into the salvage business, there is no way Lopez's Carver would work for a salvage boat."

"Lopez's Carver?" Ricardo questioned.

"Davenport ended up with Alvaro Lopez's yacht that had gold coins hidden under the floor. You know, I worked for him."

"Oh yes. I remember hearing the story."

"Why don't you look into recent boat purchases? I have a feeling our boy has bought another boat. If we can find that salvage ship, we can just set up shop nearby until we see them setting sail. We would not have to watch the airports."

"Good idea," Ricardo said. "I will do some asking around to see what I can learn."

Five days later, Ricardo discovered a small article in the Miami Herald about Dr. Gerome Russell and his salvage/research boat: *The Discoverer*. In the article, he mentioned his plans to sell his vessel to "a friend" for an undisclosed amount. When Ricardo showed the article to Luis, the two knew this had to be their target boat. After visiting the docks and seeing the ship, the two learned that Jon Davenport was to become the new owner.

With the money gained from eight robberies along the southern Florida coast, Luis and Ricardo rented a bait shop near the docks that included a small apartment in the rear of the store. They planned to make some money by doing legal business while keeping a close eye on *The Discoverer*.

****

The next day was filled with exhausting research that proved worthless. Meg figured the one valuable thing that came from the day was that they at least discovered where not to look. The highlight of her day would be her phone call to Jon. She reported everything about the day.

"Sounds like a dull day," Jon acknowledged.

"Well, Ann's day wasn't totally dull. Jose kissed her before leaving us for the evening. They barely know one another and he had the nerve to kiss her. He must really be a womanizer."

"Jose is quite the man," Jon said. "He is a decorated war hero and comes with the highest recommendations. He's not just a chauffeur. He's a bodyguard to some pretty high-up officials. I was only able to borrow him because the Princess of Asturias was out of the country with other guards."

"You mean Jose is the bodyguard of the Princess?" Meg said in shock. "That's pretty amazing."

"He's a superior soldier, Meg. He's an expert shot with both a rifle and a pistol. He's about as high up as you can go in several eastern fighting disciplines, not to mention he has two equivalents of our purple heart. You would never know it to talk to him."

"You're right about that. I had no idea. I thought he just drove a limousine."

After talking for an hour, they both agreed that Meg needed some sleep. Because of the time difference, it wasn't quite time for Jon to go to bed.

"I'll talk to you tomorrow," Meg said. "I'll be home in a few more days. I love you, Jon."

"I love you too, Meg. Sweet dreams."

They hung up the phone, and Meg crawled into her bed. A smile crossed her face as she imagined holding Jon in her arms.

CHAPTER ELEVEN

A Long Week

Ann and Meg were up early on Friday morning. They both awakened tired and dreading another day in what they had affectionately come to know as the dungeon. They dragged themselves to the hotel restaurant for breakfast and barely spoke a word while they ate.

"Let's get going," Ann quipped. "We don't want to be late to Mrs. Hitler's history class."

"Now Ann, you know Cindy's feelings would be so hurt if she heard you call her Mrs. Hitler."

"I don't think it would faze her, but you know I'm just kidding. We do need to get on down there. You never know; today could be the day."

They climbed into the familiar limousine and drove the two miles to the archives. Meg noticed that Ann had a hard time keeping her eyes off of Jose.

The two thanked Jose for the lift and told him they would give him a call when they were ready to be picked up. Cindy was in place as usual, ready to charge the gates. Meg spotted three guys against the building across the street, and figured they were laborers waiting to be hired. As on the previous mornings, the three ladies downed a cup of coffee at the café before crossing the street to the archive building at 10:00.

Just before lunch, Meg and Cindy heard Ann gasp, "Oh, my God. Oh, my God."

"What do you have?" Meg asked with growing excitement.

"Is this what I think it is? Cindy, I think I've got the manifest to the *Ambrosio*. We can't be sure because the first three letters are missing, but I'd be willing to bet on the first three letters being A, M, B. What do you think?"

Meg looked at the document. "I think you may be right."

Cindy scanned the document with great care. "It's a manifest all right."

"Do you see anything about a jeweled dagger?" Meg asked leaning toward the document.

"Let's see. No, there's nothing about a dagger, but you can see that there is supposed to be more than one page to this manifest. You can't know it for sure, but look how both columns go all the way to the bottom of the page, and this last comment has a comma beside the last word. There has to be more on another page."

Ann said, "Set it down and I'll take some pictures of it with my phone."

Cindy sat the page down on top of a black cloth she unfolded from her purse. Ann pulled out her iPhone and took several pictures. She reviewed her shots before returning her phone to her back pocket.

"We at least know what we might be looking for," Ann said. "If we could just find page two, we might know the name of our ship."

"Hey, I'm hungry," Meg said. "Let's take our lunch break. Besides that, I feel like my eyes are about to bug out of my head."

"Okay," Cindy agreed, "but let's keep it short. We wasted too much time yesterday."

The three ladies came out of the building arm-in-arm with a celebratory spirit obvious in their steps. Meg saw two of the same laborers across the street and decided the economy must be as bad in Spain as it was back home. They walked over three blocks to a little sidewalk café where Cindy ordered all of them rolls of ham and cheese on a plate with beans and rice.

After eating quickly, they headed back to the archives. Two hours later Meg felt if she didn't leave the dungeon soon, she was going to lose her mind.

"Hey, Meg," Ann whispered. "I've got to find a bathroom. I figure it will take me another hour to finish up this stack."

"I'm not feeling so good myself," Meg acknowledged, "so I'm looking forward to getting back to the hotel."

A few minutes later, Cindy found Meg. "You know, Meg, it's possible the second sheet is in one of the volumes upstairs. It wouldn't be the first time two centuries got put together accidently. The advantage to the 18th and 19th century stuff upstairs is that it is catalogued and much easier to find."

Meg breathed a sigh of relief. "Let's go check it out and then call it a day. I think something I ate at lunch is not agreeing with me. Ann went to the restroom. We can get her on our way out."

Forty-five minutes later, Meg and Cindy returned to the basement to discover Ann was not there. They looked in the restroom and all over the archives, but they could not find her.

"I'll call Jose to come get us," Meg said, "and then I'll call Ann."

****

*I can't believe they left me. Meg must have gotten sicker. I'm sure that
I can get to the hotel before Jose comes back for me. Being that I don't have
to worry about one-way streets, it's just a mile.*

As Ann walked up the street, she made out a building quite
a few blocks ahead of her that was next door to the Gran Melia
Colon. With the hotel in sight, Ann picked up her pace.
Without warning, a large man stepped out from behind a
dumpster and grabbed her as she walked by. Jerking her into
the alley, he covered her mouth.

Ann trembled and felt nauseous as fear coursed through
her body. She tried to bite his hand, but he had clamped her
mouth closed with a fierce grip. As he dragged her toward the
back of the alley, Ann heard the squeal of brakes. To her relief,
she saw Jose at the end of the alley. He started to run toward
Ann, but two other guys stepped forward out of the shadows
to meet him. Ann had never seen anything so quick and
amazing in her life. Jose moved with lightning speed leaving
the two creeps lying unconscious on the ground.

The thug threw Ann to the ground and pulled out a pistol.
He got off one shot before Jose pummeled him with both fists.
In less than a minute, the whole thing was over, and all three
men were out cold.

"Oh, Jose," Ann said as she ran into his arms. "I was so
afraid. Oh, my God, you're bleeding."

"It nothing," he said nonchalantly.

"Yes, it is something," Ann insisted. "You've been shot."

"It's not the first time, and it's just a little flesh wound. I
will be fine."

Meg came running into the alley, followed by Cindy. "Are
you okay?"

Jose glared at the two women. "I told you ladies to stay in the car. It still may not be safe."

Meg ignored Jose and wrapped her arms around Ann.

"I'm fine, Meg, thanks to Jose, but he's been shot. We need to take him to the hospital."

"I do not need a hospital," Jose said.

Two police cars rolled to a stop and the officers recognized Jose at once. They told Jose that they should return to their hotel.

"I knew those men looked like they were up to no good," Meg said. "I should have said something at lunch when I noticed them for the second time."

"This is not a good part of town," Cindy offered, "but I'm surprised someone would attempt to mug you in broad daylight."

"Maybe the police can get something out of them," Meg suggested. "I'm just glad Jose got here when he did. If he had been a few minutes later..."

"You're right," Ann interrupted. "It was very close and very scary. Jose, you were amazing. I've never seen anyone move so fast in my life. Those guys didn't have a chance."

"I was lucky," Jose replied.

Ann said, "I don't think it was luck at all. You were like Matt Damon and Daniel Craig all wrapped up in one."

"Daniel Craig?" Cindy asked.

"You know," Meg replied. "James Bond."

The group pulled in front of the Gran Melia Colon, but Ann insisted on taking Jose to the hospital. Jose seemed to know that arguing with Ann would do no good, so Meg and Cindy slid out of the limo.

"I need to get home," Cindy said as she eyed the taxi parked at the curve. "Call me when Ann gets back to let me know how Jose is doing."

"Cindy, let's not tell Jon about this until we get home. I don't want him worrying."

"That's a wise decision. Muggings happen here all the time. We should have been a little more careful. Thank God Ann wasn't hurt."

"I'll call you when I hear from Jose. We'll see you in the morning. I hope we can find that missing page tomorrow. We're running out of time."

****

Luis' cell phone began to ring. After listening for a few minutes, he let out a string of profanities. "Stupid! What an idiot! Fernando, why did you hire such idiots to help you?"

"I'm sorry, Luis. These men came highly recommended to me."

"Are we even sure these women have discovered something? They could just be visiting their friend who happens to work at the archives."

"Most people who go in the archive searching for information carry a camera phone to take pictures of documents. They're not allowed to bring anything out. The redhead had an iPhone in her back pocket."

"I know, but every hot chick has an iPhone in her back pocket. That doesn't mean anything."

"It's more than that, Luis. They said the word *Ambrosio*."

"Are you sure?"

"Yes, Luis. I'm sure. These men also said that the women looked like they had found something important."

"Okay, okay. Those losers can't identify you, can they?"

"No, they have no idea who I am."

"All right. At least we know the Davenports have found something. We'll keep an eye on them. I'll send your payment for the information as I promised."

****

The last full day of research in the archives arrived. Meg and Ann tried to embrace it with hope, but they were finding their prospects quite grim.

They took the elevator to the parking deck and made their way through town in the black limousine. Parking in an all-day parking lot, Jose, with a small bandage over his wound, walked with the two women to the archives. It was obvious he planned to watch over the ladies all day. Displaying an air of excitement that was hard to be contained, Cindy was waiting for them.

"Ann, are you okay?"

"Sure. I'm fine. Jose is the one who was shot. I'll be fine."

Cindy turned to Jose. "And you? Should you be here? Are you okay?"

"I'm fine, too. It was no big deal."

Cindy rolled her eyes and shrugged. "I've been thinking all night about our next move. While we've been looking for something that said 'Ambrosio' on it, we need to broaden our horizons. I've printed out a list of all the undiscovered Spanish galleons believed to be in Caribbean waters. I want us to get very familiar with each name over coffee. As soon as the archives open, let's look for anything with one of these four names: the *San Ambrosio* , the *San Roque,* the *Nuestra Senora de Begona, and* the *Santo Domingo.*"

"Why those four names?" Ann asked.

"I would guess these are the names of the four lost ships of the *Terre Firma* armada," Meg said.

"You are right," Cindy acknowledged. "It's possible we could find a document containing a list of general items found in the armada and not just items found on one ship. We need to expand our thinking here and not limit ourselves to such a small search criteria."

"Sounds like a great plan," Ann agreed and winked at Jose. "Since our bodyguard has chosen to keep his eyes on us all day, maybe he can help us too."

"I am happy to help," Jose acknowledged with a grin. "Just tell me what to look for."

"I assume you know that you are sworn to secrecy," Ann said with a raised eyebrow.

"Your secret is safe with me," Jose grinned.

The four studied the list and then walked across the street toward the archives at 9:55. Other than stopping for a quick lunch, they read documents nonstop. With just two hours left before they needed to leave for the airport, they discovered several documents that contained histories of a number of ships, but nothing from the *Terre Firma* armada.

"Well, we have two hours remaining to find our needle in the haystack," Meg said. "I feel pretty discouraged. We must leave by 2:00 to catch our plane."

"Don't be discouraged," Cindy said. "I've known re-searchers to spend months in the archives before they found one tiny clue. We've found some amazing information that will be quite useful. Maybe the missing page is under the next document."

By 1:00, nothing major had been discovered, and Meg was beginning to get worried. When Cindy announced that they only had ten minutes left, Meg began laying out documents and taking pictures without even reading the pages. The others began following Meg's example, and during the final few minutes, they each snapped at least one hundred pictures of what was probably worthless documents.

"Okay," Meg announced. "It's time. Ladies, and Jose, we've done our best. If there's nothing useful in these pictures, we'll just have to come back for another party."

"I like to party," Cindy grinned. "It's been great having company this week. I've loved every minute of it."

They each hugged Cindy goodbye and got into the limousine to drive back to the Seville Airport. Though Meg was disappointed with their lack of progress, she was giddy with excitement as she calculated she would see Jon in a little over twenty hours after their plane took off. She noticed that Ann seemed to be having a hard time leaving Jose behind.

Once the plane had reached an altitude where computers could be used, Meg began transferring all of the pictures of documents from her phone to her computer. Ann handed Meg her phone as well, and within minutes almost 300 pictures were saved on Meg's hard drive.

While Ann began to doze, Meg started reading through the documents on her computer. She inwardly groaned as she thought about what would probably be the wasted hours ahead of her spent looking over these pictures.

She paused long enough to eat the grilled chicken and vegetables provided to her by the flight attendant. Some six hours after takeoff, Meg slipped off to sleep. Ann, who was reading a book, saw her nod off. She reached over to turn off Meg's computer.

CHAPTER TWELVE

Home Again

Meg was out of her seat as soon as the plane came to a stop in Miami. After spending a week away from Jon in Seville, she could not wait to see him. She ran into his embrace as he stood at the bottom of the escalator near the baggage claim area. Their lips touched, and electricity surged throughout her body.

"Oh, I've have missed you so much," Meg breathed.

"Not as much as I've missed you. I hate to say it, but we need to get your bags as fast as possible. I have a trip for us to take."

"So I guess that means we're not catching our flight back to Atlanta?"

"Well, Ann is, but we have a detour to make."

"Where are we going?"

"We're going back to Nassau to take care of some business."

"That sounds wonderful," Meg replied. "I am exhausted, but I can make it."

"Did you sleep on the plane?"

"Some, but I don't sleep very well on planes. I'll be fine, but I'm just disappointed we weren't more successful at the archives. All I have is a bunch of pictures of documents. We started running out of time on the last day, so we just started snapping pictures of every document we could put our hands on."

"You never know," Jon offered. "We'll study through the photos. Something might turn up."

Meg hugged Ann goodbye before she and Jon hurried off to catch their flight to Nassau. By 6:00 pm, they were sitting down in their condo at the Emerald Isles Resort to a meal prepared by the resort staff. Meg looked around the beautiful, beachside villa with warmth at the great memories. So much had changed since the last time they had stayed at this wonderful place.

After dinner, Meg and Jon started on a walk down the beach, but Jon could see that Meg was exhausted. Silhouetted against a full moon, Jon pulled Meg into his arms.

He moved a strand of hair behind her ear. "I think maybe we should just go to sleep. A walk would be fun, but you need some rest."

"I'm fine," Meg yawned. "I am exhausted, but I've been dying to see you all week."

"You need some sleep or you won't be awake enough to enjoy my surprises I have for you."

"Oh, you have surprises for me, Dr. Davenport?"

"Sure do, and I don't want you sleeping through it. Let's get back to the condo so I can put you to bed."

When Jon kissed Meg goodnight at the door to the master bedroom, she wanted to pull him inside the room with her. Her absence from him had made her desire to be with him even greater. Jon had told Meg earlier that he was committed to making their wedding night the most memorable experience in their relationship, so Meg had to remind herself that their special day was just a few weeks away. Agreeing to start the next day on the beach at sunrise, Jon descended the stairs to get ready for bed.

First thing the next morning, Meg slipped into Jon's room without making a sound and eased into the bed beside him. She propped up on her elbow and watched him sleep for a full five minutes. The room was bright with the light of the moon that came through the open window. He was handsome, masculine, gentle, and tough all at the same time.

She leaned over and placed her lips on his. With surprising quickness, he reached up and pulled her down on top of him. Meg screamed in shock before their lips connected again. Meg reached under the covers and began tickling him.

"Stop…stop," Jon said in between gasps. "I'm incredibly ticklish. You messed up what started out to be the most perfect wake-up call I've ever received."

"No, what I did was help us keep our commitment to a memorable honeymoon."

"Okay, I give in. You win."

Meg enjoyed being held in Jon's arms for a few more moments before prying herself loose and giving him one last tender kiss. She slipped out of the room to begin making coffee in the kitchen. When Jon crawled out of bed and joined her in the kitchen, he found she had a large mug of coffee waiting for him.

Meg smiled up at him. "We had better get going, or we're going to miss the sunrise."

When they found the perfect spot near the edge of the water, Jon spread a blanket out on the sand. The couple sat together drinking coffee in the growing morning light, and watched as the sun peeked over the edge of the distant horizon. The dark water glowed with the orange brilliance of the morning sun as Jon pulled Meg against his body.

"This is our second sunrise," Meg said.

"No, it's our third. Remember? We saw one on our first morning together."

"Oh, yeah, but we both agreed to forget all about that. Is it okay to remember it all now?"

"Fine with me. As a matter of fact, you can have a cramp any time you want to, and I'll be happy to massage your legs."

Meg laughed as she remembered that special night they had together. The sun was over the horizon when Jon gathered up their blanket, and the two meandered back to the condo. They dropped the blanket on the front porch of the villa and performed a few stretching exercises before heading off for a morning run.

After showering and dressing for the day, Jon had a breakfast of fruit crepes delivered to the house. Meg did her best to get him to tell her about the surprise, but he was as solemn as an altar boy.

Meg got into the golf cart beside Jon as the fresh morning breeze blew through her hair. She loved this island and was sad they would be flying home soon. They pulled up beside the black Lexus they had borrowed on their previous trip to the island. Jon held the door for Meg to get into the passenger seat before he hurried around to the driver's side.

"Where are we going?" Meg asked as Jon pulled onto the Queen's Highway. "Can't you tell me now?"

"You'll see," Jon smiled slyly. "It's a surprise. Remember?"

After about twenty-five minutes or so, Jon took a right on a familiar beach road past Roker's Point, and Meg realized where they were going. Jon turned the engine off in the driveway of the beautiful home positioned on the bluff overlooking the bay. She saw a large, yellow bow on the front door. As she walked up the steps to the front door, she saw a note attached to the bow.

Meg pulled the note off the bow and read: "Meg, you bring more joy to my life than you will ever know. May this house be a small token of my love and commitment to you. I love you with all my heart. Jon."

Meg began to shake and big tears flowed from her eyes. She couldn't speak but just hugged him close. Her life had moved into warp speed since running into Jon months ago on the island of Nassau, and now, she found such joy and hope for the future.

"I, I don't know what to say," Meg said.

"Just say that you love me and that you accept this small gift."

"Of course I love you," Meg said as she kissed him. "Small token? This is huge. Does this mean we're moving here?"

"I told the realtor we would want to do some remodeling, but I thought you might want to make the color choices. That will give us something to look forward to when we come back from our honeymoon. I thought we might be spending some time here looking for our wreck, and we would need a home base."

"You don't have that kind of money to spend on this house?"

"Yes I do. In fact, I've made offers on the lots on each side of the house as well. I thought I had better have a place to go if you kick me out of your house. I told you my investments have done very well, and you are worth every penny."

"You are unbelievable," Meg said before kissing him again.

"I thought we could have our wedding out here in the back yard."

"Oh, Jon. That would be so perfect. You are so good to me."

"Meg, I loved you when you were a teenager. I know I was married later, and I loved my wife with all my heart. I didn't think I could ever love again. When you came along, I found a deep love for you rekindled. Now it is a blazing fire."

Jon kissed Meg again as he held her body close to his for several minutes. She was filled with joy and peace. When Steve died, she had thought she could never again find real contentment, but she had been so wrong. So much happiness filled her heart that Meg thought she might explode with elation.

"Well, we had better go." Jon urged. "I want to go into town to make a few contacts about remodeling the house. Why don't I take you back to the condo? I'll be back after a while, and we can go to the closing together. Your signature needs to be on the document as well."

They walked through the house before leaving, and Meg pulled out her iPhone. She took pictures of all of the rooms from every possible angle. Jon dropped Meg off at the condo before driving on toward George Town. After deciding to take a morning swim in her new ocean, she slipped into her bathing suit.

Meg stepped out onto the beach and looked out to sea. She loved the feel of the white sand between her toes. Feeling the light breeze kiss her face, she stared out over the calm, turquoise ocean.

About two-hundred yards off shore, Meg could see the outline of a white sail making its way northwest up the coast of this island paradise. The thrill of being back sent chills up Meg's back. She walked down the beach a while before stopping to pick up a perfect sand dollar that had been bleached white by the sun and surf.

Meg couldn't imagine a more perfect place, and it was hard to believe she was about to own a beautiful home just fifteen or twenty miles up the beach. She could feel the warm sun embrace her body as the sea gulls seemed to be welcoming her home. She was in heaven.

After going for a brief swim in the warm, tropical waters, Meg knew she had better head back to the condo. As she bent down to pick up her towel from the sand, she saw out of the corner of her eye a young guy staring at her. Meg passed by the man lying on a towel and wondered why he would be looking at her. As far as she was concerned, she was just a plain looking girl with not much to offer in physical beauty. Regardless of whether or not she thought of herself as much to look at, Meg knew Jon thought she was beautiful. His opinion was the only one that mattered to her.

At 1:00, Jon was back at the condo so he and Meg could go to the attorney's office for the closing. They grabbed a quick bite to eat then drove to the lawyer's plush office. After penning their signatures enough times to give them writer's cramp, it was official—they were owners of a beautiful

Bahamian home that was situated on a deep, protected cove facing the Atlantic Ocean on the north side of the island.

Jon drove them out to their new home where they met with Bernard, an architect, and Marc the contractor. The two agreed to begin work on the drawings and the initial demolition phase of the renovation right away. Marc told the couple he believed he could have the main house completed in about a month by using two crews working twelve-hour shifts. He would just need Meg to pass along her ideas for the remodel as soon as possible.

Meg showed Marc where she would one day like a pool and asked him to prepare a spot when he was doing the other clearing for the guest house. Jon suggested they wait until after the wedding to start on a pool. He said he didn't want a big hole in the yard when all of their guests arrived, but he asked Marc to get the yard landscaped before the wedding day.

Meg could imagine the entire scene. Chairs for the guests could be set up in the cleared area while she, Jon, and the pastor could stand under a trellis in what would one day be her tropical flower garden. While they had hoped to make a dive before returning home, they ran out of time. After enjoying a relaxing evening together that included a wonderful dinner and a romantic walk down the beach, Jon suggested an early bedtime.

On Tuesday morning, they returned to Nassau and took a flight back to Miami. Before heading back to Atlanta, Jon wanted to show Meg their new salvage ship. They also had to stop by a lawyer's office to sign the papers that would make *The Discoverer* officially theirs.

He rented a car and drove them to the deep-water marina where the research ship was docked. As the couple walked down the street paralleling the wharf, they walked right past a bait shop. They failed to notice a Cuban man staring at them.

"Oh, Jon, she is beautiful," Meg said as she stood staring at the gleaming ship. "Can you take me aboard and give me a tour?"

"I thought you would never ask."

Jon took Meg's hand as they walked aboard. He first took her from bow to stern on the main deck. He showed her the space and shared some commentary on the equipment that would be brought aboard for the recovery effort. He took her below to tour the next level down with its offices, labs, and bunks for the crew. The lowest deck was reserved for storage.

They climbed the steep stairs to the captain's quarters to what Jon called "the Love Nest." Jon already had a full size bed delivered, and the cabin had been redecorated. He had an interior decorator follow a nautical theme and included a picture of the two of them at the Emerald Isles Resort on Great Exuma Island that Meg had never seen.

"I wondered what happened to that picture," Meg said as she stood gazing at their picture with the sun rising over the ocean before them. "I remembered the man taking our picture before breakfast that morning, but I never saw the print."

"I hoped you had forgotten about it," Jon said. "I wanted it to be a surprise."

"See how your arm is around me? You appeared to be trying to keep your distance, but I think even then, you loved me."

"No doubt. I was just fooling myself."

"This cabin is beautiful. We even have our own personal bathroom and shower."

"It's called a head," Jon said.

"Oh, yeah. I never have quite figured out why it's called the head. Show me the bridge. You would think it would be called the head."

They climbed up a level that contained the main wheel house, computers, and weather equipment. It was so high tech Meg marveled at all she saw. Jon showed her the top level that was really more for looking out than for steering the ship, even though Meg noticed a large, beautiful steering wheel mounted at the front of the platform.

"Jon, the whole thing is amazing. I can't believe she's ours. I can't wait to begin our search."

"I've still got to sign the final papers, but she may as well be ours. The first thing I would like us to do is take up Dr. Russell's offer to use it for our honeymoon," Jon said. "I think that would be a nice way to break her in. Just imagine the things we could see and the fun we could have while we're getting used to our new ship."

Meg grinned. "All I want to see are your beautiful brown eyes looking into mine. I would be fine with renting a room somewhere and not coming out for a week."

"That sounds tempting, but you've got to admit that sailing through the Caribbean on our own boat while we take our sweet time does sound appealing."

CHAPTER THIRTEEN

Needle in a Haystack

Jon and Meg stood on the top of the research vessel and kissed while Luis watched them through his telescopic camera lens. He had asked enough questions around to find out that Jon was not only the new boat owner, but he was also in the process of purchasing some salvage equipment to go onboard. He also learned the couple planned a cruise for their honeymoon. It was odd that he thought they had been married all along.

He had already started making connections with people who might be able to join the staff. He determined that if he could have someone aboard who reported to him, he could learn everything he needed to know. He had made some headway with a young woman who had been interviewed for a position with the kitchen staff. Maybe she would be hired for a small salary, and he could sweeten the deal for her in return for a little information.

She was a real fine girl too, so he hoped to get more than just a spy out of the arrangement. Being careful not to be seen, Luis put down the camera as the two lovebirds walked by his bait shop. The brunette was a real looker, and he couldn't help but stare.

My day will come. You'll see, Meg Davenport.

****

Meg and Jon drove away from the docks toward the Miami International Airport. They boarded the next flight to Atlanta and pulled into the driveway of the ranch a little after 7:30 that evening. Meg's whirlwind tour of the world had come to an end.

"I am so tired," Meg said. "I think I can sleep for a week."

"You can't sleep for a full week," Jon corrected. "You've got to be awake at the dinner next Monday so we can make our big announcement."

"Oh no, I forgot all about the dinner in the craziness of the last seven days. I've got so much to do to get ready for it."

"Like what?" Jon asked. "There is just one thing you need to do."

"What's that?"

"Show up and look beautiful. That won't be hard for you to do at all."

"Give me a break," Meg sighed with a sound of disbelief, but deep down she treasured Jon's compliments.

Jon parked the truck and walked around to Meg's side to open the door. He pulled their luggage from the back seat, but Meg grabbed her carry-on bag. As they climbed the steps to the large front porch, Judy came out to hug them both.

"Welcome home," Judy gushed. "I have missed you so much. I can't wait to hear all about your trip."

"It was wonderful," Meg said. "The best part is coming home. I've missed you too, Judy, and I have a lot of stories for you. One is that I think Ann is in love."

"In love? You've got to be kidding. Who is she in love with?"

"His name is Jose. He was our driver in Seville and is quite the specimen. I'll tell you about it over dinner. I'm starved."

Meg and Jon followed Judy into the kitchen where they sat together around the kitchen table. The fried chicken was delicious, but the peanut butter pie was the highlight of the meal. Meg filled them both in on the events of the week by describing the architecture of old Seville along with great detail about the amazing food. She told about their daily research at the archives, including how they would take pictures of documents that they deemed potentially useful.

"When we had about thirty minutes left," Meg said, "we just started taking pictures of as many documents as we could. I guess I thought we might find a needle in the haystack after we left the place. Ann and I called it the dungeon."

"Did you take pictures of *Jardines de las Reales Alcazares*?" Judy asked.

"Yes, I did," Meg replied. "Judy, your Spanish sounds almost native."

"I studied Spanish for years and spent some time in Spain when I was a wild, young woman. I would love to see your pictures."

After dinner, they sat together in the family room, and Meg hooked up her laptop to the huge flat screen television on the wall. One by one she showed them the pictures she had taken throughout the week and offered commentary on almost every shot.

When Meg was skimming through the photos of the documents in order to find the final picture taken at the archives, Judy shouted, "Stop."

Meg was so startled by Judy's abruptness the computer almost fell out of her lap.

"What is it, Judy?" Meg asked.

"I saw something on one of those document pictures. It would be several back from where you are now."

"Wow, Judy. I was just skipping through them. Let me see if I can go back slowly. You tell me when you see whatever it was you saw."

Meg started reviewing the pictures in reverse order. It took a few minutes, but Judy stopped her on a picture that looked like every other document Meg had spent the week reading.

"That's it," Judy said. "Look at the third line. Do you see it?"

They all said in unison, "*Terra Firme.*"

"Oh my God," Meg said in shock. "That looks like a manifest."

Judy scanned the document. "That is the manifest of the whole armada, I think. Didn't you say the *Ambrosio* was in that fleet?"

"That's correct," Jon said. "She was the smallest ship, but we think that may be the one sunk off our island."

"Well, if I'm reading this right," Meg said, "this manifest will contain a list of everything all four treasure ships carried, which will include the *Ambrosio*. You did it Judy! We spent all week studying these crazy things, and you spot it in about two minutes. You're my hero!"

"I was just lucky," Judy replied. "Some of this is tough to read."

"We should send it to Cindy for her opinion," Meg offered.

"Include the pictures of the documents taken before and after this one as well," Jon said. "I'll get Cindy to translate it all for us so we can have the details of the cargo."

They sat around the family room drinking coffee while they tried to read the smudged print of the old Spanish document. An hour later, Meg stood up and stretched.

"I think it's time for me to go home," Meg admitted. "In addition to this big dinner for a bunch of rich people, I do have a wedding to plan."

"Why don't we meet for lunch tomorrow," Jon suggested. "Better yet, why don't you meet me at Ruth's Chris in Buckhead for a celebration lunch?"

"I would love that. I could be there around 1:00 or maybe before."

Jon walked Meg out to her Honda. The moon was full, and the air was beginning to feel a bit cool and crisp. A wisp of hair blew into Meg's face, but Jon pulled it aside. Meg gazed up at Jon as he lowered his lips to hers. They stood still in the moonlight for several minutes holding one another. Promising to see Jon at lunch the following day, Meg lowered herself into her car. She drove home knowing that soon, home would be with this wonderful man.

****

Luis kissed Carla again before pouring her another drink. Carla was a beautiful Hispanic woman with an amazing body, jet black hair, and huge, dark eyes. They were celebrating Carla's new employment, but Luis was trying to decide when he would offer her a little bonus. He was fortunate to meet her at Mango's Tropical Café and glad that they hit it off right away.

He was thrilled to hear Carla would be working in the kitchen of *The Discoverer*. She told him that when the ship was not at sea, she was to help Chef Marceau with his catering business. Luis planned to take the girl to a fancy restaurant a few times, buy her some nice jewelry, and then offer her a side job. He was sure there would be no problem.

****

As Meg stepped out of the dress shop, she couldn't help but feel like a weight had been lifted from her shoulders. The sky was clear blue, and the sun was hot on her face. She held her arms out as if to embrace her new life. Her dress was ordered. Now all she needed to do was line up the caterer, florist, and minister in George Town.

Later that evening, Jon and Meg sat together on the front porch of the ranch long into the night. Meg leaned her head on his shoulder as he questioned whether or not their fate was determined by chance or had God brought together two bleeding hearts.

Meg squeezed Jon's hand. "I've learned through my experience that God knows what he's doing, and he doesn't make mistakes. I also don't think I believe much in chance anymore."

Jon yawned. "For whatever reason he brought us together, I'm sure happy."

Since Meg would be busy making preparations for the fund-raiser for the next few days, not to mention finalizing wedding plans, she broke the hypnotic spell she seemed to be under to tell Jon good night. They both needed their rest, so Meg once again began her long drive home.

Monday's fund-raiser passed without a hitch. The dinner was a huge success by raising several million dollars for the Johnson-Robertson presidential campaign, and Jon's friends and associates were thrilled with the introduction of his fiancé. Not only were his friends happy with the announcement, but news agencies from around the country bit into the story like a starving man's first taste of a home-cooked meal. The story of Meg's deceased military husband, Governor Johnson's daughter's death, and the Governor's son-in-law's engagement was perfect fodder for reporters.

Jon kissed Meg to the cheers of the crowd and to the flashes of the reporters' cameras. Because of Jon's relationship with Governor Johnson, their plans for marriage became talking points for every news agency in America.

As Meg dragged herself out of bed the next morning, she heard her cell phone buzz. She saw a new text message from her mother: "Nice picture on front page of the paper."

Meg ran to the front door to find her copy of the morning newspaper. Right on the front page was a huge, color picture of her and Jon kissing while the Governor smiled in the background. It was classic, and deep down, Meg loved it. She went back inside, picked up her phone and dialed Jon's phone.

"Good morning, beautiful," Jon said on the other end of the phone.

"Hey, you crazy man. What do you mean having your way with me in front of all of those photographers?"

"What do you mean?" Jon asked, not having a clue as to what Meg was talking about.

"Have you seen the morning paper?"

There was a pause while Jon walked down the stairs to look at the paper.

"You're a great kisser," Meg heard Jon say.

"Well, I suppose the whole world knows now."

"How can anyone know you're a great kisser?" Jon teased. "I'm the only one who knows that."

"I don't mean that, silly. They know we're getting married."

"That was the plan. I want the whole world to know that you are mine. Looking at the Governor reminds me of another thing we need to add to our to-do list. We've got to go to the courthouse to complete an absentee ballot. It looks like Randall will win the presidency without us, but I want to be as much a part of this as possible."

"I like your father-in-law. I think he'll make a great president. I was thinking about driving out to talk with Judy about the food for the wedding. Would you save me a cup of coffee?"

"Sounds great. I'll be waiting."

Jon had Meg a cup of coffee as promised and they settled on the couch in the family room. Jon sat his cup on the end table. "What have you heard from Cindy about the latest pictures?"

"She sent me a note saying she wanted to translate all the documents around that one picture. She said we should hear from her today or tomorrow. I know the document was in bad shape, but it sure seemed like a manifest."

"I have no doubt, Meg. I was hoping to find a manifest for just the *Ambrosio*, but I guess this will have to do. I don't see us going back to Seville."

"It's frustrating that the archive officials do not take better care of the basement documents. A lot of the manifest was messed up by moisture."

"That's true, but I've seen Cindy do some miracles in translating old documents."

They ate breakfast together before Jon left for his office. Meg stayed with Judy so she could put the final touches on the wedding plans. She told Judy that she wanted it to be a simple but beautiful outdoor wedding on their piece of tropical paradise. She hoped to use flowers from the island, but planned on having a lot of additional flowers and plants sent in to supplement. October twentieth was just around the corner, and she had so much to do to be ready for the most important day of her life.

Meg's phone buzzed again, but this time the text was from Ann: "What a kiss from one of the richest men in Georgia! Now the whole world knows." ☺

"The whole world knows indeed," Meg thought, and she could not have been happier.

CHAPTER FOURTEEN

Great Exuma

Feeling almost dizzy with excitement about being so close to her island home, Meg stepped off the Delta flight at Lynden Pindling International Airport in Nassau. She turned to look at Ann to see if she shared the excitement of being in the Bahamas. Ann seemed to be more excited about her change of careers than being in this wonderful island paradise. She smiled at the thought that Ann was now the Vice-President of Operations for Jon's new salvage enterprise.

The final leg of the trip would require the services of a small plane that would take them from Nassau to Great Exuma Island. They would be in George Town within the hour, and Meg would see her newly renovated home for the first time. She knew there would still be work going on after the wedding, but for now, the house and grounds should look like a finished project. For one thing, she wanted a swimming pool surrounded by a garden. Meg knew that she was acting like a spoiled, rich girl, but she had always dreamed of owning a swimming pool that looked like it was placed in the middle of the Garden of Eden.

Meg could hardly be contained as she and Ann climbed into the F-250 that was parked at the George Town airport terminal. Jon had purchased the truck for their salvage company's use, and had it shipped to George Town. The vehicle had been left for them in the parking lot near the terminal.

Meg had assured Ann that she could stay at the house while they were on their honeymoon. The guest apartment above the garage should be completed before long and would offer Ann a more permanent place to live.

Ann had talked nonstop about the possibilities of finding the *Ambrosio*, but Meg knew that she was most excited because Jon had agreed to hire Jose as a diver. It was obvious that something was going on between them. He called her at least two or three times a week from Spain.

Ann drove while Meg served as copilot. As the two friends pulled into the driveway, Ann stopped the truck and gasped at the beauty before her. The stucco house was surrounded by a large porch with astounding, open views of the beach and ocean just below the house. The house sat about fifty or sixty feet above sea level on a bluff overlooking the calm waters of a protected bay.

Jon had determined the bay would be a perfect place to anchor their new salvage ship, *The Discoverer*. As Meg took in the surroundings of her beautiful home, she wondered why she had been so blessed to have the privilege of living in this little corner of Wonderland. She thought back to being called Alice in Wonderland when she was a kid and decided that maybe having been named Margaret Alice wasn't so bad after all.

Marc, the contractor, had told Meg the landscaping around the house would not be completed, but as far as she was concerned, it looked like a postcard. Ann pulled forward to a three-car garage located beside the house.

"Welcome to your new home," Meg said as they stepped out of the garage. "At least it's your new temporary home. I can't believe the incredible job Bernard and Marc have done in such a short time. This doesn't even look like the same place. Marc extended the porch around the house, and the yard looks like a dream come true."

"I thought they were going to do the landscaping later," Ann said.

"Well, they are, but this must be phase one of the Garden of Eden. Let's go inside."

Meg and Ann walked through the house and marveled at the beauty all around them. The rooms were open and bright. Meg loved the colors that she and Ann had picked out from pictures on the Internet. She reverently rubbed her hand along the granite countertop in the kitchen and realized this kitchen and living room were bigger than her whole house back in Georgia.

Ann could not keep quiet about how impressive the huge picture window was in the main living room that overlooked the bay. Meg looked down to the sandy beach below and saw a new dock that Marc had built out into the water. It would provide a perfect place for their boat. She wondered if the water was deep enough for *The Discoverer* but knew that Jon had already considered that issue.

"Well, you will be Mrs. Jon Davenport in just four days," Ann said.

"I almost can't believe it," Meg admitted. "Isn't it something how life takes twists and turns?"

"You can say that again," Ann said. "I thought I would be spending the rest of my life doing investigations for DFACS."

"You and me both," Meg laughed.

"So, what's up with Jon? Why isn't he here?"

"He had some work to finish up at his office in Atlanta. When that's done, he'll fly to Miami to pick up his boat, or I guess I could say *our boat*, before coming on over. He had someone remodel the interior, so I'm sure it's going to be beautiful. He'll arrive Friday morning along with the rest of my family."

"I'm so glad Jon is flying your mother and the rest of your family down," Ann said.

"I'm not sure who is more excited," Meg replied, "my mother, my sister, or my niece. All Lacy can talk about is meeting a Bahamian boy down here."

"How old is Lacy?" Ann asked.

"She turned sixteen in July. She's a beautiful girl, and I'm just concerned she might be a little…crazy. We better keep our eyes on her. If we're not careful she'll be behind a sand dune with some boy."

"Is she that wild?" Ann asked.

"She's a good girl, but I don't know if she's boy crazy or just likes leading them on. I don't think she would do anything, but she has the looks that will grab the boys' attention. She's quite a knockout."

"So your sister has a sixteen year old daughter? She must have gotten pregnant when she was young."

"Liz married while she was in college, but she is six years older than me."

"So that makes her…thirty-eight?"

"Yep, thirty-eight, and she had Lacy when she was twenty-two. I can't imagine having a kid when I was that young."

"I'm not sure I can imagine having a kid at all," Ann acknowledged.

"I just wish her marriage was stronger."

"What do you mean?"

"Well, she and Rick have had a rocky marriage for a long time. I think he's unfaithful, but honestly, Liz may not be living right either."

"That must be tough on Lacy."

"She acts totally oblivious to her family problems, Ann, but I can see a volcano of anger and bitterness that will one day erupt."

"I'm so sorry, Meg. What does your family think about their rich family member?"

"You know, I was worried about that, but so far, no one has hit me up for money or anything. Everyone seems to be pretty cool about it. I think they're pumped about having a relative with a house in the Bahamas they can visit at any time. My brother-in-law is a big time fisherman, and I think he wants to try out scuba diving. Lacy wants to at least try snorkeling, but I have a feeling she'll want to be a certified scuba diver once she sees the reef. They're going to stay for a week after the wedding, so you'll have some company."

"How long will your mother be staying? Her name is Elizabeth, right?"

"Yes, Elizabeth. My sister is named after her. She plans to fly back home on Sunday. I don't know why she's not going to stay longer, but she said she would come back for a visit later."

"You do remember that Jose is coming for the wedding too, don't you?" Ann asked.

"Oh, yeah. I had nearly forgotten that incidental fact," Meg teased. "You've only mentioned it thirty times in the last two hours. Lacy might not be the only one I need to keep my eye on. You're a beauty too who may be a little crazy, and I'm not sure about Jose's intentions."

"He is nothing but a gentleman," Ann said with a big grin.

Meg went upstairs to the spacious, master bedroom suite. The room overlooked the bay with large windows in both the bedroom and bathroom. She loved the whirlpool tub in the bathroom that was more like a small swimming pool. She looked around at all of the granite and tile that surrounded the shower and whirlpool. It was so beautiful. The window in the bathroom would give her a panoramic view of the bay while she sat in the whirlpool. It was more than she had even been able to imagine.

She unpacked her things and placed them in the Coaster Dubarry dresser. She wondered if she would miss her old bedroom suite she had gotten for quite a bargain at Goodwill. It pleased her to think of her young neighbors back in Georgia enjoying the lovely furniture. She fell back on her incredible new bed and admired the detailed carving in the wooden headboard. It was the most gorgeous bedroom furniture she had ever seen.

Ann whistled as she walked into the room. "Wow! What an amazing bedroom! You look like a princess lying there or maybe more like a pirate's wench."

"I like princess better," Meg laughed. "Your room's not so shabby either."

"I do like it, a lot, but I might have to come to your bathroom to go swimming," Ann teased as she admired the whirlpool.

"I guess we better quit gawking and get busy. We need to meet with the caterer and the florist, just to make sure everything is okay."

"I thought your coordinator would be doing all of that," Ann wondered aloud.

"Well, she is, but I just want to make sure everything is ready."

"What about your dress?"

"Oh, I'm glad you reminded me. Margaret, the coordinator, told me to pick it up at the cleaners downtown. Let's run our errands, and then I want to take you by the Emerald Isle Resort for dinner. I'd like to show you the condo we stayed in the first time we came here. It is like a fantasy."

****

On Friday, Jon pulled his Carver yacht up to the dock as Meg ran down to meet him. He wrapped Meg up in his arms and kissed her. He acted like he hadn't seen her in a year when it had just been a few days. Ann came slowly down the steps to allow the two lovers a moment alone. Jon took the two women aboard the yacht to show them the improvements made to the interior.

"I think you're going to like it, Meg. I took your advice and had all of the appliances replaced."

"I can't imagine why the oven was broken, but it made you think that maybe the microwave or refrigerator would be next," Meg commented.

"I think we'll find that the new appliances are a lot better quality. It's amazing that someone would design this yacht with such detail but put cheap appliances in the galley."

Meg loved the kitchen, and in particular liked the living room feel of the dining area. She also liked the comfortable chairs added that she had not seen in some of the pictures they had looked at while planning the remodel.

"It's perfect," Meg insisted with a smile. "You have great taste."

"No, you have great taste," Jon corrected. "You're the one who picked out everything."

"Well, I did have some help from Ann and Judy. Have you checked to see if there's anything else of great value hidden away on the boat?"

"Checked and rechecked," Jon confessed.

"I think it's perfect," Ann offered. "Are you sure you don't want to take it on your honeymoon?"

"No, we can't," Jon reminded her. "We have to pick up the crane in Honduras. That's part of Dr. Russell's agreement. Besides, I think we're going to enjoy spending our honeymoon on *The Discoverer.*"

CHAPTER FIFTEEN

The Big Day

Luis rolled on his back as he thought about Carla. His weeks with her had been amazing, and she had followed through with not only getting the job on *The Discoverer*, but was also more than willing to share any information he wanted. He considered spending time with her to be a fringe benefit of the business venture.

She was a beautiful woman in every way imaginable, and he had never enjoyed being with someone as much as he had enjoyed Carla. He knew he would have to kill her before it was all over with, but in the meantime, she was his. The disturbing thing was that every time he was with this beautiful creature, he couldn't help but imagine what it would be like to be with that American woman. As hard as he tried to focus on Carla when they were together, every time he looked in her eyes, he saw the beautiful face of the woman who haunted his dreams. One day, his dreams would come true. He would kill her jerk of a husband, and Meg would be his for as long as he wanted.

Luis coached Carla on how to get information without being detected. He showed her pictures of what she could expect the divers to find on the sea floor. He did everything possible to prepare her for the task of bringing down the Davenport couple. Because Luis had knocked off a drug dealer in Miami and took over his beat, he had a good income. He purchased nice things for Carla that bought her silence and cooperation.

Luis discovered Jon had a wireless Internet system installed on the ship that must have had a satellite hookup, so he purchased a laptop for Carla to use for communication. She was to send him a daily report of everything she encountered throughout her day. He told her that he even wanted to hear about the kitchen gossip. It was critical that he make his move at the right time or the treasure could be lost to him forever. In the meantime, he would continue selling bait and pushing crack, patiently waiting for the day he would become a very rich man.

"So you leave tomorrow," Luis said as Carla walked back into the room with a cup of coffee.

"Yes," she agreed as she sat Luis' coffee cup on the bedside table. "We are to sail at 8:00 in the morning, but I have to be onboard tonight. Oh Luis, I am going to miss you so much."

"Yes, but if you will pass everything along to me that you see or hear, we will soon have more money than we could spend in ten lifetimes. I will buy you the biggest diamond you have ever seen."

"Maybe you can come see me sometime. I know you can't come on the ship, but I can meet you on land somewhere."

"Maybe we can do that. It's important you gain the trust of the crew onboard–especially Jon. I thought they were married when we first met, but I understand that this first time out will be for the honeymoon."

"Yes, we are to sail to Great Exuma first thing, take the couple around the islands, and go on to Honduras. We are supposed to return home before Thanksgiving."

Luis got out of bed and wrapped his arms around Carla. He kissed her before opening a drawer to the bedside table. He pulled out a necklace with a heart shaped diamond and placed it around Carla's neck. She squealed with delight while admiring the necklace in the mirror. Admiring the twinkle of light that was reflected from the gem, she fingered the diamond.

"Oh, Luis, it's beautiful. You are so good to me."

Carla kissed Luis hard before picking up her duffle bag. She ran her fingers down Luis' cheek looking longingly into his eyes. After giving Luis one final kiss, she pulled up the handle of her suitcase and walked out the door.

****

Meg looked down at her bouquet of daisies, and a tear rolled down her cheek. She found it hard to believe that in another hour, she would become Mrs. Jon Davenport. The daisies made her think of Steve and the flowers he had arranged for her to receive at the Bayview Resort. She was still amazed that her husband had made such elaborate plans for their reunion before he had been killed in Afghanistan.

A smile crossed her face as Meg thought back to her botched trip to Nassau. She went to the island to find the gift her deceased husband had planned to give her, but instead of finding a gift, she found Jon. It had only been two months ago and so much had happened; so much had changed. She did miss Steve, and would always miss him, but now God had brought a new man into her life. She knew that if Steve could see her, he would be happy. She briefly wondered if God allowed people in heaven to see what was happening on the earth. Meg marveled that she had once again found such happiness.

Meg smiled as she thought about Jon's protest over not seeing her on the day of the wedding. She was a bit old fashioned, but it was important that Jon's first glimpse of his bride be as she walked down the aisle.

Meg's mother watched the tears sliding down Meg's face and pulled a tissue from the nearby box.

"You're so beautiful, sweetheart. I'm very happy for you."

"I'm so happy too," Meg said as tears began to flow again.

"You're going to have to stop that, or we're going to need to redo all of your makeup."

"I know, Mama. I'm just so happy and blessed. Do you think it's okay for me to be this happy? I mean, I feel a little guilty."

"Honey, you should not feel guilty. You know Steve would want this."

"I know," Meg replied. "I was just thinking about that a moment ago. I never thought I would be able to love another man, but here I am."

"Here you are," Elizabeth agreed with a smile. "I've got to admit that when you told me you were getting married, I was afraid you had lost your mind. After all, you've only been engaged for such a short time. You didn't get reacquainted until just a month or so ago."

"Two months, Mama, but you're right."

"Let me finish," Elizabeth said patiently. "Though I first had concerns, I don't have any now, after seeing you two together. You are both happy and right for each other."

"Thank you, Mama. I do love him."

"I know you do. I love him too. You're going to be very happy together."

"We will. You look beautiful, Mama."

"Thank you, sweetheart," Elizabeth said as she slowly twirled around and allowed her light pink, knee length dress to billow out slightly. "I was so glad to have an excuse to go shopping."

"Glad to be of service," Meg said with a laugh, and then she became quite solemn. "I love you, Mama."

"I love you too, sweetheart," Elizabeth said as she pulled Meg into an embrace. "You are the most beautiful bride. Your husband is not going to be able to keep his eyes off of you."

"Oh, Mama. I never would have made it this far without you. Thank you for always being there for me."

"You're my baby girl," Elizabeth said as a tear rolled down her cheek.

"Now, Mama. You can't start that. We don't have time to fix us both back up."

"I'm going to slip over to the guest room to check on your sister. You just call me if you need me."

"Okay, Mama."

"You know that it all starts in about thirty minutes."

Meg smiled. "I know. I'm going to stay here until five minutes before the processional."

Almost thirty minutes later, Meg stood at the back of the crowd where she watched Jon, his brother who was the best man, and the minister take their places. The arbor was covered with allemande and bougainvillea. Meg thought how funny it was that Jon suggested the allemande. He didn't know that they were also called wild unction. Marrying Jon seemed like a wild unction, but Meg knew it was one of the most right things she had ever done.

Jon and the pastor stood under the arbor that was on the edge of the bluff. The scene was the most beautiful thing Meg could imagine as the calm, turquoise, tropical waters gently lapped upon the shore beneath them. Governor Johnson slipped his arm around her shoulders and kissed her on her cheek.

Meg had decided to wear a white wedding dress. She felt like a wedding was not right unless the bride was dressed in white. After all, Vera Wang said "every bride deserves to wear white." Meg and Jon had worked hard to maintain their commitment to make their wedding night a special occasion in every way, so if anyone deserved white, it was her. Though Meg considered several Vera Wang dresses, she ended up wearing a custom made Oscar de la Renta gown.

She was inspired by a picture she saw of Jenna Bush on her wedding day and decided she wanted one similar to Jenna's. It was a beaded, organza dress with a small train that made it perfect for an outdoor wedding. Mrs. Bush had described it as "simple, sophisticated, and elegant," and Meg decided that was just the look she wanted. She chose not to wear a veil because she had no idea what the wind would be doing on her wedding day that high up on a bluff.

The days leading up to the wedding had been memorable as she spent a lot of time making final plans with her mother. Her mother had loved every minute of it, and Meg knew she would cherish this time for the rest of her life. Her mother now sat on the second row smiling back at Meg.

Offering his arm to Meg, Governor Johnson stepped forward, and she smiled up at this gracious man who had stepped in to be her father on this special occasion. She couldn't believe he flew to George Town during the busiest part of his presidential campaign. The people in charge of his campaign were putting an election spin on his commitment to his family, but Meg knew his presence had nothing to do with politics.

As she thought about the fact that Randall Johnson loved her, a tear began to flow down her cheek. Pulling out his handkerchief, the Governor gently wiped the tear from her cheek. He kissed her forehead with great tenderness before turning to escort her down the aisle.

Though Meg had decided not to use flower girls, Margaret, the wedding coordinator, had decorated the green, grassy aisle with daisy petals. It all appeared to be so dreamy that Meg wondered if she needed to pinch herself to make sure she wasn't dreaming. She seemed to float beside the Governor before magically appearing next to the most handsome and gracious man on this wonderful planet.

Jon stood before her in a sharp looking, black tuxedo and a pastel, yellow cummerbund. He wore a daisy in his lapel and a beautiful smile upon his face.

The ceremony was short but meaningful. As the minister told Jon he could kiss his bride, Jon pulled Meg into his arms and kissed her with both gentleness and passion. Meg felt the flow of Jon's tears running down her cheeks, which caused her to lose control. She hugged him close as the small crowd clapped with satisfaction and joy at the marriage of these two special people.

Meg knew there was no way to keep pictures of her wedding out of the papers because of Governor Johnson's participation, so she had instructed her photographer on which pose she would want shared with the world. Meg was finding it difficult handling her overnight fame and knew all of the society papers would be writing about her wedding the following week.

One leading society magazine paid her a lot of money to have one of her wedding pictures on the front cover. Meg was afraid that the events leading to the renewed friendship she found with Jon would make it into the tabloids. Much of the story would be very sweet, but if the world knew about the attempted attack on the Republican National Convention, Homeland Security was afraid there would be copycat attacks.

Although the attempted terrorist attack would be kept under wraps, Meg knew that the story might eventually come out about her soldier husband being killed in battle. She was sure this would stir the patriotic hearts of Americans. Though she didn't like the sudden fame, she knew that if Governor Johnson was going to be the next President of the United States, she had better get used to the limelight.

The ceremony was followed by a wonderful reception filled with dancing, laughter, and enough food to feed the whole population of the island. Meg enjoyed spending the time with her family. She couldn't help but notice that Jose couldn't keep his eyes off of her best friend. Ann didn't seem to mind one bit.

She also noticed that the seventeen-year-old son of the manager of the Emerald Isle resort danced with Lacy more than once. Lacy didn't seem to mind that either. Meg made a mental note to warn her sister about Lacy's apparent raging hormones and the doting boy who seemed to have a similar problem.

Meg regretted she didn't have more time to spend with her family. She was so happy to have them present, and she was thrilled that Jon's brother, Mike, could fly down from Raleigh to stand with Jon. She remembered Mike from her childhood, but he was three years older than Jon. He had not hung around much when she was a kid. Meg figured she would have many years to get to know Mike better.

As the sun began to go down in the western sky, Jon and Meg ran through a barrage of birdseed as they made their way down the dock to the waiting ship. The newlyweds walked up the gang plank and stood on the deck to wave goodbye to their friends and family. The ship pulled away from the dock, and Captain Buffington blew the loud fog horn from the bridge.

Jon held Meg tightly in his arms. "You are the most beautiful woman in the entire world."

Meg smiled before she stood on her tip toes to kiss his cheek. "You know, just a few months ago when Ann was badgering me about our relationship, I told her that I would at least hope for tomorrow. I had no idea that tomorrow was going to be so wonderful."

Jon picked Meg up and carried her to the bottom of the stairs to their cabin. "I love you so much, Mrs. Davenport. I wish I could carry you up the stairs, but I don't think these stairs were made for two."

Meg climbed the stairs ahead of her husband and reached out for his hand when he got to the top stair. He picked her up again.

"I love you, Dr. Davenport. I am the luckiest woman in the world. I give myself completely to you for the rest of my life."

"You did that earlier today, sweetheart."

"True, but I'll do it again every day for as long as I live."

"I know that we are going to find that sunken treasure, Meg, but as far as I am concerned, I hit the mother lode about two months ago."

Jon opened the door to their cabin and walked inside with his bride. Meg traced his jawline with her forefinger before kicking the door to the cabin with her foot. As the door closed to their wedding suite, *The Discoverer* motored south toward the Caribbean.

CHAPTER SIXTEEN

Celebration Cruise

At the end of the second week of their honeymoon, Meg and Jon flew from Puerto Rico to Richmond, Virginia to be with Governor Johnson on Election Day. Though neither wanted to put their dream voyage on hold, both agreed that Richmond was the place they needed to be on November sixth.

Tension rose that evening as the Johnson family watched exit polling numbers coming in from around the country. Meg had enjoyed the day with Mrs. Johnson, who now insisted on being called Gina, and now the family gathered with their supporters at the Richmond Hilton. Meg had never experienced such excitement and anticipation.

Just after 11:00 p.m., the Democratic senator conceded the election, and Governor Randall Johnson made his public appearance to give his acceptance speech. At the conclusion of the speech, Gina, Jon and Meg joined the President Elect on the platform to the wild cheers and applause of an excited nation.

Jon and Meg's picture appeared in every major newspaper in the country the following day as they were recognized as part of the first family. After the election was sealed, Don Best flew the newlyweds back to Puerto Rico to pick up their cruise in the southern Caribbean. Meg was exhausted and slept for most of the flight back to their ship.

The four weeks spent on their honeymoon cruise ended all too soon. Their last stop had been Honduras, where they picked up the crane and made some inquiries as to what happened to the *San Roque*. There were a number of rumors as to where the captain had buried the treasure some four hundred years earlier, but no one had ever found the first piece of gold.

"Just imagine all of that treasure hidden away where no one will ever find it," Meg said wistfully.

"Someone will find it," Jon said. "One day this area will all be commercialized. Someone will come along here and find it while digging a foundation for some huge resort hotel."

"Maybe we should go into the resort building business," Meg teased.

"I think we have enough businesses going for now. Besides that, I'm a bit preoccupied at the moment. I think if we find the *Ambrosio*, we'll be doing pretty good."

Jon and Meg went scuba diving every available opportunity as Meg was becoming quite an expert diver. They agreed their favorite spot was about thirty miles north of Honduras in an area called *Islas de las Bahia* or the *Bay Islands*. This area did not contain the tourist traffic of places closer to the states, and the couple loved diving the shallow reefs and deeper wrecks. They spent a lot of time diving the Meso America Reef, which Jon had told Meg was the second largest living reef in the world. He showed her sponges as large as refrigerators, manta rays, and even a whale shark.

One day short of four weeks after the wedding, *The Discoverer* docked in what Jon often called Pirates' Cove. There was some folklore about pirates hiding out in the Exumas, and Jon decided their cove would have been the perfect place for a pirate's ship. Even though there was no evidence of pirates ever being on their part of the island, Jon was convinced this was their main hideout. He decided he would call it Pirates' Cove.

The trip had been a dream come true for Meg as she not only enjoyed being with a man who loved her deeply, but she also experienced a lifestyle aboard her own ship that only the rich and famous get to experience. She met some wonderful people along the way and experienced a taste of island life she would never forget. Meg also enjoyed meeting the staff of *The Discoverer*. She especially hit it off with a young woman named Carla, who worked in the kitchen.

Meg had misplaced a diamond necklace Jon had given her as a wedding gift, and Carla found it. Meg had noticed it missing but couldn't imagine why it wasn't on the dresser in her cabin. She searched everywhere in her room and was becoming quite frantic. Jon never told her how much the necklace was worth, but she knew it had to be quite valuable. One afternoon, Captain Buffington dropped anchor just off Barbados, so Jon and Meg took their small boat in for shopping. When they returned, Carla met them at the bottom of the stairs leading to their cabin. She held Meg's necklace in her hand.

"Is this yours?" Carla asked. "I found it dangling on the fire extinguisher mount near the dining room door."

There was a large fire extinguisher mounted to the wall near the entrance leading to the dining area. Though it hung securely against the wall, Meg could imagine her necklace dangling in the space created behind it. It was a strange place for this expensive necklace to be; she figured it must have fallen from her neck and become lodged there.

"Oh, Carla. Thank you so much. I have been frantically searching everywhere for this."

Meg took the necklace and hugged Carla. She was amazed that Carla had returned such a valuable piece of jewelry. She could have sold the necklace for thousands of dollars, which would have been a big help to her. Meg knew Carla was not well off, so returning such a valuable necklace must mean she was a person of integrity. After this exchange, Meg mentioned to Jon how wonderful the ship's staff was and that the Captain had done a great job in choosing people of such impeccable character.

As the newlyweds stepped off *The Discoverer* onto their own dock, Ann ran toward Meg with her arms held wide. Jose was not far behind her. Meg was so happy to see her best friend she became a little emotional at the reunion. Ann was smiling as big as the world, and Meg could tell that spending a month together on the island with Jose had moved their relationship to new levels.

The two friends walked arm in arm up the dock toward the house while Meg talked nonstop about their trip. After she unpacked, Meg and Jon went to see the progress on the guesthouse. They were amazed to see that it was dried in and looked complete from the outside.

When Jose took them through the building, there was still work to be done inside, but it was coming along. It would be a very nice addition to what was becoming their compound. Jon designed the house to offer four bedrooms downstairs and four upstairs. Each bedroom would also include a bathroom, and Jon included two private showers per bathroom in the plans. A den area was included on both floors plus a kitchen on the downstairs level.

Jose informed Jon that he had negotiated the purchase of an additional five acres of land adjacent to Jon's property, as Jon had instructed him to do. Adding the extra acreage would be helpful as Jon sought to turn their property into what Meg had called a "research resort." Most of the additional acreage would not be oceanfront, but they would gain another couple of hundred feet along the bluff.

Some of the equipment that had been ordered before the wedding had arrived, including a small bobcat that would be useful in loading gear on and off *The Discoverer.* Jose reported to Jon that someone would need to make a trip over to Miami for a couple of days in order to have what he called the seavac system installed. It was a huge vacuum cleaner that would pull the sand off the bottom of the ocean. It would help them to locate items buried under the sand. The loose sand would be pulled off of the bottom and dumped in a location about a couple of hundred yards away in order to keep the working area clear of silt. All in all, things seemed to be going well.

As the four friends sat down together at dinner, Jon asked, "Other than ordering materials and strengthening the dock for heavy equipment, what else have you guys been doing?"

Jose looked at Ann with a grin. "Well, we've been busy overseeing construction, and I took Ann out for scuba training. She learns fast. Thanks for leaving me the keys to your boat."

"You are welcome to stay here in the main house for as long as you want," Jon said. "I'm assuming the apartment in

the guesthouse will be completed in another month or so. I'm
sure it will be ready by the first of the year at the latest."

"So, what are our plans?" Jose asked.

Jon replied, "I'm thinking we can do some initial diving on
suspected sites before Christmas, but I want it to look like
we're just sport diving. I would rather locate the wreck before
making our official claim of the site. Let's assume we'll find
something in the next month. We can file the paperwork with
the Bahamian officials and start in earnest on January second."

"I think that sounds great," Ann agreed. "Believe it or not,
I'm getting the hang of scuba diving. Meg, I did sign us up for
the certification class this weekend, like you said. Once that's
done, we'll be all legal."

Ann walked over and put her hand on Jose's shoulder.
"Jose and I were kind of thinking of going to the States on
December twenty-second for Christmas with my family. We'll
plan to be back on December thirtieth, if that's okay with you."

"Sure, that's fine," Jon acknowledged. "We'll be going
home for Christmas as well. We need to find a caretaker to live
on site while we are gone."

Jose said, "I met Diego Rodriquez. He is the father of
Pedro, who works at Emerald Isles."

"Yes, I remember Pedro," Jon offered.

"Diego is honest and a hard worker," Jose continued. "I
think he'll be open to work for us."

Jon reached to refill his glass of iced tea. "That sounds very
good. Could you look into hiring him to live on site full-time?"

"Yes. I'll see him tomorrow," Jose answered.

"I'll pay him a full-time salary plus provide a place for him
to live. We can build a caretaker's home on the new property as
soon as it's ours. Can he build?"

"Yes. He built the house he lives in now, but it is small."

"Tell him I'll provide a bigger house, and he can oversee its construction. I'm sure we'll need someone to keep the grounds along with doing repairs from time to time. Also, we'll need a person on-site when we're traveling."

The team talked on into the night planning, scheming, and dreaming. Jon sent word to Captain Buffington that he would need to take *The Discoverer* and the crew back to Miami the following day where they would stay until after Christmas. He asked that the ship return with minimal staff on Wednesday, January second. After the fifth cup of coffee, Jon told the group he was exhausted.

"While you young people can stay up all night acting like teenagers, I have to get my beauty sleep."

****

Carla was so excited about getting back to Miami to see Luis. She had reported to him by e-mail about her trip, but she looked forward to telling him all about her experience face-to-face. As soon as she was able to get a cell signal for her phone, she called him.

"Luis. I have missed you so much."

"Hey, baby. Did you get anything else for me?"

"I learned a lot of things about the Davenports. They are very nice people. Meg and I became friends on the trip."

Luis laughed aloud. "Is that a fact? How did you manage that?"

"I arranged to find Meg's missing necklace."

Carla reported to Luis how she had taken Meg's diamond necklace and returned it a few days later as if she found it. Carla had been amazed that Jon and Meg left their cabin unlocked when they went ashore. Taking the necklace from the dresser was like taking candy from a baby, and Carla could tell that Luis was pleased. It made her so happy to know that she had handled that situation well.

Carla felt like she deserved an acting award for the role she played. She knew it would at least win her respect from Meg and love from her man. Getting close to Meg would help her gain information to pass along to Luis. It had been tempting to keep the necklace, but knowing Luis would be proud of her was even more enticing.

"You did real good," Luis said. "So what's everyone doing next?"

"Jon is sending me back to Miami until after Christmas. That means I get to spend Christmas with you, Luis. Isn't that wonderful?"

"Yes, that's wonderful. Just gather as much information as you can before leaving. The more I know, the better everything will be."

"Okay, Luis. I'll see you tomorrow. I…I can't wait to see you."

"Oh, I'm looking forward to seeing you, too."

CHAPTER SEVENTEEN

Our Reef

First thing on the Monday morning before Thanksgiving, Meg, Jose and Ann lined up on the dock as Jon prepared to lift a sheet off the back of the boat.

"I just figured this was the best name for the yacht, considering our new life sort of started aboard her."

"Go ahead and lift the sheet," Meg encouraged. "We're all dying to know her name."

With one jerk of the sheet, Jon revealed the name that had been painted on the back of the yacht.

They all said in unison: "The *New Beginnings.*"

Meg put her arms around Jon. "I love it, sweetheart."

"I think it's perfect," Ann agreed.

"Well, let's get aboard the *New Beginnings*. I recorded the coordinates to that location Meg and I discovered months ago. I say it's time we go check it out."

Even though it had not been that long since August, Jon felt like it had been an eternity because so much had happened during those three months. He remembered seeing what could have been a coral encrusted mast sticking out from the main reef when Meg was driving the yacht on their second day together.

He smiled when he remembered standing on the bridge, wrapped in a towel, and looking at the depth monitor. Jon was positive there had been an irregularity in the reef. He couldn't believe it had taken them so long to get back to that spot.

Jon dropped anchor on the beach side of the reef and explained to Jose and Ann what they had previously discovered. The group donned their equipment and made one last check before stepping into the crystal clear water.

As many times as Jon had fallen over the side of a boat to descend into the depths of the ocean, he never tired of it. Every dive was a new experience, and even the same reef would appear different from the way it had looked the previous day. He and Meg held hands as they kicked their way down to the sandy bottom about thirty feet below the surface.

From the bottom, the reef rose four or five feet up but then fell on the other side to about seventy feet deep. It created a wonderful wall of reef that dropped straight down into the depths, which made for exciting diving. Jon was thrilled that even the ocean floor on the deep side of the wall was only one hundred feet deep. While that would require careful planning, it was still shallow enough that he and Meg could enjoy diving it for many months and years in the future. As far as he was concerned, this was their reef. While hovering near the base of the shallow side of the reef, three huge amberjacks swam just overhead. An eerie shadow was cast on the small group of divers.

With one easy kick, Jon led the way by sailing along the top of this rock-like structure that was cascaded in color. Though the sponges weren't anywhere near as large as the ones in Honduras, the reef was still covered with them. Once again, the familiar cherubfish and queen angelfish swam over the top of the reef.

Meg grabbed Jon's hand and pulled him down toward the sand on the shallow side of the reef. She pointed to a tiny fish hovering near the base of the reef. Jon recognized it as the unusual mandarin fish. Though this type of fish wasn't that rare, they were so small and therefore easy to be missed by divers who were intent on larger finds. Its bright blue, orange and yellow colors were intoxicating, and Jon wished he had brought his camera along to capture the beautiful sight.

He pointed the unusual find out to Ann, who seemed to be quite impressed and didn't want to move on to other discoveries. He prodded them forward as the group returned to the crest of the reef. When he saw that he only had 600 psi of air left, he motioned for them to return to the boat. Even though they had not stayed down past their limit, he stopped at the ten-foot mark on the anchor line for a few minutes just to begin developing the habit in the other divers.

The divers dropped their gear inside the boat, and Meg stepped out of her shorty wetsuit. She had grown quite tan over the weeks in the tropics, which stood in stark contrast to her bright yellow bikini. Jon looked at her and winked, which caused Meg to blush a bit. Jose and Ann seemed oblivious to their antics and were headed into the galley to get a drink.

"That was so incredible," Meg said as she tried to shake some water out of her ear. "I love the reef. I couldn't help but feel like it's all ours."

"I felt the same way."

"What was that blue and orange fish?" Ann asked as Jon and Meg walked into the air-conditioned galley.

"That was a mandarin fish," Jon said. "You don't see them very often because they are so small and typically swim away when you come close."

"It was so cute," Ann said. "I wanted to catch it and bring it home."

"Well, I was disappointed we didn't find the mast to our Spanish galleon," Jon acknowledged. "I know this is where we saw it last time. I think we need to ride up and down the reef to see if we can spot it on our monitor again."

"You probably need to stand naked on the bridge or we'll never find it," Meg teased.

"Naked on the bridge?" Ann asked in shock.

"Don't ask," Jon said. "I wasn't naked anyway."

"Sounds kinky to me," Ann teased. "What were you two up to?"

"What happens in the Bahamas stays in the Bahamas," Meg said solemnly.

"Why don't we rest a while, eat some lunch, and then make another dive?" Jon said.

"I will grill hamburgers," Jose volunteered. "Special recipe."

"Sounds good to me," Jon agreed. "I think I'll pull up the anchor and coast along the reef. Meg, why don't you join me on the bridge and see if you can spot that irregularity again?"

"Aye, aye Skipper Sir," Meg giggled before saluting.

Jon pulled the boat toward the anchor line in order to provide enough slack to get the anchor loose from the rocks on the bottom. He pressed the button to engage the motor, and the anchor began rolling up into the bow of the boat. Following the direction of the reef, Jon moved forward slowly while Meg focused on the monitor. After about twenty minutes, Jon turned the yacht around to go back to the original coordinates.

"Nothing," he said. "I would have sworn this was the spot. I wrote it down, and I saved it in the GPS."

"Go west," Meg suggested. "Or, I guess it's northwest. Maybe we were just a little off."

Jon took the boat in the other direction for about ten minutes, but still nothing. Ann's head popped up at the top of the ladder.

"Dinner is served," she said with a French accent.

"Good because I'm starving," Meg said as she looked at Jon.

"Oh please," Ann said. "You two act like fourteen year olds."

"Fourteen year olds better not act like this," Meg said as she and Ann climbed back down the ladder.

"I did," Ann responded.

"For some reason, I'm not surprised," Jon faintly heard Meg reply as they walked into the galley.

Jon dropped the anchor again before heading down to the galley. He hoped that after lunch they would discover the ancient mast just below the yacht. The smells of the grilled ground beef was making his stomach growl as he walked into the dining area.

He joined the other three at the table and accepted his plate from Meg. She had already placed a burger, chips and beans on the plate. He thanked her as he reached for the ketchup and mustard. Over lunch, they discussed the possibilities of the location of that spot Meg had previously seen on the sonar fish finder.

Jon insisted he could not have made a mistake in plotting the current coordinates months ago, but he acknowledged that they could have drifted a little by the time he put pen to paper. They decided to start slowly working the reef in both directions and hoped to eventually find the spot.

After lunch, the four made a second and third dive but had no luck in locating the mast. Though everyone was discouraged, they refused to give up. That night over the dining table, Jon drew out a map of the reef, and the group developed a search and rescue type strategy to explore it. The next four weeks were spent diving the reef, searching for what Jon called an "irregularity," but nothing of interest was located. Christmas was now ten days away, and the group would soon be heading back to the states for the holiday.

"Let's go diving," Meg said one night at about 10:00. "We haven't done a night dive since that first time in our secret lagoon."

"If you want to," Jon hesitated. "I have learned through thirty-six years that to have a happy marriage requires a happy wife."

"Hmmm. I'm glad to know you've learned something that important. That piece of information could come in handy."

They went upstairs to change into their bathing suits. Meg put on her black one-piece while Jon pulled out his old familiar faded red swim shorts.

Jon pulled Meg into his arms and kissed her. As Meg's arms slid around Jon's body, he considered forgetting the night dive.

Jon said. "How was I so lucky to get to have you as my wife?"

Meg smiled, bent over to pick up her towel, and began walking away from Jon. Jon grabbed her around the waist while she giggled and squirmed.

They headed down to the dock to untie the *New Beginnings*. Within fifteen minutes, Jon dropped the anchor over the reef, and they stepped into their neoprene wetsuits and pulled on their scuba gear. He found two strong flashlights before turning on Meg's air. She turned on his air, and both divers sucked through their regulators to make sure everything worked as it should.

When Jon fell over the side of the boat into the dark waters, he experienced a momentary rush of adrenaline that he always felt in the first few moments of a night dive. He knew that Meg would be uneasy about falling into the pitch-black ocean, so he turned on his strong flashlight as he hoped to assuage some of her fears.

They swam toward the reef, and Jon was once again in awe at the indescribable beauty of a night visit to this strange, underwater world. He smiled to himself when he saw Meg looking at a six-foot nurse shark trying to hide its head under an overhang in the reef. The sight of a harmless shark no longer frightened her. After about thirty minutes of bottom time, he motioned for Meg to follow him back toward the boat.

"That was so amazing," Meg said as their heads broke the surface.

"I never cease being in awe of this incredible beauty," Jon agreed. "I'm so glad you insisted on doing this."

Jon took Meg's fins so she could climb up on the platform along the back of the boat. Once he handed both pair of fins to Meg, he joined her aboard the boat, and the two of them began stowing their gear. Meg unzipped her wetsuit and stepped under the freshwater shower on the back of the boat. Taking her into his arms and holding her against his body, Jon joined her under the spray. After showering, they spread a towel out on the front of the boat and lay side-by-side and stared up at the stars while their bodies dried in the ocean breeze.

CHAPTER EIGHTEEN

Night Dive

An hour passed by quickly as the two enjoyed the quietness and romance of the moonlit night. Jon finally stood to help Meg to her feet. The couple leaned against the front railing of the boat as tears rolled down Meg's face.

"I can't explain to you how I feel," Meg began saying. "You have made me so happy."

"You have made me happy too," Jon agreed. "My heart had become so hard and calloused with pain, but you somehow broke through the hardness that had encircled it. Do you know that song that says 'loves like a hurricane?' Well, I feel like I went through a storm, and now your love has helped me find a new life."

"Do you realize what you just said?" Meg asked.

"I know it sounded a little corny, but I really mean it."

"No, I mean you said something about a hurricane."

"Yeah. It was a song I heard."

"No, Jon. Listen to what I'm saying. That ship was encrusted in the reef, and a hurricane came along while we were hiding out in the cave on Conception Island."

"Meg, you may be onto something. That storm could have dislodged the mast, or whatever that thing was that we saw."

"So much has happened since that hurricane blew through here that night that it just wasn't on our minds," Meg said.

"I bet our coordinates were right all along. It's just that the mast was broken loose. I'm sure that hurricanes create some mighty rough seas. How about another night dive?"

"Sounds good to me," Meg said. "Have we stayed out of the water long enough? I'd hate to get the bends when we're on the heels of finding the treasure."

"Let's give it another fifteen minutes. You make us some coffee, and I'll move us back to the spot."

Jon fired up the engine and began moving the boat slowly northwest to the original coordinates. He dropped the anchor and climbed down to the galley for a cup of coffee. While drinking the warm brew, Jon pulled out a copy of Duncan Matthewson's *Treasure of Atocha*. He scanned through some of the pictures of what the original treasure looked like when the Fisher family first brought it up from the sea floor. He showed the pictures to Meg commenting on how the gold coins looked as bright and shiny as ever in the light from underwater flash photography.

He reminded Meg that the gold would not look that bright in the deeper waters without some type of artificial light. He pointed to a picture of the ballast stones and explained to her that these were placed in the lower part of the ancient ships to keep them from being top heavy.

When they had finished their coffee, Jon and Meg stepped back into their gear and fell into the water. Because the ocean floor was about one hundred feet deep on the north side of the reef, Jon knew their bottom time would only be a few minutes before needing to return to the surface. He and Meg were not prepared to spend time decompressing, so it was important that they time the dive with precision.

The dark water embraced them like a tight, winter's glove. The creatures all around them seemed to recognize the humans as foreigners to the strange underwater world and the undersea creatures of the night swam quickly out of reach of the divers.

Once on the bottom, they swam around for a couple of minutes when Jon suddenly felt Meg jerk his fin. He looked behind him and saw her shining her light on a long tubular piece of coral. When Jon looked at one end of the tube, he could see it had broken off something, and the core of the tube was wood. It had to be part of the mast from a Spanish galleon. If he had not been one hundred feet underwater with a regulator in his mouth, he would have shouted for joy.

Jon looked all around the sea floor for anything that might be treasure. He and Meg started picking up every little round object they could find and put it in their net bags attached to their belts. Meg even placed a larger piece of coral in her bag that could have been construed as being rectangular, if one looked at the object with a great deal of creativity. Jon pointed toward the surface, and the two kicked their way back to the boat.

When they broke the surface, Jon yanked his facemask off and removed Meg's as well. He pulled Meg into his arms and kissed her. Climbing aboard the boat, Jon heaved the heavy net bags aboard and reached down for Meg's hand. They once again went through the routine of rinsing in the fresh water. When the gear was cleaned and stowed, Jon pulled up the anchor, and the *New Beginnings* sped back to the dock in Pirates' Cove.

"See what a little poetry on the high seas will get you," Jon said as he pulled Meg into his arms while being careful to keep one hand on the steering wheel.

"Maybe you should try some more poetry right now and see what else we can find," Meg teased.

"I know this. I don't care if Jose and Ann are sleeping; we're getting them up right now. We've got to tell them this news."

Once back at the dock in the safety of Pirate's Cove, Jon tied up the boat while Meg ran to the storage building for a cart. They put their net bags in the cart and hurried toward the house. Once they came to the steps leading up the bluff, Jon grabbed one end of the cart while Meg grabbed the other end.

"You know," Jon said to Meg as they dragged and pushed the cart up the steps, "we're going to have to come up with a better way to get heavy things up and down this bluff."

"You can say that again," Meg grunted.

They placed the cart in the foyer of the house and ran up the stairs. Jon pounded on Jose's door while Meg ran into Ann's room shaking her out of her sleep-filled stupor. Jose came to the door in his boxers wiping his eyes. At the sight of Jon, a concerned look came over his face.

"Get dressed; and come to the dining room. We have something to show you."

"What's wrong?" Jose asked in confusion.

"Nothing is wrong," Jon said. "In fact, something is quite right. Come on downstairs."

Within a few minutes, the four were gathered around the dining room table where Meg had spread out some blankets to protect the beautiful cherry wood of her tabletop. One by one,

Jon pulled out the encrusted items from the net bags, which they had taken from the sea floor. He laid them on the table.

"Where did you get this?" Ann asked.

"Let's just say that we went night diving and had an inspired revelation," Meg said.

Jon and Meg told their friends the story of the night dive, leaving out some of the details of their time on the bow of the boat. Jon told of finding the broken off mast and how they decided to just gather up anything that could be something of value. His plan was to place the items in the electrolyte solution, and hopefully in the morning, there would be something of value underneath all of that crust.

"It hit us, in a rather profound way, that Hurricane Lynn must have caused whatever we had seen to shift or break off. When we dove straight down the reef at the coordinates we had written down back in August, the mast of what I assume to be the *Ambrosio* lay on the bottom of the ocean. Well, it wasn't exactly straight down. It had moved a little ways from the bottom of the reef."

"I can't believe it," Jose said in astonishment. "It was there all along."

"Yep," Meg answered. "Right under our noses."

"I suggest we put these things in the bath and make plans for another dive first thing in the morning."

Meg was so excited that she had trouble going to sleep. She was amazed that her sexy husband lay beside her snoozing away. Before she knew it, however, she was opening her eyes to a rising sun through her bedroom window. When she jumped out of bed, Jon sat up and grabbed her arm.

"Wait just a second young lady," he said. "You can't go look at it without me."

Pulling her arm away, Meg raced for the door of their bedroom. Jon ran after her only to be stopped by Meg at the top of the stairs.

"Hey, Tarzan," Meg said, "you might want to put on some clothes. We're not the only ones in this house."

Jon ran back into the room and grabbed his gym shorts as Meg hurried down the stairs. When Jon returned to the stairs, he saw Jose's door open up, and Ann was already on the bottom step just behind Meg. Jon and Jose hurried to the mudroom where Jon had placed the items in a ceramic tub. Meg was already on her rubber-gloved hands and knees, inspecting each item in the bowl.

"I believe we have something," Meg said with excitement in her voice.

She held up one of the clumps of crust and pointed to where the solution had eaten away the crust. Peeking out from under hundreds of years of thick coating was a smooth, round stone. She pointed to a few other stones that appeared to be exactly like the one she held in her hand.

"Ballast stones," Jon offered. "There's a ton of them down there."

Ann raised an eyebrow. "Ballast stones?"

"They were river stones placed in the bilge of a ship to help keep the ship steady."

Meg picked up the rectangular object, but it was still bound by crust. It had to be something of significance, but it needed more time in the solution.

Jon said, "I suggest we get some breakfast and go make our dive. It's going to take a while for that stuff to break loose. No doubt we are onto something."

Meg said, "I think we should alert Diego to be more diligent in watching the house. Don't let him know there's anything in the house, but let's tell him we're going out for a while."

After a breakfast of waffles and sausage, Jon covered the tub with a piece of paneling and some loose clothes in the mudroom before he locked the mudroom door. Meg called Diego to tell him of their plans to be gone for a while, and the friends descended the stairs to the *New Beginnings*. Within minutes, they were headed to the reef.

After dropping anchor, all four divers were in the water kicking their way down to the sea floor 104 feet beneath the surface. Even though it was a bright, sunny day, the ocean was darker at this depth because the water filtered the rays of the sun. Meg noticed Ann's yellow wetsuit was not nearly as bright as it was on the surface.

Jon pointed to the mast in the sand, and hoping to find treasure, they all began picking up objects from the seafloor. While a few items were placed in the net bags attached to their belts, Jon had suggested caution in bringing up a lot of the stuff. If it wasn't treasure, there would be no need to haul it up from the bottom. He informed them there would be a learning curve, or if they weren't careful, the result of their labor would be nothing more than a ton of rocks aboard their boat.

Jose picked up what had to be the hilt of a broken sword. Although much of it was covered with barnacles, the outline of the handle was unmistakable.

While Jon and Ann were admiring Jose's sword, Meg noticed a rectangular outline in the sand. She fanned the sand away and pulled a golden bar free from its sandy tomb. Though the color was faded at this depth, there was no doubt it was a bar of gold. She held it up in triumph, which made the sword quite insignificant.

They returned to the boat after twenty minutes, because Jon didn't want to worry with decompression. One by one they pulled the items from their net bags and laid them on the deck of the boat. Pulling up the anchor, Jon powered back toward their home. Once in the house, Meg hurried to the mudroom to see if there was any progress. She could see a little more smooth ballast stones on some of the objects. Because the tub was full of items brought in from the previous night, they would be unable to add anything from their most recent collection.

"It's going to have to sit in the bath for twenty-four hours before we know anything," Jon said. "It's coated with a thick crust. Maybe we need to busy ourselves doing other things and agree not to look until dinner time."

"Right," Ann said, sarcasm laced her voice. "I can't just walk around all day like there's nothing in there. I'll go crazy."

"Okay, you can sit in the mudroom all day staring at the stuff, and we'll all get busy on the building we're working on down at the docks," Meg suggested

"You're right, smarty," Ann remarked to Meg with a playful smirk. "Maybe if we all get busy with the project, we won't think so much about the treasure."

"I'm not sure we can call it treasure yet," Jon said. "I guess we at least have a gold bar, but we need to get the shell of our building up before we leave for home this week."

After grabbing a bite for lunch, the men picked up their tools and walked toward the docks. Meg and Ann worked together to carry a cooler of water to the work site. They discovered Diego was already working on the structure and had made some pretty good progress by himself. Jon wanted a workstation closer to the docks that could also be used for extra storage. The spot for the storage building was ten feet above the ocean line, but it still had easy access to the dock. Jose had suggested they plan to build a ramp from the dock to the building so it would be easier to move items to and from the boats to the storage building.

"Since Judy's not here yet, I suppose Ann and I should go work on dinner," Meg suggested after working for a while.

"Yeah, and I'm sure you're not going to peek at the tub," Jon said wiping sweat from his face.

"Of course not," Ann said innocently.

Meg and Ann walked up the steps to the house while Jon, Jose, and Diego continued working away. While Meg washed her hands to start preparing dinner, Ann walked straight into the mudroom.

As Meg filled a pot with water for spaghetti noodles, she heard Ann gasp loudly. "Meg…You are not going to believe this."

CHAPTER NINETEEN

Awestruck

About an hour later, Meg called down the bluff, and the three men put away their tools. Diego had declined the invitation to join them for dinner, so only Jon and Jose began the climb toward the main house. Meg glanced down the stairs to see Jon looking up as if he dreaded the climb. It wasn't that far, but Meg had a feeling Jon would be creating a cart path for an all-terrain vehicle before long.

When Jon and Jose sat down for dinner, there was a gleaming, ancient gold coin lying on their plates. The two women were about to burst with excitement.

"We couldn't help but look," Ann blurted out.

"Why am I not surprised?" Jon stated with mock exasperation.

"One of the objects was a small container with five gold coins," Meg revealed. "The rest was either trash or ballast stones. There is one more thing in there, but it is going to have to sit for a while. It's the biggest item we brought up. It may be nothing, but at least we found some gold. That should mean something."

"It does mean something," Jon said with excitement. "It means we are onto what could be our wreck. I think this calls for a celebration."

"We figured you would say that," Meg said.

"What do you mean?" Jon replied.

"Once we saw the gold, we put dinner away because we thought you would want to take us out."

"You little sneak. And what have you been doing up here all this time?"

"We took a shower," Ann said. "I don't suppose you noticed how sweet and clean we happen to be?"

"As a matter of fact," Jose chimed in, "you did catch my eye."

"It's settled. Jose and I will get dressed. We're going to the Bonefish Lodge."

The group enjoyed an amazing Bahamian style fish dinner while celebrating the beginning of something they all hoped would be a memorable experience. While driving to the restaurant, Jon had warned them not to mention the basis of their celebration or not to even say the word "treasure" or "gold."

The meal was wonderful with an air of expectancy. They spoke about their next move while being careful not to say anything about what they were doing. The excited little group arrived back at the house on the bluff around midnight, and all four dragged themselves up the stairs to get ready for bed. Jon collapsed back on the bed with exhaustion and didn't even remove his clothes. Meg put on her gown before crawling into bed beside Jon.

"Jon. Jon!"

"Huh?" He mumbled.

"Don't go to sleep. You've got to take off your clothes."

"I don't have the energy."

Meg got Jon to at least take off his jeans. She lay down beside her beautiful husband and fell into a deep sleep.

Meg opened her sleepy eyes to a room filled with the early morning sun. She had slept hard but still felt exhausted. She heard the shower going as she stepped into the bathroom.

"Is it okay to dump that solution in the grass or do we need to carry it away from the yard?" Meg shouted over the noise of the shower.

"It needs to be carried off," Jon said. "I have a feeling it could kill the grass we are trying to grow. If you're dressed, why don't you go pull out whatever is left of the rocks. I'll get Jose to help me carry the tub out to the edge of the yard before breakfast."

"Okay," Meg said. "I'll get rid of the rocks, but I'm keeping the ballast stones. I'm going to get some coffee going first. Boy, I miss Judy. It's not just that I hate the fact I have to fix breakfast, but I miss her being with us."

"Yeah, I miss her too," Jon agreed as he stepped out of the shower and grabbed his towel.

"You're too fast. I wanted to bring you coffee and the paper so you could sit out on the balcony while I prepare breakfast."

"You're so sweet, honey. Why don't I fix breakfast? I'll make us some eggs, grits and bacon. I'll even bake biscuits from scratch."

"Now you're trying to make me look bad," Meg teased.

"There is not a thing in the world I could ever do to make you look bad," Jon said as he kissed Meg tenderly.

Meg walked down the stairs and into the kitchen to put on some coffee. She couldn't help but pause at the picture window over the sink that revealed a great view out of the side of their home. Meg thought the sunny morning was beautiful as she watched a parrot land in a branch of the large banana tree just outside the kitchen window.

She could never get used to looking out her window at a bunch of bananas waiting to be picked. The parrot just sat there looking at Meg as if the two met at the window every morning for a brief chat. The bird's brilliant colors were beautiful and were one of the many things Meg loved about living in this region. She wondered if she would ever tire of paradise. Meg pulled the plastic bag of trash out of the trashcan so she could use the can to carry out the debris left in the rubber tub. She walked into the mudroom and screamed.

Ready to encounter a snake or some large island rat, Jon ran down the steps at the sound of his wife's scream. Instead of a snake, Meg was on her knees looking into the tub. The final large object was no longer covered in barnacles or coral, but sat in the solution at the bottom of the tub. It was a small, rectangular chest that was about sixteen or eighteen inches long and maybe a little over a foot tall. Jon grabbed a rubber glove from the floor, reached into the tub, and pulled out the chest.

"Oh, my God," Ann said as she walked into the mudroom.

Jose joined the group in the small room, and they all sat and stood in silence. All of them seemed to be hypnotized by the chest and were unable to even move, much less speak. Jon held the chest up to the light of the sun and inspected it from every angle.

"Well, ladies and gentleman, I believe we have found some treasure," Jon laughed. "It's quite heavy."

"I...I can't believe it," Meg said. "What do you suppose is in it?"

"I have no idea," Jon acknowledged. "We need to open it, but I don't want to hurt the historical value of this chest."

Meg stood and inspected the chest. "The clasp is gone, so the lid should come straight off."

"We better set up the video camera," Ann suggested. "This discovery needs to be recorded for posterity sake."

"Good idea," Jon agreed. "Dr. Russell would be quite disappointed if he did not have footage of our initial find."

Meg laid out some towels on the kitchen table as the thought of setting up an old wooden table somewhere for future treasure finds drifted through her mind. This was the second time in two days they were risking damaging her good table. Ann put the video camera on the tripod and pressed the record button as Jon set the chest on the tabletop.

When Jon tried to remove the lid to the box, it held fast. Jose hurried to the tool shed and came back with a small, prying tool. Jon worked the tool around the lid of the box as he slowly broke the grip of hundreds of years of corrosion.

A hush settled in the room as the lid was removed with great care. Lying on top was a mound of beautiful pearls. Meg was awed by the pearls, but she was hoping for gold. Jon was cautious as he removed the pearls to see a layer of smaller emeralds that surrounded two of the largest emeralds Meg had ever seen. They were brilliant green stones that were at least two inches square.

Light reflected from the gems and radiated around the room. It was like the priceless stones were celebrating the light for the first time in over four hundred years. Jon removed the precious stones one at a time and laid them on the table beside the pearls.

"Oh, my," Jose said in reverence.

Meg was speechless as she saw that beneath the gems was a line of small, rectangular bars of gold. When Jon worked one of the bars out of the chest, they discovered that there were three layers of bars that were each about two inches thick.

"Since there are six bars across, there must be eighteen little bars of gold. Look at the King's emblem stamped on each one. This should at least verify it's from a Spanish galleon."

"What are we going to do with it?" Ann whispered.

"Whatever we do," Jose responded, "we better be careful."

"You're right about that," Jon said. "The emeralds alone are sure to be worth over a million dollars. I once read of emeralds discovered by the conquistadors, and I know that some of the more famous ones are considered to be more valuable than gold. For now, I'll put it all in the safe, but I think we should take it to our deposit box at the bank. We cannot even speak of this outside of the house or beyond the privacy of our boat. This kind of discovery gets people killed."

Meg picked up one of the large emeralds and held it up to the light. It was magnificent and heavier than she had anticipated. She remembered reading about a famous emerald that was discovered near Columbia that sold for over two million dollars.

"I'm concerned that people have already seen us doing a lot of diving on the reef," Meg said as she pulled her eyes away from the beautiful stone. "Maybe we need to do something to remove suspicions."

"I think we ought to spend today creating a ruse," Jon agreed. "Let's go down to the marina to buy some bait. We can spend the day fishing. With any luck, we can bring in a big catch when we go back to the marina to fill up with fuel. When people see us, they'll think we're just fishermen."

"And fisherwomen," Meg added with a grin.

"I'll pull down the dive flag before we get to the marina," Jon continued. "Though we'll have to put it back up before we dive, we can at least lead others to think we're out here just to fish."

"We could still slip overboard for a dive or two," Jose suggested. "Maybe two of us could fish while two of us dive."

"Maybe we should go south from the marina first and fish some before we slowly make our way back to the spot," Ann offered.

"I like that idea," Jon said. "Okay, first of all, we celebrate with my famous biscuits and then head out."

"Famous biscuits?" Meg asked sarcastically. "I thought you were teasing earlier. Since when can you make biscuits?"

"My dear, there are many mysteries about me yet to be discovered," Jon declared with a grin.

Chapter Twenty

Let's Go Fishing

After breakfast, the group hurried down to the dock, got into the *New Beginnings*, and set out for the marina at George Town. The marina was dotted with small fishing boats and a couple of sailboats. A tidy, little store containing basic food items, fishing gear, and bait was located at one end of the docks.

The two women went to the restroom while Jon and Jose browsed through the tackle section of the store. Jon had already met Al, the big man behind the counter, from his previous gas purchases. Al was a transplant from South Georgia, was around one hundred pounds overweight, and always wore a tank top that was about two sizes too small. He already had significant body odor, even though it was just 9:00 in the morning. Jon bought some shrimp and lures while Jose picked up a new rod and reel.

"So what seems to be biting this time of year?" Jon asked the big man as Meg stepped out of the restroom.

"The wahoo are pretty active," Al answered before spitting a mouthful of snuff juice into a cup. "Ya'll could even get into some yellow and black fin tuna. If you go deep enough and are patient enough, you might even snag you a blue marlin."

"I don't think I want a marlin today," Jon said, "but wahoo sounds good. That's a lot like a king mackerel, isn't it?"

"Simlar'," Al said. "They're bigger, faster, and better eatin'. That pole ain't goin' to do you much good, though."

"I have some more poles in the boat that I'm sure are more suited," Jon said.

Al continued as if Jon had never spoken, "You're goin' to need at least 80 pound test line with a four foot steel leader. You could use this lure. It's a Rapala Magnum 26, and she's a beauty. I know you're thinkin' it's too big. She's bigger than…Oh, good morning Ma'am."

"Meg, this is Al. Al, this is my wife, Meg. She's not fished much in the ocean, so I was hoping we could find a good catch today."

"Well, ma'am," Al said after he emptied the contents of his mouth into a Styrofoam cup. "I've caught many a wahoo on this lure."

"Thanks for the advice, Al. Just add the lure to our stuff, and don't forget your boy is filling up my tank."

Al rang up their purchases as Ann walked up, and he spoke to her before giving Jon his change. After leaving the dock in the marina, Jon guided them into open water where they headed south to start their fishing expedition.

It wasn't long before Meg was surprised with a hit on her pole that about pulled her overboard. She screamed while Jon jumped down from the bridge to help her with the pole. Whatever she had on the line had pulled her hands down to the side of the boat and pinned her hands against the railing. Jon took the pole from her grasp as he whistled at what had to be a big one. He gave the fish plenty of line so it could run for a while, but after thirty minutes of fighting, Jon pulled a wahoo, weighing close to ninety pounds, to the side of the boat.

"Ol' Al wasn't kidding," Jon said as he held the fish still so Jose could shoot the thing with the pistol.

Jose gaffed the fish so he could pull it aboard. Meg gave Jon a high five, and Ann aimed her camera at Meg standing beside her catch. Jose climbed back up to the bridge to move the boat toward the spot of the wreck.

On occasion, they stopped to fish over various spots where Jon could see fish on his fish finder. After a couple of hours, the boat was settled over the place in the reef where they had discovered the mast, and while Jose and Ann fished, the Davenports slipped into the water for another dive.

Once on the bottom, Jon and Meg scanned the area to locate other pieces of the wreck, but they didn't spot anything of importance. They picked up several pieces of what looked like fist sized coral and placed them in their net bags. Jon was hoping to find more gold bars, but he was unsuccessful. On their way back up to the boat, Jon looked for where the mast had broken off during the storm.

He and Meg had discussed the possibility of the ship being covered in coral closer toward the surface, but neither was able to spot anything. Jon looked around one last time to make sure no other boats were in the area and also to make sure they weren't about to be caught by any fish hooks. The two divers surfaced at the back of the boat before crawling aboard.

"Any luck," Jose asked, his voice hopeful.

"I can't tell, but I doubt it," Jon admitted. "I picked up a few things, but I don't think any of it is gold."

"Maybe we'll have better luck," Jose maintained.

The Davenports pulled out their fishing poles while Jose and Ann put on scuba gear. As Jon sent his line flying forward in the direction of shore, the second shift of divers slipped beneath the water to begin their search for treasure.

Ten minutes after throwing the first cast, Meg leaned her pole against the side of the boat so she could retrieve a chair. She sat down in the chair and pulled her hat further down on her head.

She picked up her pole and checked the tension on her line. "I don't think fishing is a lot of fun unless I'm catching something."

"That's why it's called fishing instead of catching," Jon laughed. "You've got to be patient if you're going to be any good at this."

"I think I'll stick to diving. It's a lot more exciting. Hey, Ann is back."

When Meg hurried to the back of the boat, Jose had surfaced behind Ann and was helping her remove the tank from her back. Jon reached down to retrieve the gear while Meg helped Ann aboard. Although both divers enjoyed the dive, neither found anything of significance.

Jon moved toward the ladder to the bridge. "I think we're done for the day. Let's go back by the marina so Al, and anyone else who is watching us, gets a look at our fish. We don't have a bad catch."

"I'm glad you guys caught a few while we were diving," Meg acknowledged. "This is a pretty good haul."

"No doubt you win the prize," Ann said as she patted Meg on the back.

"We'll let the items we brought up stay in the solution overnight," Jon suggested. "I don't think it's anything, but I suppose you never know."

It was late when the group pulled into Pirates Cove and they were ready for dinner and bed. Meg decided that while fishing might be a fun sport for some people, she didn't care if she ever picked up a fishing rod again in her life. What she wanted most now was a hot shower and her bed.

The two couples discovered the following morning that the items recovered from the bottom of the ocean were nothing more than rocks of barnacle-covered coral. All four were quite disappointed, and Jon told them that they would need to study the pictures of what the treasure looked like more carefully. He had been meticulous in taking pictures of each item they had discovered so far in an attempt to catalogue their progress.

The group reviewed the pictures in detail as they compared the actual items of worth to the rocks from the previous day. After spending the next three days diving the site in a covert way, the divers were disappointed to discover nothing new.

On Friday, Jon told everyone that there had been enough treasure found to indicate this was indeed a good place to start after Christmas. He made plans to gain permission from the Bahamian officials to start their salvage efforts in that location, but he decided to wait until they returned after Christmas to tell anyone about a possible find.

Jon took their new treasure to the bank and added it to his safety deposit box. Now the box contained the jeweled dagger, seven gold pieces of eight, pearls, diamonds, emeralds, and eighteen small gold bars. It was enough to get the *New Beginnings Salvage* team pretty excited, and they all agreed that it would be hard to go through Christmas without thinking about the treasure all the time.

On Saturday, four days before Christmas, all four of the treasure hunters drove to the airport together. Ann's family lived in Birmingham, so she and Jose planned to fly to Birmingham from Ft. Lauderdale.

Jon and Meg were going back to the ranch where they would meet up with Judy. The group agreed to get together on December twenty-eighth for a big dinner at the ranch before taking off for the Bahamas on the twenty-ninth. New Year's Eve would be celebrated in their island home so that the group would have time to be in place before *The Discoverer* docked.

CHAPTER TWENTY-ONE

New Year's Resolution

Carla held her hand to her face as she felt the burn of Luis' slap. This was not the first time he had slapped her, but this was the hardest she remembered being hit. She had done nothing wrong, but she made the mistake of mentioning Jimmy's name. She didn't mean anything by it because Jimmy was just her friend, but Luis was very jealous. He seemed to be getting more violent as it came closer to time to head back to the Bahamas.

Carla decided she would go all out that night to give Luis a good time. Maybe a night out would make him forget about whatever seemed to be bothering him. As soon as he was sober, she was going to have to remind him of how important it was that she not arrive at the ship with a black eye. That might ruin the whole thing.

"Jimmy better just be a friend or I'll kill him," Luis screamed. "I mean it. I'll kill him. You're all mine. Got it?"

"Luis, he's just a friend. You are the only man I want. I promise. I don't want anybody but you."

"Okay. I've got some business to take care of," Luis said. "I'll be back tonight. Maybe we could get some dinner and go by the club afterwards."

"Why do you want to go to the club, Luis? I'm good enough for you, aren't I?"

Luis raised his hand to slap Carla again, but Carla cried out, "Luis, I can't have bruises when I go back to work. That would mess up everything."

Luis grabbed Carla and pulled her close. Carla could smell the alcohol on his breath as he stared glassily into her eyes. It seemed that he enjoyed hitting women, especially when he was drunk. Luis kissed Carla and patted her face.

"You are fine, baby, real fine. I just want to stop in and see the guys. I got some business to do with the owner. We'll do some business, smoke a little, and come back to the apartment. Sound good?"

Carla answered, "That sounds good Luis. Whatever you want to do."

Not only did Luis seem to be getting more violent as *The Discoverer's* departure grew closer, but he also stayed out more and more each night. Carla was tempted to think that he was seeing another woman, but she was confident that he loved her. She was certain he was not spending time with someone else. They were going to get married as soon as all of this was over. She was sure of it.

"Listen," Luis said, "there's nothing more important than getting on that boat and learning everything you can learn. You got to contact me every night. Got it?"

"I got it, Luis. I did good the first time didn't I?"

"Yeah, you did good. That necklace thing was brilliant."

Carla felt real guilty about tricking Meg that way. Somehow, she would make it up to Meg. Ever since Carla had begun working for the Davenports, they had done nothing but treat her nice. She would just do this job for Luis, and then they would leave Jon and Meg alone.

"Thanks Luis. I did it for you. You're not going to hurt Meg, are you?"

"No way, honey. I don't hurt people unless they need to be hurt. You just do your job like we talked about."

"I will, Luis."

"I know you will. This will all be over soon."

******

The Discoverer pulled up to the dock in Pirate's Cove on the morning of January the second, and Jon climbed aboard to greet the staff. The deck was clean and spacious, but he noted the small crane that had been attached near the stern of the ship. Standing next to a yellow, two-man submarine, a crew member peered into the window at the small compartment. Further down, he spied a large box that he knew contained the main part of the sea vacuum he had read so much about. He wasn't sure where the hose was stored, but it could not fit in the box. Jon pictured vacuuming up the sand from the bottom of the ocean and dumping it away from a potential wreck site. He was sure he would find hundreds of feet of hose stored somewhere else aboard the ship.

Captain David Buffington stood at the gang plank to meet Jon when he came aboard. The captain reached out to shake his hand as he stepped onto the deck.

"Welcome aboard, sir," the captain greeted with a broad smile. "I can't tell you how wonderful it is to be back on a ship. Your honeymoon voyage was a real treat. Now, I'm looking forward to the next assignment. Thank you for the opportunity to serve again."

"You are welcome. You were given the job because you are the best in the business. I'm glad you're on our team."

"Thank you, sir."

Jon looked beyond the captain's broad shoulders to see only a few staff members coming toward the gang plank. Buffington had agreed to a streamlined staff for this project because Jon didn't want too many people knowing about possible treasure. Other than the captain and two assistants, there was a kitchen staff of only two.

"You remember Chef Marceau?" Buffington questioned as a short man with a goatee came toward the pair.

"Chef," Jon said as he offered his hand, "it's a pleasure to have you aboard. The food on our honeymoon cruise was exquisite. I've heard your catering business has become quite successful in Miami, so I am amazed you want to stay with *The Discoverer.*"

"It is my pleasure to be included on your team. I have always had a great fondness for the ocean, and I love to travel. It's a perfect fit for me at this stage of my career. My new assistant, Carla, has proven to be quite valuable in the kitchen. You will be pleased, I'm sure."

"I'm sure I will. My housekeeper, Judy, may also want to help out in the kitchen some, if you will allow her. She is a very good cook."

"I would be delighted to have her serve alongside of me."

All in all there would be ten people onboard for this phase of the project. If they needed to hire more, Jon was sure there were plenty of willing people around to help out. He also knew at some point he would be bringing experts aboard to determine the source of the treasure, and he planned for Cindy to be one of those experts.

After lunch, Jon met with the whole crew to explain the planned agenda. The ship would set sail that afternoon for a nondescript place north into the Atlantic where they could do a practice run. Meg, Ann, and Jose would work the vacuum and then practice with the sub.

As the meeting adjourned, Jon picked up a file from the table, and an application form slid to the floor. Though his wife and two partners knew he would be working on filing the official papers with the Bahamian government in Nassau, no one else knew that they were close to discovering gold.

Meg retrieved it from the floor and handed the form back to her husband. "Are you trying to spill the beans before we get started?"

"I didn't even mean to bring this with me," Jon grimaced. "I'm going to complete the form, but I plan to leave off the coordinates until the last minute. I plan to call Jose from Nassau as soon as the paperwork is filed so we can all meet at the wreck site."

"I'm assuming you'll meet us there in the *New Beginnings?*" Meg wondered.

"That's the plan. We'll probably need the small boat for transport anyway."

Jon prepared to leave for the Exuma International Airport where he would charter a plane to Nassau. *The Discoverer* set sail for the practice run, and Jose, Meg, and Ann worked hard to make it appear that the crew planned to stay out for several days. Jon anticipated sending word to Jose within twenty-four hours to head back to the wreck site where they would soon begin their first recovery attempt.

Jon wrapped his arms around Meg and pulled her close to his body. "I hate leaving you. I know it's just twenty-four hours, but I'm not ready to be away from you for twenty-four minutes."

"Oh, Jon," Meg teased, "you've taken morning runs without me that were longer than twenty-four minutes."

"True," Jon grinned, "and you should have been with me on those runs. I'm sure you're going to be busy. Besides that, you have Ann and Carla. You and Carla got pretty tight on our honeymoon cruise."

"I do like her, and I'm looking forward to Ann getting to know her too."

Before walking toward the truck, Jon lowered his lips to Meg's. She wrapped her arms around him as if she didn't want to let him go.

"I should be meeting up with you tomorrow," Jon whispered. "I love you."

"I love you, too. Please be safe. Who's flying you to Nassau?"

"One of the guys with Island Air. I'll tell him to be careful with me."

"You do that," Meg said before kissing him on the cheek one last time.

Jon first met with a lawyer in Nassau, who would help him work through the legal tangle to gain the rights to excavate the site. Had this wreck been in the waters off the United States mainland, the Abandoned Shipwrecks Act would have governed their decisions. This act turned the ownership of abandoned ships over to the United States government thereby making the government the owners of any treasure that was discovered.

The Bahamian government had not enacted such a law, and therefore Jon would have to negotiate a potential percentage with government officials before he could begin the salvage effort. Because there was no known wreck in the area and the officials anticipated the amount of the recovery to be negligible, Jon's lawyer, Samuel Jennings, informed him that he thought he could negotiate an agreement.

"What kind of agreement do you anticipate?" Jon asked.

"I think if you offer them thirty percent, they will jump on it."

Jennings educated Jon about the whole process while Jon considered the possibilities of gaining seventy percent of the treasure. The lawyer told him that ownership of property stopped a few feet above the sea line, and anything beyond that line could be claimed by the Bahamian government.

"If you find a diamond ring in your yard, the ring is yours, but if you find a ring in the ocean, in theory, at least part of it belongs to the government," Jon's lawyer informed him.

"I'm sure the government is not too interested in diamond rings, but they would be interested in a Spanish galleon full of gold."

"That's for sure," Samuel said. "You can also be sure that someone higher up will want a good percentage of the historical items you bring up, like canons and stuff like that. They may want most of that to create a money-making enterprise through their government sponsored museums."

"I'm fine with that," Jon agreed. "I think a seventy/thirty split is okay too, though I wish we could keep more. Just make sure you downplay everything. For now, let's just tell them we have found a broken mast and two pieces of eight. That should be enough to indicate there's a ship somewhere below."

CHAPTER TWENTY-TWO

Ready, Set, Go

The Discoverer set sail for a spot just south of Cat Island. Jon and Jose had picked a place in the shallow waters south of the island because it would be far enough away from the wreck site so as not to draw undue attention, and it was close enough where they could return as soon as the paperwork was completed.

Captain Buffington slowed the engines as the ship came within sight of Springfield Bay, and he began monitoring the ocean floor. When the depth gauge read ninety-seven feet, he killed the engine and ordered the anchors to be dropped. Jon wanted the vacuum and submarine tested in waters resembling the conditions of the reef where the ship wreck was located.

When the large ship came to a stop, Captain Buffington's first mate, Jeremiah Ingleman, assisted Jose in getting the vacuum ready for testing. Jeremiah was a tall, well-built young man from Germany who had made his home in Miami. Meg knew Ann must have loved Jose because she never made an offhanded comment about the "the blond German hunk." Meg had noticed Ingleman giving her and Ann the once over and then returning to Ann to allow his gaze to linger. Ann was a real beauty, and Meg consoled herself by saying Jeremiah knew she was a married woman after all. Ann had to know this gorgeous guy was checking her out, but she didn't care. Amazing!

Meg pulled on her bathing suit and poured powder on her legs and arms to make it easier to slip into her wetsuit. Though the water was plenty warm, the last thing she wanted was to get a chill one hundred feet below the surface five minutes into their experimental run with the sea vac. She joined Jose on the back deck, donned her scuba gear, and stepped over the side into the beautiful blue water.

Meg felt the familiar jolt as a thin layer of water entered her suit, warming to her body temperature. She swam over to the floating coil, grabbed a metal handle situated on the end of the hose and kicked her way to the bottom. Jose took hold of the hose behind her to help hold it in place as she pressed the green button, which would engage the motor.

The hose came to life and began sucking up the sand from the bottom of the ocean, just like her Kirby back home. Meg thought she had almost this much sand in her carpets at home and smiled inwardly at the thought of borrowing the seavac for a couple of days for a little house cleaning. Jeremiah had sent the other end of the hose off the far side of the boat so the sand would be filtered down to the ocean bottom some distance away.

It took practice, but Meg became quite good at sucking up the sand and avoiding the shells, rocks and debris that lay on the bottom. After working with it for a few minutes, she and Jose switched places to give him a chance to guide the seavac through the process of sifting the sand in search of treasure. Though no treasure was found, nor did they expect to find any, the divers gained some valuable experience on using the system. After close to twenty minutes of bottom time, the two finned their way to the surface and climbed aboard the ship.

After showering and getting dressed, Meg walked to the dining area for dinner. As she went through the food line, she smiled at Carla who served her plate. Meg and her new friend chatted briefly about the experiences of the day and the excitement of being underway with their first salvage project. Meg was careful not to reveal too much about what they were going to search for, though Carla seemed to be very interested.

Meg appreciated the opportunity to sit with Judy for the first time since Christmas break as they enjoyed eating their meal together. Though Judy had said she would rather stay at the house in Pirate's Cove, Meg was not surprised to see her aboard *The Discoverer*.

"I guess you are missing your man," Judy said with a smile on her face.

"Yeah. This will be the first night since we met back in August that we have not spoken together at least by phone."

"You are so pitiful," Ann joked as she pulled out a chair and sat down at the table.

"I am pitiful because I am in love," Meg said hitting Ann on the arm.

"Hey, watch it," Ann chided, "or you're going to make me spill my tea."

"I remember the heartache of missing my man," Judy said with a wistful look in her eye.

Meg had never heard Judy speak of a man in her life, though Jon had told her Judy had once been married. Meg assumed they must have divorced or something. She didn't want to encourage a sad conversation, but she was quite intrigued.

Meg sat her coffee cup down on the table. "Judy, I know you were once married. Is your ex-husband still around?"

"No, he died a long time ago, and I don't think of him as my ex-husband. For some reason watching you and Jon has made me think of him a lot these last few months."

"I'm so sorry," Meg said.

"Oh, don't be. I've had my sad moments, but I decided years ago a pity party was a lonely affair and not worth the effort."

"How long were you married?" Ann asked.

"We were married for a little less than a year. I met my husband on the night of my eighteenth birthday. He was tall and handsome–a real looker. I was head over heels in love with the guy right away. I had gone down to the town hangout with my friends, and I noticed Bob as soon as I sat down. He noticed me too and came right over to my table."

"We danced together, and he kissed me right there on the dance floor after wishing me a happy birthday. We spent the whole evening together and went out every night for the next seven days. The seventh day was his last night before heading out to boot camp in North Carolina. We went to the drive-in and watched a movie about Pearl Harbor. The truth is I don't remember a lot about the movie because we spent the whole night making out in the back seat. My mother would have killed me."

"If my mother knew everything I have done, she would disown me," Ann chimed in.

Judy continued, "After the movie, we drove out to this beautiful hillside just out of town, and I pulled out a blanket from the back of Bob's '57 Chevy. We spread the blanket out on the ground and lay down looking at the stars. I knew Bob would be leaving the next day, and I was so afraid I would never see him again. I know it's hard to believe, but I loved him, and I knew he loved me."

"He rose up on his elbow, looked me in the eyes and told me he loved me. I was thrilled and couldn't catch my breath. I'm ashamed of all that happened that night. I soon discovered that I was not going to be able to hide anything from anyone for long because I was pregnant."

"Pregnant?" Meg gasped. "I didn't know you had any children."

"Well, I did. Bob went off to war, and I discovered I was pregnant. You would think I would be horrified. Though I was sad for my indiscretion, I was overjoyed to carry his baby. My mother was so ashamed of me, but I decided to make the best of it. I made the decision, however, not to tell Bob through my daily letters that I was pregnant. I didn't want him to feel like he had to marry me because we had a child."

"He came home on army business when our daughter was about a year old, and he called me. My mama kept Susan while Bob and I went out on a date. He took me back to that hillside and proposed to me. I told him about Susan, and he cried. Can you believe it? He cried. We left the hillside, found the preacher, and got married right there. I got to spend a whole week with him before he headed back to Vietnam. That was the last time I ever saw him. His helicopter was shot down by the Viet Cong, and the army never recovered his body."

"Oh Judy," Meg cried. "I'm so sorry. I had no idea."

"Susan was all I had, and I never married again. When Susan was nineteen, she was killed by a drunk driver one Friday night while coming home from school. She was determined to leave the university to spend the weekend with me for my birthday. Her death almost killed me."

Meg hugged Judy as tears flowed down the cheeks of all three women.

"It took a long time, but I pulled myself out of depression and began giving myself to help others. That's what saved me. I took care of my mother for the next fifteen years until she died, and then I began working for hospice. It was there that I met Jon.

I took care of his first wife, Julie. After Julie died, Jon asked me to work for him. He was a mess, and I couldn't bear to see him left alone. I quit my job and moved to his ranch. The last five years of my life have been some of my best years. Jon is like a son to me and has treated me like royalty. Meg, the day he brought you home was one of the happiest days of my life, other than my time with Bob and Susan. You have brought such joy to his heart."

Meg could not stop crying. Judy hugged her, and they all started crying again. The rest of the crew left them alone in the dining area as the women cried and hugged.

"I think we better go up to my room and tell jokes or something," Meg said. "If we don't, I'm going to be a cry baby all night. Ann, why don't you get Jose, and the four of us can play Spades."

They spent the evening together playing cards, telling funny stories about their pasts, and everyone headed to bed close to midnight. Meg hated going to bed alone that night and could only think of Jon as she drifted off to sleep. She dreamed of

Jon crashing in the jungles and fighting off the Viet Cong as his helicopter burned in the background. She jerked awake crying and crawled out of bed for a drink of water. She walked out on her balcony overlooking the side of the ship and stood looking out into the night. She was the luckiest woman alive.

CHAPTER TWENTY-THREE

Interesting Find

Jose, Meg, and Ann took turns taking the submarine down the next day, and Ann proved to be quite the submariner. She picked up on the nuances of maneuvering the sub faster than the other two. After lunch, she and Meg took their first dive together while Jose stayed aboard the ship. Jose was trying to stay close to the satellite phone in case Jon called for him, but the phone remained silent all day.

Jon called later that night and Jose put the phone on speaker so Meg could listen, too.

"I should be done by noon tomorrow," Jon stated. "I think the authorities will want to finish the process since it's Friday, and no one wants this issue to be in limbo until next week."

Meg could tell that he was as excited as a Little League baseball player the day before the opening game. "So, do you think you'll be back by tomorrow night?"

"I don't see why not. I can't imagine these guys dragging their feet on this."

"We took the sub down today, and it worked like a charm. It's sort of like playing a video game. Ann is quite the expert."

"That's excellent," Jon exclaimed. "I have a feeling that will come in handy some day."

"The seavac isn't that big of a deal either," Meg continued. "You have to hold it just right, though, or you'll end up wrestling with it the whole time."

"I'm not surprised with that," Jon acknowledged. "There's a lot of pull with that thing. I figured it would take us a while to get the hang of it."

Jose leaned toward the satellite phone. "I know we need to work with it some more, but I think we're doing pretty good with just a little practice."

"That's great news. I better turn in. I'll see you guys tomorrow. I love you, Meg, and I miss you."

"I love you, too. Be careful."

The group made an early morning dive on a reef just off the point of French Bay and then started slowly making their way back toward Great Exuma. At 11:35, Meg jumped at the sound of the phone. It had to be Jon with good news.

"Hello."

"Hey, sweetheart. Great news! Everything is finalized. I'm headed back to the airport now and should be at the site in a couple of hours."

"That's wonderful. Hold on and let me ask Captain Buffington how far away we are." A moment later Meg returned to the phone. "He said we were about thirty minutes away from the wreck site."

"I'll see you shortly."

When Captain Buffington dropped anchor over what was hoped to be the *San Ambrosio*, Jose looked in all directions, and there was not another boat in sight. Smiling at Ann, he gave her a thumbs up.

Meg zipped up her wetsuit. "Jon's going to kill us for not waiting on him, but I have a feeling he'd do the same thing."

Jose, Meg, and Ann dropped into the ocean and pulled the seavac to the bottom. Uncovering numerous shells and rocks, Meg controlled the tube as she slowly sucked up the sand from the ocean floor.

Jose picked up a round object from the ocean floor and held it up for Ann's inspection. Shrugging her shoulders, she took it from Jose, and put it in a nearby crate. When the crate was full, Jose pulled a pin on a small tube on the side of the crate, and two cylinders filled with air. The crate floated toward the surface with ease while someone onboard pulled the slack out of the rope.

After twenty minutes of bottom time, they had removed four crates of what they hoped contained valuable objects, though everything was covered with barnacles and hardened sediment. By the time Jon arrived on the *New Beginnings*, all of the items were in the lab soaking in the chemical solution.

When Jon climbed aboard *The Discoverer*, Meg couldn't contain her excitement. A huge smile crossed his face as she hurried toward him, and he pulled her into a passionate kiss as if no one was around. Meg pulled away when she heard the dinner bell and was not clear if it was time to eat or if someone was just trying to mess up the moment. When she looked around, she realized it was dinner time.

As each of the team members went below for a celebration dinner, they all clapped Jon on the back as if he had just scored a touchdown in the Super Bowl. Meg smiled at her husband as she realized that you can't keep a lot quite on a small ship like *The Discoverer*. Everyone seemed to know that something significant had happened during Jon's absence.

When everyone was assembled in the mess hall, Chef Marceau got the team's attention so he could introduce the meal.

"Tonight, we celebrate new beginnings," Marceau said as he winked at Jon. "May God shine his grace upon our endeavor, whatever it is."

Everyone laughed and raised their glass in a toast. The chef served a wonderful meal of filleted grouper over rice. Jon told Jose, Meg and Ann about his experience in Nassau. The authorities worked hard to get the coordinates out of him before the judge got involved, but Jon had refused to tell them anything. The judge told Jon it would take about a month to process until Jon inadvertently left one thousand dollars lying on the judge's bench.

"It's amazing what a little money can accomplish," Jon said.

Meg and Ann told Jon about their experiments and gave him more details on how they had become quite proficient with the seavac and the submarine. After dinner, Meg led Jon to the lab where he looked over the day's find.

"I expect most of it will be coral or something insignificant, but you never know. This task will be tedious, but if we will be patient, I think sooner or later we will find the mother lode."

"Hey, Carla," Meg said as she saw her friend from the kitchen walk down the hallway outside the lab.

Meg thought that it was a little odd for Carla to be at this level. She had never seen her friend anywhere near the lab.

"Hey, Meg. I'm just finishing up and thought I'd try to get some exercise by taking a walk."

"That's a good idea. It might take a lot of laps, but you could create a walking track on the ship. I've got a pedometer in my room at home. When I go back to the house, I'll bring it back with me so we can figure out how many laps are needed to make a mile."

"That sounds like a great idea. Did you find anything today?" Carla asked.

"We'll have to see," Jon said. "I think it's all coral. We'll know for sure in the morning."

By the following morning, nothing was left in the cleaning tanks except smaller rocks and a cloudy solution. Jon scooped out the solid stuff, and the group readied themselves for round two.

Before the divers could prepare themselves for the day's work, a thirty foot fisherman pulled up beside *The Discoverer*, and Jon recognized Dr. Gerome Russell of the National Underwater and Recovery Agency. Jon had called him, as promised, from Nassau before finalizing matters with the Bahamian officials. Dr. Russell had full video rights to any discovery found by *The Discoverer*. So, while Jon and his crew would begin what he hoped to be the salvage of a Spanish galleon, Dr. Russell's camera crew would be getting it all on film for a documentary.

Gerome had gambled on selling *The Discoverer* to Jon for such a cheap price in hopes that Jon's discovery would net him a nice prize through a televised documentary. Over the next months, these underwater videographers would float in and out of their lives putting their discoveries on video for future editing. One videographer would be placed full-time on *The Discoverer*.

Jon established a schedule where he and Meg would work together and be followed by Jose and Ann while he and Meg rested on deck. By allowing short breaks in between the dives, they found the group could make a total of four dives in three hours.

Crates of objects from the sea floor came up nonstop throughout the morning, and after lunch, Jon and Meg made a dive to look for the place where the mast may have broken off. They had no luck. Over the next five days, the divers brought up crates of material from the ocean floor before hitting pay dirt.

"It's gold," Meg said giving Jon a hug and a kiss.

Sure enough, there were two pieces of eight lying in the bottom of the cloudy mix in the tubs on the morning of the sixth day. Jon had been surprised the coins had been covered in crusty sediment, but after thinking about it, he decided the gold must have been secured in some type of container.

"I don't understand your confusion," Meg said.

"Gold is not going to tarnish or even be covered in hardened crust. It just sits on the bottom of the sea floor waiting to be discovered. It would be covered in sand, but the coins should be recognizable once the sand is removed."

"So that's why you think these coins must have been in some type of container that did get covered in barnacles and sediment. Over time, most of the container was destroyed as crust and coral formed around it."

"I think you're right. I had expected to just discover the gold on the sea floor, which may still be the case. The wooden chests, or whatever the Spaniards may have stored the gold in hundreds of years ago, would have just deteriorated and the gold would be easy to recognize."

Meg was careful to write in her journal their first treasure was found on Tuesday, January eighth, after diving for five straight days. They were all excited and couldn't help but express their enthusiasm when everyone gathered for breakfast.

"You must have good news," Captain Buffington said to the four team members.

"We haven't gotten rich yet," Jon said. "But we have found something that says this is the place to keep searching. We found two coins. I'd say it's worth around $5,000 or so, but it's a great start."

"That's good news," Carla said as the others turned, surprised that anyone else was listening to their conversation.

"We hope to find more," Meg said, "but we're at least excited to have something to write home about."

"I wouldn't write anyone yet," Jon warned, even though he knew his wife was just using a figure of speech. "We need to keep what we're doing silent for as long as we can. We should get the crew together and remind them to keep all of this off of social media."

Jose nodded his head. "The last thing we want right now is competition."

"Not to mention that people get a little crazy when there's treasure involved," Jon added. "We should also take the videographer down to the spot where the gold was found. I'm sure he'll want that on film."

"Let's just hope that our gold trail doesn't stop with just these gold coins," Meg said. "I'm sure there's more down there somewhere."

CHAPTER TWENTY-FOUR

Exciting News

That night, Carla pulled out her laptop to write Luis a note. She logged into the ships WI-FI and thought for a moment.

> Luis, I miss you. I hope you are doing well. The Davenports found two gold coins today. Jon said that it's worth about $5,000. Can you believe it? $5,000! He's expecting to find a lot more, so he must think we are over the treasure ship. Just think. We will be together soon, and have all of the gold we could ever want. I'll be in touch. Carla.

She felt a twinge of guilt as she hit send, but she brushed it away. She thought back to the diamond necklace and passionate kiss Luis had given her before she had sailed away from Miami. After all this was over, they could leave this place on their own yacht and live together forever.

Who would have thought that Carla Ramirez would have ever amounted to anything? I wish my father could see me on my yacht with my diamond necklace. He would have to take back all of those ugly things he said about me.

Carla began searching on the Internet for island property. She imagined what it would be like to own a beautiful home, just like Meg. She was shocked at how expensive it would be to purchase such a house, but she decided that the cost didn't matter. She and Luis would be able to afford anything they wanted. They could live in their island paradise and fill up the house with kids. Her children would always be loved and treasured. She would make sure they would never have to grow up like she did.

As she was about to log off of her computer, Carla heard a ding. She couldn't believe that Luis was returning an e-mail. If she had not spent a few minutes looking for her dream home, she wouldn't have seen until the next day.

Great news, babe. We are onto something. I'm going to move my base so I can be a little closer. Maybe I'll move to Nassau or Great Exuma. I want to see you. I'll come to George Town soon so we can meet. We'll spend the night together. You're doing a good job, baby. A real good job. I'll write back to let you know where to find me.

Carla was so excited and couldn't wait to see him. She was not sure how she would get away from the ship, but somehow she must see her man. *He called me baby. He's coming to see me. I know he loves me.* She dreamed that night of being held in Luis' arms.

****

Wednesday morning started with excitement and anticipation as the four treasure seekers returned to the task of searching the bottom of the ocean. They had pulled up a number of crates the previous day, but nothing else of value had been discovered. Even though no gold or silver was brought up from the depths, Jon and Meg found what looked like the place where the old mast had broken off.

It was located by sheer accident as they were making a dive for lobster. The sea offered great visibility as the couple sailed down the side of the reef, which was alive with color in the morning sun.

While scanning the sides of the reef for the spiny creatures, Jon felt Meg pull his hand. He looked up to see two dolphins swimming by and Meg seemed intent on going after them. They chased the playful twins that seemed not to be the least bit afraid of the two divers. Jon was surprised when one of the dolphins nudged Meg. The other one let him touch its head. He couldn't believe that they seemed so tame.

When the dolphins took a nose dive into the depths down the side of the reef, Jon stared after them in amazement. As he allowed his gaze to drift over the reef, he saw it. About fifteen feet below the top of the ridge, there was a short, rounded piece of coral sticking out about a foot. Jon motioned for Meg to follow him.

When Jon stopped at the suspected place, he inspected the area with great attention. He pointed to the center of the projection and was sure that it was made of wood. This had to be the other end of the mast that now lay on the ocean floor beneath them. It must have broken off during the storm and fallen down the wall to the bottom. Jon thrust his fist upward in slow motion like he had just won the Tour de France.

Swimming back to the ship, Jon counted his kicks so he would know how far away the original mast lay.

"We think we have found it," Jon said excitedly to Jose as Jon helped Meg remove her gear.

"Found what?"

"We were chasing a couple of dolphins and came across the other end of the mast still buried in the side of the coral wall."

"That's incredible," Ann shouted as she hurried over to the group. "So do you think the ship is covered in the coral?"

"I think so," Jose agreed. "It's not unusual for anything to become a reef once it's been underwater for a while."

"This means we've been searching in the wrong place," Jon concluded. "We're not far off, but our focus has been in this area straight below us and to the west. We need to move *The Discoverer* south. Maybe two of us can continue vacuuming the sand while the other two can try to get undeniable proof a ship lies inside the coral. If we can prove to the government a treasure ship is in the reef, I think we can get permission to somehow get inside the reef to retrieve the treasure."

Ann brushed a strand of hair out of her eyes. "Do you mean the reef is hollow?"

"If the *San Ambrosio* is in the reef, there's a good chance a hollow cavity was formed by the coral growing around the ship."

"Jon, didn't you tell me we would need to know the name of the ship before the authorities would allow us to dig into the reef?" Meg asked.

"I think we can use the picture of the *Terra Firme* armada manifest to prove we have treasure from one of the ships. That should be good enough. Why don't we confirm beyond doubt there is a ship in there and then go back to Pirate's Cove to get in touch with Cindy. She can study through the document to find something that will at least be convincing for the officials."

"That sounds good to me," Ann said. "I'm looking forward to getting off this ship for a night or two. I miss your hot tub."

"I knew I shouldn't have let you use my hot tub," Meg teased. "Now you're worthless."

Jon instructed Captain Buffington to move southeast down the reef to the new spot he and Meg had discovered. The four divers stepped into their dive gear, which was now becoming as familiar as an old pair of tennis shoes, and slid into the warm, tropical water. Within a few minutes, Jon located the short piece of coral encrusted mast again and motioned for the others.

Jose and Ann inspected the spot, and Meg knew that they must share the excitement she felt. Jon had mentioned that he hoped to discover gaps in the reef somewhere so he could find some old timbers. Though nothing looked promising at first, the divers surfaced with a renewed hope, dressed, and made their way to the dining area for dinner.

****

Meg and Ann spoke with excitement about their plans, and the small crew couldn't help but note that something had changed. Though Carla could not pick up on any specifics, she knew there would be some good news to share with Luis that night and wondered if he might already be on the island. Carla could not think of an excuse to leave the boat, but she decided they would have to dock soon. After cleaning up from dinner, Carla slipped into her private room and pulled out her laptop.

My dear Luis. She paused and wondered if using the word *dear* was a little too much. After all, Luis had never told her that he loved her, but she knew he did. He bought her gifts, and they had shared intimate moments. She was sure that he loved her. She chewed on her nail a moment and then continued.

Something has happened. Jon and Meg took a dive today and returned to the ship real excited. I'm not sure what happened, but the ship was moved to a different place–not far from our original spot, but we moved. I watched the group at dinner tonight, and it seems like something is going on. I hope to have good news for you tomorrow. Are you nearby? I miss you. I'm hoping to have shore leave soon. Maybe we can spend a few days together.

Carla hit send and longed to be with him in person. She knew she loved him. She was positive the man wanted her to live with him and even marry him. He was so strong and confident. He seemed rough, but she could help him change. She hated that she had to help him steal gold from the Davenports, but they had so much gold already. Meg would be fine without finding more treasure.

They were rich before they started searching for this sunken ship. It won't hurt them to give up some of their gold. Maybe Meg will one day forgive me. She doesn't even have to find out that it was me.

She closed her computer and decided to do her walking routine around the ship. Luis didn't like fat women, so it was important that she not gain any weight.

CHAPTER TWENTY-FIVE

Terror

Meg watched Jose and Ann glide effortlessly over the top of the reef and disappear into the deeper water. Snaking along behind them was the hose of the seavac. Because they would be diving as deep as 100 feet below the surface, Jose and Ann would not be able to stay down as long. There were advantages to staying in the shallower depths, but it would make synchronizing their dives a little more challenging. However, dividing up the team would bring about greater progress.

Meg was sure that Ann was in love. She had watched the two bantering back and forth on the deck before making the dive, and Jon had even picked up on the obvious change that had taken place in their relationship. If not in love yet, Ann was at least moving toward love at a break neck speed. She figured they would make a wonderful couple and would have beautiful children.

Jon and Meg began searching the reef for holes or caves. Though they found numerous holes in the coral, each one appeared to be the normal little hole in a reef occupied by lobsters or moray eels. After twenty minutes, Jose and Ann swam by with several crates tied together floating to the surface.

It was apparent Ann had not allowed the balloons on one of the crates to fill completely with air because she was able to hold it still as she stopped her ascent. She reached inside the crate and pulled out an object that had to be a cannon ball. It was covered with crust and barnacles, but there was no doubting the familiar round shape. This was another sure sign that they had discovered the site of the wreck.

Ann surprised them when she reached back into the crate and pulled out a brick-sized object. When Meg swam closer to inspect the object, she saw right away that it was not gold. It was silver. She took the bar from Ann and rubbed her finger over the seal of the king of Spain. She wanted to shout and cheer.

Meg pumped her fist against the resistance of the water before she and Ann did a slow motion high-five. Ann gave her a "thumbs up" sign as she turned to continue her ascent toward the surface. Because Jon and Meg were so shallow, their air would last longer, and they did not have to worry as much with decompression issues. The Davenports stayed down for another fifteen minutes and swam for the boat.

Jon led Meg into the lab where Jose and Ann were looking over the morning's find. Jon held the round object in his hand and agreed with Jose that it was a cannon ball. He held the dull, silver bar up to the light, and Meg gasped at the incredible success of the morning. They were excited and felt confident that they were about to find the lost treasure of the *San Ambrosio.*

After lunch, Jon and Meg took their turn on the seavac while Jose and Ann were required to make a shallower dive to avoid a longer period of rest. Meg was amazed at the whole process of bypassing decompression sickness, or the bends. She had learned in her scuba classes that air embolism was a killer, and it was best to carefully plan your dives so it would not be an issue. Air embolism was sickness that developed when air bubbles formed in a person's blood stream that would cause strokes and possible death. Jon had shown her from his decompression tables that Ann and Jose either had to sit out for almost an hour before being able to dive to the deeper side of the reef, or they could dive the shallower depths a lot sooner.

Both couples regrouped at dinner to discuss their progress. Jon and Meg had pulled up a few more crates of potential treasure from the sea floor, including several more cannon balls, while Ann had almost gotten her hand bitten off by a moray eel. Had she not been holding her knife, Jose insisted the thing would have gotten hold of her hand or wrist. The shiny knife had drawn the creature's attention, and the thing probably needed some false teeth now after biting into the metal blade.

Meg's mouth was watering just from the wonderful smell of the spaghetti. The chef called it his secret recipe. Meg had never tasted spaghetti sauce so good and told the chef he was a genius. Chef Marceau smiled and kissed her cheek, but he refused to give her the recipe.

The next morning, Meg leaned against the cleaning tank while the others looked on. "It's a cannonball just like we figured."

"And look at how shiny that silver is," Ann added.

Meg picked it up and admired it in the bright light coming through the lab window. The object creating the most excitement, however, was a small, jewel studded crown. Jon held it up for everyone to inspect. It would take some more cleaning, but everyone realized it was a very valuable discovery.

Jon also stated that this could be an identifying mark for the wreck, assuming the crown had been properly logged in the manifest. With anticipation, the two couples returned to the ocean in search for more treasure.

Jon and Meg took their turn searching the reef while Jose and Ann made their way down the wall on the deeper side. Jon had commented that all of their searching had been on the wall side of the reef, and maybe they should try the shallower side. Meg continued around a piece of coral that jutted out like a long, rock finger and didn't notice Jon stopping to investigate a dip in the reef. As she swam along the bottom just above the sand, she saw a shadow pass over her.

Meg assumed the shadow was Jon swimming up to join her, but when she looked up, she saw what had to be a ten foot hammerhead shark. Panic coursed through her body as she looked around for Jon. He was nowhere to be found. Just ahead was what looked like an indention in the reef that may have even been a swim through cave, so she hurried toward it.

Meg swam into the opening so fast that she banged into the wall of coral and cut her shoulder. *Oh no! It's blood. I can't believe I cut myself.*

The huge creature at the mouth of the cave began shaking and gyrating. Meg knew her life was about to end. She backed as far as possible into the cave and saw Jon coming toward the cave behind the shark. Dread coursed through her as she thought about the possibility of having a front row seat to watch her husband being mauled to death by this man-eating creature of the deep.

Jon pulled out the small bang stick he had attached to his leg that was armed and ready. He had explained to Meg that the stick held a forty-four magnum bullet that could be fired by ramming it into the side of a large fish or shark, but she had never seen how the stick worked.

As the huge beast turned toward Jon, he raced toward it and rammed the stick into the shark's side just below its head. Meg heard a muffled pop as a huge hole formed on the opposite side of the shark. The creature writhed in pain and blood filled the water. The shark stopped moving and just hung suspended at the opening of the cave. Jon hurried into the cave, grabbed Meg's hand and pulled her toward the boat. He left her at the ladder and swam down toward Jose and Ann. Meg figured he was getting them out of the water before more sharks showed up.

As Jon strapped his tank into place behind the bench, Jose and Ann were stepping out of their gear. Meg just sat down in shock with all of her gear still in place.

"I was afraid the water would become a feeding ground for sharks," Jon admitted.

When Meg heard him say "feeding ground," she turned ashen and trembled violently. Tears began to flow from her eyes, and Jon sat down beside her.

"Everything's okay, sweetheart. You're going to be fine. Let's get your gear off."

"I know," Meg said between sobs. "I just thought...I just thought that shark had me...or you."

Jon sat Meg's tank on the deck of the ship and pulled her into his arms. "He didn't, thank God. Why don't you take a day or two off?"

"No," Meg pulled back. "I can't. If I don't get back into the water, I may be afraid for the rest of my life. I'll be fine."

Jose informed Jon that he and Ann had filled up a couple of crates when Jon had motioned them back to the boat. The crates had been left on the bottom, and there was at least one pretty interesting find. It was a strange shape that had several possibilities. Jon suggested they eat some lunch before he and Jose returned for the crates. Meg insisted that the salvage work go back to business as usual after lunch. She was determined to return to the cave where she had hidden from the shark.

They waited until late in the afternoon to go after the crates. While Jose and Ann retrieved the crates and added a few more items, Jon and Meg swam back to the cave. The shark's body was nowhere to be found, so they were sure something had eaten the large creature. Jon started to swim by the cave, but Meg pulled him inside. Once in the darkened hole, Meg pulled out a small flashlight and shined it into the crevices and cracks. She saw the spot where her tank had banged into the coral and could make out a distinct shine of what was either brass or gold.

Jon pulled out his camera and took a few pictures. They searched the area some more and found that by digging in the sand at the base of the coral, they could reach under the edge of the reef. Though neither could tell what they were feeling, they were positive they were touching something other than coral.

They swam back to the ship for the seavac system, returned to the reef, and began removing the sand. Within a few minutes, Jon was able to look under the edge of the reef and see the unmistakable shape of a brass latch attached to some old timbers. The two divers returned to *The Discoverer* with the news that they had found the *San Ambrosio* hidden in the reef.

CHAPTER TWENTY-SIX

The Ambrosio

The excitement grew inside Carla as Jon called for a toast and swore the entire staff to secrecy. Everyone lifted their glass in recognition of the solemnity of the moment. Though she made the vow to secrecy, Carla felt ashamed because she knew Luis would soon be privy to the news she was about to hear.

"Ladies and Gentlemen," Jon said in a very formal, official sounding voice. "We have found the *San Ambrosio*."

Everyone cheered, clapped one another on the back, hugged and kissed. Carla was standing next to Jeremiah Ingleman and was more than a little surprised when the handsome German pulled her into his arms and kissed her soundly on the lips. Though Carla was shocked, she enjoyed it more than she should have, considering the fact she was in love with Luis.

"I must admit to you that we are calling it the *San Ambrosio*, but we don't have evidence it is indeed that ship," Jon continued. "We plan to gain permission from the Bahamian officials to begin removing some of the reef to salvage the ship, but it may take a few days before permission is granted. To celebrate this occasion, I am giving you some days off, though you can't go far. We'll keep the *New Beginnings* anchored over the wreck, and *The Discoverer* will dock in Pirate's Cove for three days. During these three days, you are welcome to stay aboard or go into George Town or whatever you want to do. I hope we will have the government's agreement to take out a piece of the reef in three days and will be able to get back to work."

As the cheering resumed, Jeremiah inched closer to Carla. She had no doubt the gorgeous German was making a move on her, and for some unknown reason, she had a deep desire to be with the man. He was such a nice guy and gorgeous with blond hair and sapphire blue eyes that crinkled when he grinned.

"What a wonderful day," Jeremiah said with a beautiful smile on his face.

Carla was captured by his eyes. "Yes, it is. It's hard to believe we found it so fast."

"It is amazing. What do you plan to do with your days off? Would you like to spend them with me in George Town?"

"Uh…well…I'm planning to meet a friend. I told her that as soon as I had a day or two off, I would visit her."

"I'm sorry to hear that. I would have enjoyed spending time with you."

Carla was flooded with regret, but then chided herself for being so weak. She loved Luis and he loved her. For her to even entertain the idea of spending three days with Jeremiah was tantamount to cheating.

"I…I have a boyfriend, and we are going to get married."

"Well, that's good to know. Congratulations."

"Thanks. Hope you enjoy your days off."

As the noise in the mess hall diminished, Carla could hear Jon speaking to the other three partners.

"I'm hoping to explore the rift in the sea floor with the sub when we return. There seems to be a line of possible debris leading to the edge of a significant drop off about one hundred feet from the reef. Even if it takes more than three days to get permission to dig into the reef, we can explore with the sub and continue sifting through some of the other stuff scattered around."

Carla saw Meg turning toward her, so she stepped forward to give her an awkward hug. She could tell that Meg was sizing her up and probably wondering why she was hanging around eavesdropping.

"I'm so excited for you," Carla blurted. "This is a dream come true."

"It is," Meg agreed. "What do you plan to do with your time off?"

"I'll go into town and shop around. I've never been to George Town before. I'm sure there's plenty to do. I'm looking forward to standing on solid ground again. I guess you'll have to stay out here on the boat?"

"I think we will do it in shifts," Meg agreed. "I imagine I'll be here part of the time, but I'll go home some too. I need to wash clothes and do some things around my house."

After dinner, Carla went back to her room feeling grateful she had privacy. Though two beds occupied the small cabin, Carla was the only one staying in the room at the time. She pulled out her laptop and began typing an e-mail.

"Luis. I have missed you so much and find myself thinking of only you."

Carla paused as her mind drifted toward Jerimiah. After the fit Luis threw over Jimmy, there was no way Carla would ever mention Jeremiah.

I am excited about the treasure, but I look forward to our life together more. I have good news. Jon has found the San Ambrosio, or at least some ship, buried in the reef. We are going to dock at Pirate's Cove for three days, and I have shore leave. Are you on the island? Can we meet?

She thought long and hard about how to end her note and felt butterflies in her stomach. *I love you. Carla.* She pressed the send button before she could change her mind, and shut down her computer.

The following morning, Chef Marceau had already begun preparing breakfast before Carla arrived. "Am I late?" Carla wondered.

"No, dear. I just started early today. This will be our last meal until breakfast on Tuesday."

"Really? What about the crew?"

"Jon is going to have meals catered so we can all have three days off."

He's got to be the most considerate man I've ever met. He's handsome and rich. What a catch he was for Meg, but she's beautiful too.

Carla thought Meg was the most beautiful woman she had ever seen. They were a striking pair, but neither acted rich. They were just normal people who had a big heart and a lot of money. She liked them both a lot.

Relieved to be back on land again, Carla walked down the dock at Pirate's Cove. Jon had made arrangements for a shuttle to take some of the crew into town, so she caught a ride. It didn't take her long to find an Internet café, and within minutes she was reading an e-mail from Luis.

Her heart nearly leapt out of her chest when he told her to meet him for the night at *The Dunes at Palm Bay*. She felt the heat rising up her neck as she considered Luis' plans for the evening. *I'm sure he's also planned a romantic dinner for us.* She was disappointed that Luis had not concluded his note with *I love you.* He had not even typed his name.

Carla noticed the shuttle van in the parking lot across from the café. "Excuse me," she stammered to the driver. "Are you going back to the Davenports?"

"Yes, ma'am. Do you need a ride?"

"No, thank you. Could you give Meg a message for me?"

"Sure. Whatever you need."

"Please tell her that I'm staying in town with a girlfriend from Miami. I'll be back by Tuesday."

Carla hated lying to Meg, but she thought that would be best. She didn't want Meg worrying about her not returning to *The Discoverer* that night.

She walked into the main office of *The Dunes* to the smells of fresh flowers and a pipe. She pulled out a wad of cash and paid for a room, just as Luis had instructed her to do. She hoped Luis would pay her back, because $160 a night would break her.

She reached into her purse for her cell phone and sent Luis a text with the directions to their small cottage. Within thirty minutes, Luis walked through the door of her two-room house, and Carla ran into his arms. She felt so secure in his arms and buried her head into his strong chest.

"So, tell me about the find," Luis said after a few minutes.

Carla was disappointed. Why couldn't he say something nice to her? She had fixed her hair and even wore some perfume. All he could think about was the stupid boat. Maybe once they had the money, he could be all hers.

"The Davenports think it is a Spanish treasure ship. I know they have found some things that make them think that."

"Like what?"

"Well, I saw some small rectangles of gold, gold coins, a brick of silver, and a beautiful jeweled crown. Meg said they think there's a lot more inside the reef, and Jon believes there may be treasure down in some deep crevice. He plans to take his submarine down to check it out."

"Okay. That's good. We'll have to play this just right, baby, and we'll be rich. They've already found enough to set us up for years. You just need to be careful, and don't get caught. You gotta watch out for the woman. She's pretty sharp."

"Do you mean Meg? She's real nice and treats me nice. We've become friends, sort of."

"That's good. Being her friend is good. Just don't blow what you're doing. It won't be long and we'll be out of here. We'll have enough money to buy our own island. I'll buy you a diamond necklace for every day of the week."

After telling Luis the details of the last couple of weeks, Carla sat down on his lap and began rubbing his shoulders and back. Though Luis seemed to be thinking about something else, Carla felt so happy to be with her man.

The next morning, Luis told Carla to enjoy herself, and he would be back later on that evening. He said he had some things to check into, and he gave Carla $500 so she could buy something nice.

Dreaming about what she would do with a million dollars, Carla spent the day walking through the tourist areas of George Town. She bought a black bikini that looked a lot like the one she had seen Meg wear. She also bought some clothes and a real pretty necklace. She would pretend Luis bought it for her, which in a way he did. When Luis did not return by dinner, Carla ate alone at *Splash Restaurant* just down from her cottage, went back to her room, watched television, and fell asleep on the couch.

She heard the door squeak as Luis entered the cottage. Why was he coming in so late? This was their time to be together, and Luis didn't seem to care. He never talked to her about anything of importance except that stupid treasure, and she wondered if he even loved her.

"Hey, baby. I got tied up," Luis said.

"Where have you been?" Carla whined.

"I had some things to do, and it took me longer than I had planned," Luis said evasively.

Luis pulled Carla into his arms and began kissing her passionately. Her frustrations evaporated as Luis told Carla about his dreams of spending the rest of their lives together. She said she didn't care so much about the diamonds and money, even though that would be nice. What she wanted was a man who loved her and took care of her.

"I've got to get some sleep, baby. I'm wiped out."

"This is our last night together, Luis. Do you have to go to sleep right now?"

"I'll make it up to you. We just got to make sure we're doing everything just like we planned. Once we get the gold, we'll have the rest of our lives to live like kings."

Luis headed toward the bedroom and crawled into bed. In less than two minutes, Carla heard Luis beginning to snore.

The next morning Luis did not seem to be the same person she met in Miami, but Carla assumed he was nervous about what she preferred to call their "project." He had rushed her out of the bathroom by telling her that he had called her a cab. He kissed her goodbye and told her to stay in touch.

As Carla pulled away from the cottage in the taxi, she stared out of the back window at Luis. She was so torn over what she was doing. She knew that betraying the Davenports was not right, but she loved Luis and wanted him to be happy. Was there any way that all of this could turn out good?

CHAPTER TWENTY-SEVEN

Wishes and Dreams

Meg pulled the sheets tight on her bed and picked up the bedspread from the floor where she had dropped it minutes earlier. Although Judy insisted on changing the sheets, Meg figured that she outranked the dear housekeeper, so she opted to change the sheets herself. Judy was more like a mother than a housekeeper, and Meg wanted to do everything possible to make housework easier on her.

As Meg walked down the stairs into the kitchen, she saw Judy hugging Carla at the side door. Carla sat her bags down in the mudroom and looked up to see Meg standing in the kitchen.

"Hey, Carla," Meg said with a smile. "I'm surprised to see you back early."

"Well, my friend had to leave, so I thought I would just come back."

Carla had sent word to Meg to tell her that she was staying in George Town with a girlfriend. It seemed so mysterious that she had just said "girlfriend" that Meg had thought about it for a long time. She saw Carla brush off Jeremiah two days earlier and had a fleeting question as to whether or not Carla was gay. Jeremiah was a very good looking man and was one of the nicest guys you would ever want to meet. Meg had concluded that if Jeremiah wasn't her type, then maybe guys weren't her type at all. Maybe there was more to Carla's friend than she was saying.

"I was just preparing some lunch for us," Judy said. "Are you hungry?"

"I am a little," Carla answered. "I didn't eat much for breakfast."

Filling three glasses with ice, Meg sat them on the table and turned toward Carla. "Has your friend been to George Town before?"

"Friend?" Carla questioned, and then quickly nodded. "My friend had a great time. She has never been here before but said she might like to come back."

"Have you known her long?" Judy asked.

"We went to school together," Carla lied. "Her parents are from Mexico too, so we became close friends in elementary school. She works for the airlines, so she can fly for free. I told her to come back next time I had shore leave."

"That sounds nice," Meg said. "Maybe next time we can meet her. You two would be welcome to stay here."

"So, what's next?" Carla said, changing the subject before more questions could be asked about her "friend."

"I'm hoping to hear some good news from Jon today. He called last night and said our lawyer was afraid the authorities might not act as fast as we want them to act, so it might take a bit longer. I'm thinking that if we still do not have the go ahead by tomorrow, we might just go back out and resume where we left off. Ann and I could take the sub down and check out the ravine, or whatever you call that place."

"Is that safe?" Carla asked. "I mean, can you two handle that submarine?"

"Ann is quite the expert. I know that sub looks like a big bubble, but it's quite easy to control. It's supposed to be able to go over 3,000 feet deep. I don't think it's that deep in the crevice. The edge of the drop is about 125 feet deep. Jon swam right up to the edge of it on our last dive on that side of the reef."

"Sounds scary to me," Carla said. "What if something happens to the submarine? You would be stuck."

"That sub is brand new," Meg said. "I can't imagine anything going wrong with it right now. We'll be careful."

The three ladies enjoyed homemade chicken salad sandwiches. Carla had never eaten anything but store-bought chicken salad before; this salad, with the grapes and nuts added, was delicious. Over their meal, the conversation turned to children.

"Do you and Jon plan to have children?" Carla asked.

Meg replied wistfully, "Oh, I don't know. I would love to, but I think Jon is not too interested in babies. I lost a baby once, and I may not even be able to get pregnant."

"I would love to get married one day and have two children—a boy and a girl," Carla said.

Meg placed a mental check mark on the question of Carla's sexual preference.

"Is there a man in your life?" Judy asked.

"Well, I do have a man back in Miami," Carla acknowledged. "There's nothing permanent, but one day something might work out. Were you ever married, Judy?"

"I was married as a young woman, but my husband was killed in Vietnam. I never found anyone else after that. I do love seeing happily married couples. Meg, you and Jon sure do seem to be happy."

"Oh, Judy, we are! I have never been so happy in all my life. Jon is the most wonderful man. He is kind, gentle, and compassionate. I never thought I would have such a man after my husband died. I think Jon is one of the most selfless men I've ever met."

"I think you're right about that," Judy agreed. "I've known Jon for a number of years now, and he's a keeper. I'll tell you the secret of a happy marriage. Build your relationship on friendship and love, not on sex. The couples that seem to be the happiest to me are those who are good friends first and lovers second."

"I agree that sex is better when it grows out of friendship," Meg said. "Jon seems to love talking to me and listening to what I think. We've enjoyed working on this project together. I look forward to every day with him. It makes me so sad when he has to be away like this."

"I hope I can have a relationship like that one day," Carla said. "I'm so tired of men who don't understand what having a relationship means."

They agreed and left the table to begin cleaning up from lunch. Meg showed Carla around the house and told her she was welcome to visit anytime she wanted. They also walked over to the guest house, which was nearing completion. Meg told Carla that Marc just had a few things left to do before the house was finished.

The guest house was made of stucco, matching the main house, and it had a big front porch on the first level, matched by a balcony above it on the second level. One end of the house was a two-level apartment for Ann. The other end contained a full kitchen, living room, and three bedrooms on the lower level with four bedrooms and a sitting area on the upper level. Instead of hot tubs in the house, Jon planned to build an in ground hot tub beside the pool he hoped to complete once they found the treasure. Meg invited Carla to spend the night with them, and they could all return to *The Discoverer* the following morning.

After the three ate dinner together, Carla heard the side door close and Ann's voice rang out from the mudroom. "I hope you like what I got you, Meg."

"What did you get me?" Meg asked as Ann walked into the kitchen.

"I got you a new iron. I'm so tired of using your cheap one. I don't know how you can stand it."

"My iron is not cheap," Meg defended.

"Yes it is. It's feather light. I can't stand a light-weight iron. You have to work too hard at it. I got you a real iron."

Ann pulled it out of the bag and opened the box. Meg took hold of the iron and acted like it was too heavy to lift.

"Gracious girl, I'm going to have to work out so I can iron my clothes," Meg said with a grin.

"Good. A little exercise does a girl some good. Not only does it help you with ironing your clothes, but it also improves every part of your life."

The ladies played Scattergories until 10:30. They agreed it was time to turn in so they could get an early start the next day. As Meg was about to get into bed, her cell phone rang. She looked at the caller I.D. and saw it was Jon.

"Hey, gorgeous," Meg said into her phone.

"Hey, babe. I sure do miss you."

"I miss you too. When will you be home?"

"Well, true to form, things are taking longer than we had at first anticipated. I don't think I'll be back tomorrow, but I should be back on Wednesday."

"Oh, Jon. I don't know if I can stand you being away that long."

"I know, honey. It's just two more days. I was thinking about Jeremiah and Jose out in the Carver and wondered if they might need to be relieved."

"Why don't we just take *The Discoverer* back out tomorrow like we had planned? Ann, Jose, and I can dive while we're waiting on you to return, or at least we'll be keeping post over the wreck."

"I guess that'll be okay. I've been thinking that we need to purchase a small boat to use for the trips back and forth. It will be useful when we're using the Carver to stand guard over the wreck. We can't use *The Discoverer* as a shuttle. Besides that, I wouldn't mind having a little fishing boat our guests could use when they come to visit. We could pull our kids behind it on an inner tube one of these days."

"Do you mean your nephew, Jason? He's not ours, you know. Besides that, isn't he too big to be pulled on an inner tube?"

"He might like it, but I was talking about our future kids. You said you wanted to have children. I would love to have a son or daughter, as long as she looks like you."

Meg was speechless. She just held the phone to her ear and couldn't say a word. Her eyes began to mist over, and a tear rolled down her cheek.

"Meg. Are you there?"

Meg finally found her voice and said, "Yes…I'm here."

"Are you crying? Oh, babe, what's the matter?"

"I didn't think you would want to have any children. I didn't think I could be any happier, but …Oh Jon. I love you so much."

"Sweetheart, I want to have as many children as you want. You are going to be a wonderful mother."

"I don't know about that, but you are the most wonderful man in the world. I'm so lucky to be your wife."

"I'm the one that's blessed. We're going to have an awesome family. In the meantime, I'll get Jose to pick up a boat for us. We can trust him with that decision, and maybe I can get home soon."

"I'm ready to have a child, but we should probably wait until we get the treasure up," Meg laughed. "I'm ready for you to get home, though."

"I'll be there as fast as I can. When you see Jose tomorrow, tell him to bring the *New Beginnings* in and go pick up a good boat at the marina. I know there's a boat dealership just off the marina. Tell Jose what we're thinking about, and tell him to let the guy at the dealership know I'll be by to make payment as soon as I'm back in town. As a matter of fact, I'll just call them in the morning and work out the details."

"Okay. I love you. Please be careful."

"I will. You be careful too, sweetheart. I can't let anything happen to you. You are the love of my life, and will one day be the mother of my children. Goodnight."

"Goodnight."

Meg lay down in her bed and began crying all over again. She had long ago buried her desire to be a mother because she thought it would never be a possibility, and even after falling in love with Jon, she assumed he didn't want any children. Then Meg sat up with the sudden realization that Jon's desire for children came out of his deep love for her. He knew that she wanted children, so therefore he wanted them too.

Meg wondered if having a child would cause her love to be divided or would it cause it to be multiplied? What would her life with Jon be like with a new baby? She lay in her bed imagining a happy home where she and her wonderful husband played together with their little baby…boy. She decided a boy would be best. She knew Jon would love having a son. What if she had a girl? Meg didn't know anything about raising a little girl. For that matter, she didn't know anything about raising a boy.

She got out of bed to go to the bathroom. She stood staring at herself in the mirror and began to laugh. She looked like a mess. Here Meg was thinking about their child when she didn't even know if she could get pregnant again. The last experience was horrible.

She would never forget the beginning of the pain that did not go away for a long time. The physical pain was nothing compared to the pain she felt in her heart over losing her little girl. It all started with a complication that didn't seem to concern the doctor too much. He told her to slow down and spend a lot of time resting. As much as Meg had rested, the problem not only continued, but worsened.

One day Meg was so sick, and the pain in her belly was severe enough to cause her to double over. She thought she was going to be sick and went to the bathroom. Before she got to the toilet, she lost the baby right on the bathroom floor. The child was almost five months along, and she was so developed Meg could tell right away her baby was a girl.

During counseling, Meg was encouraged to name her little girl, so she chose the name Courtney. She needed Steve during all of this, but he had been away on maneuvers. Without warning, Meg was filled with fear about what might happen to her. She didn't know if she could go through it all over again. She picked up her phone and called Jon.

"Hey. Are you okay?" Jon asked

"I'm okay," Meg replied sheepishly. "No, I'm really not."

"What's wrong, sweetheart?"

Meg began to cry into the phone while trying to speak at the same time.

"What's happened? Is everything okay?"

Meg finally got control of her emotions and said, "What if I can't get pregnant? What if I lose the baby again?"

"Oh, sweetheart. You're going to be fine. For starters, I'm sure you can get pregnant. A lot of women have miscarriages, and it has nothing to do with their ability to get pregnant. I've heard that sometimes it's God's way of taking a baby who would not be able to live a normal life because of some problem. We'll do this together, honey. Of course…I'm not sure how you could get pregnant if we didn't do it together."

Meg laughed and said, "Oh, I wish you were here right now. I'm just afraid, Jon. I went through such a bad experience last time."

"I'm so sorry for all of that. You'll be fine this time. We'll be careful and make sure you're under the best of care. You just wait and see. We're going to have so many babies running around our house; we're going to have to buy a school bus to haul them all over the island."

"I don't know if I can handle a school bus load," Meg said with a smile. "I would like maybe one or two."

"All I know is that I am not far from forty years old, so we better get started."

"I love you, Jon Davenport. You are so good to me."

"I love you too, sweetheart. You are going to be the most beautiful and the sexiest mother in the Bahamas. You need to get some sleep. It's two o'clock in the morning."

"I know. I just started thinking about how wonderful it will be to have a child and got all scared. I'll be all right. Goodnight."

"Goodnight. I love you, Meg."

CHAPTER TWENTY-EIGHT

Into the Deep

The Discoverer pulled away from the dock on Tuesday morning and dropped anchor over the wreck within thirty minutes. Meg climbed down a ladder and jumped aboard the Carver yacht to speak with Jose.

"Jon wants you to go to the marina to pick out a smaller boat for us to use as a shuttle. He said he would call ahead and speak to a salesman at the dealership, but he trusts your judgment. We're looking for something to use for fishing around the islands, but also something that would be small enough to pull an inner tube."

"Okay," Jose agreed. "That's a good idea. It would be easier to have a smaller boat. I'll call Jon once I look over the inventory at the dealership."

As Meg and Jeremiah climbed back aboard *The Discoverer*, Jose pulled away to head for the George Town marina. On the way to the treasure site, Meg had thought about what they could do that would be productive while waiting on Jon's return. The most intriguing thing that might lead to something significant would be to explore the ravine. Jon had said it looked too deep to dive and would have to be explored with the submarine. Meg pulled Ann aside and spoke with her about the possibility of going down together to take a look around.

Ann was quite good at handling the sub, and they could at least find the bottom of the chasm.

"Why don't we make a dive first," Meg suggested, "and try to get our bearings. We could come back up, eat some lunch, and take the sub down into the hole this afternoon."

"I'm game," Ann said. "I love that sub. I feel like I'm floating around in a big bubblegum machine."

Meg said, "It reminds me of one of those kid's toys. You know, the see-through balls filled with things that move around when you roll it around?"

"Well, let's hope this one doesn't roll around. I'm fine with going down, but I'd be a little afraid to go too deep. If it gets too deep, I'd want to come back up. I don't want to discover some huge sea monster down there."

"You're crazy, but I don't think I'm game to go too deep myself. We can watch the depth gauge and come back up if we start getting deeper than two hundred feet or so."

The two women went to their cabins to change into their bathing suits. After donning their scuba gear, they fell over the side and started kicking their way down the wall to the sea floor far below. Meg never tired of seeing the multi-colored fish that always covered the reef.

Meg stopped and grabbed Ann's hand. She pointed to a ledge sticking out from the reef and saw a grouper that had to weigh at least one hundred pounds. She had to remember to tell Jon about the fish. He would love spearing something that big. They resumed their descent to the sand and swam over to the edge of the drop off.

Meg shivered as she looked over to what seemed to be a bottomless pit. It was true that there was some debris littering the sand that could be something from the wreck. The two women began filling their net bags with a few items that looked promising. After a few minutes, Meg pointed toward the surface. She knew they had not been down that long, but they had gone about 125 feet deep. She stopped at the ten foot mark on the anchor line and waited for five minutes, and then they swam to the ladder hanging off the platform on the back of the ship. Jeremiah was there to help them out of the water.

After lunch, Meg and Ann went out on the deck to ready the submarine. Ann suggested they wait until Jose returned so he could man the communication base on *The Discoverer*. They didn't have to wait long as a bright, red boat came skipping across the top of the ocean toward them. Jose pulled up beside the salvage ship in a brand new, twenty-four foot Robalo R247 skiing and fishing boat. It was a dual console boat with a fiberglass hard top providing protection from the elements. Fishing rod holders were mounted along the back of the boat, and it had a 300 horsepower Yamaha motor. It was pretty, and Meg could picture herself behind the wheel as Jon yelled encouragement to their little boy.

"Jose, it's beautiful," Meg shouted down to him as he threw a line up to Jeremiah.

"I got a great deal. It's last year's model, but she's brand new. I think it will be perfect for what we need."

"Ann and I are thinking about going down in the sub. How about manning the communications for us?"

"Are you sure you want to go down? Are you ready for that?"

"We all agreed that Ann was the best with the sub. We'll be fine. We're going to explore for a few minutes. If it gets deeper than 200 feet, we'll come back up."

"All right. I'll help get it ready."

Meg and Ann climbed into the sub and sealed the hatch as it bobbed up and down on the gentle seas. The sub was quite simple and reminded Meg of playing a Nintendo game because it was controlled by a joystick. They sat in their seats, and Ann pressed the button turning on the motor. The sub's ballasts began filling with water, and they slowly slipped beneath the surface.

Ann guided the huge bubble with great skill right down to the edge of the crevice and began descending down into the darkness. Meg reached over to flip on a switch that turned on the head lights, and the two women began looking around in awe. Neither had ever gone this deep, and it was quite an adventure. Ann watched the depth gauge and held the sub steady at about 175 feet.

"Turn on the light underneath and let's see if we can see the bottom," Meg said.

Ann pushed a lever down as Meg peered beneath her into the never ending darkness. She strained to see if she could make out the bottom, but it seemed to be bottomless. Suddenly the lights went out and the two women sat in darkness.

"Meg, what's happening?" Ann said in a panicked voice.

"I'm sure we're fine, Ann. Let's not lose our heads. I bet it's something minor. Is there a battery operated light in here? Call Jose. He'll know."

"The radio is dead," Ann whimpered after being unsuccessful in reaching Jose. "I don't know of any emergency lights in here. I never even considered losing power. I get the sensation we're sinking."

Meg felt around her seat and all around the sub hoping to find a flashlight. Nothing. Then she reached into her back pocket, where she found her cell phone. She remembered putting it in her pocket earlier and had forgotten to take it out before submerging in the sub. She pushed the button and the phone's screen came to life. The bubble was lit up with an eerie glow, and Meg held the phone in front of the depth gauge.

"250 feet and sinking," Ann squeaked. "What are we going to do?"

Something very large swam right by their bubble and bumped the side of the sub. Both women screamed with fright as the sub jerked a bit toward one side.

"Ann, we've got to calm down," Meg said trying to gain control of her own emotions. "We shouldn't be surprised that some large creatures live down here. Let's see if we can figure out how to get this thing started again."

Meg looked at all the controls along the panel and saw everything was turned on. She scanned all around the sub and then looked under the control panel. She saw a yellow wire dangling and another wire lying on the floor.

"Look at this," Meg said. "It looks like this wire somehow came loose."

"It doesn't look like it came loose," Ann said. "It looks like someone partially cut it."

"We've got to somehow get this wire back together. I need to cut some of this rubber housing away so we can splice the wire."

Ann reached into her pocket and said, "Here. Try these fingernail clippers. Maybe you can cut the rubber with that."

Meg took the clippers and after a minute had the rubber cut away and the bare wire exposed. She pulled the two wires together and started twisting the bare wires together.

"Ouch," Meg shouted as the lights came back on for a few seconds and electricity surged through her body. "That hurt."

"Just hold the wire by the rubber and keep the two bare parts touching," Ann suggested.

Meg held the wires together without trying to twist them, and the lights came back on. The engine purred back to life. Ann looked at the depth gauge and saw they were almost four hundred feet deep. They didn't take time to enjoy the view, but rather began their ascent to the surface. Ann called Jose and told him to have the crane ready.

As the sub surfaced next to *The Discoverer*, both women breathed a prayer of thanks. Jose dropped the line from the crane, and the two women climbed out of the hatch. Meg attached the cable to the hook on the sub before they climbed up the ladder hanging over the side of the ship. The submarine was hoisted back onto *The Discoverer*.

"This wire was cut," Jose said after inspecting the submarine. "Someone tried to sabotage our efforts."

The whole crew had gathered to hear about what had happened. Meg noticed that Carla was standing right by the sub with her face as white as snow. Captain Buffington crawled aboard the sub to inspect the wires and agreed with Jose's conclusion.

"Someone not only tried to sabotage our efforts, but they also tried to kill you," The Captain said. "We need to call the authorities."

"Let's call Jon first," Meg said. "He'll know what's best to do."

Meg and Jose climbed aboard the new twenty-four foot Robalo and sped back toward Pirate's Cove. For some reason, there was no signal on the satellite phone out over the wreck, so they were forced to return to land in order to get hold of Jon.

Meg was still shaken by the near death experience and was unsure about how the group should proceed. She knew Jon didn't want to bring too much attention to their operation, and if they called in the authorities, their project may be halted all together. As soon as Meg's feet were on the dock, she dialed Jon's number.

CHAPTER TWENTY-NINE

Manifest Destiny

"Hey, babe," Jon's voice immediately came over the phone. "I've got great news."

"I've got news too," Meg said with a little edge in her voice

"What's wrong?" Jon asked.

Meg started at the beginning and told Jon the story. She ended with Jose's conclusion about possible sabotage.

"How could it be sabotage? No one knows what we're doing." Jon confessed.

"I don't know, but someone tried to kill us today," Meg acknowledged. "What do we do? Should I call the authorities?"

"Are you okay?"

"Yes. Ann and I are both fine. We had the daylights scared out of us, but we are fine. I think you would have been proud of us."

Jon paused for a moment and said, "No, don't call anyone yet. I'm getting ready to fly back now. We have permission to dig into the reef. Thank God we're not in U. S. waters or this never would have happened. We'll figure out what to do when I get back. Just meet me at the airport in about an hour."

An hour later, Meg and Jon embraced and kissed at the door leading to the deplaning area. Meg was so relieved that Jon was back. She felt Jon's lips upon hers, and Jon could not seem to hold Meg close enough.

On the drive back to Pirate's Cove, they agreed to a full-scale checkout procedure before ever using any of the underwater gear again. No one should trust the gear to be safe until it was closely studied. Then they went about trying to figure out who would want to sabotage their project. There was only one conclusion: Luis.

He was the only one still alive who might try something like this. There was the possibility of someone doing it that was connected to the terrorists, but Luis sounded like a better possibility. Jon decided not to call in the authorities yet, but rather to hire a couple of guys to help guard the boat at night whenever it was docked in Pirate's Cove.

As Jon climbed up onto *The Discoverer*, everyone gathered around to hear the news. He filled them in on the legal procedures and how the courts gave him permission to "strategically" cut into the reef. He had to agree to take photographic evidence of their recovery efforts so as to prove the salvage company did everything possible to preserve the reef. Jon had ordered equipment to be delivered to Pirate's Cove that would help them get to the wreck behind the coral. When Jon, Meg, and Jose had returned to the salvage ship, they brought the *New Beginnings* back out so *The Discoverer* could leave to pick up the new equipment before dinner.

The next morning was overcast as a storm was making its way through the Bahamas. Jon knew there would be a few short hours to work before having to call it a day due to the weather. The four partners suited up after breakfast and got right to work. The new equipment that was so vital to reef preservation resembled a hydraulic concrete splitter, and this tool would enable the team to remove only the necessary parts of the reef. The progress was difficult as Jon and Jose were deliberate in working the reef inch by inch while Ann removed debris, and Meg took pictures of the progress with Jon's underwater camera. Dr. Russell's videographer worked silently in the background filming every move.

They climbed back aboard, after going through two tanks of air apiece, and the rain was beginning to fall. Jon sent Jose and Ann back to Pirate's Cove to get the Carver Yacht back to the security of the bay before the storm became severe. He and Meg planned to spend the afternoon reading additional books on ship wrecks he had purchased from Amazon. The storm had moved through by dinner time.

"I'll just tell Jose that they should return first thing in the morning," Jon suggested. "There's no need for them to come back tonight."

"I don't know if we can trust them at home alone without a chaperone," Meg winked.

Jon laughed. "Judy's there. She'll keep them in line."

The group worked every waking hour for the next two days before finding something worth reporting from the wreck. On Friday afternoon, Jon attached a flotation device to an old, crusty cannon. While the timbers were no longer in place, the barrel of the cannon was very obvious. On Saturday morning, a large piece of the reef came loose and a hollow cavity was discovered inside the reef. Within this cave, numerous objects were uncovered that were obviously plates and what looked to be personal affects. They also found several gold coins.

After inspecting the tub in *The Discoverer's* labs on Sunday morning, Jon and Meg discovered plates, cups, swords, and what looked like pieces of old muskets. While there was not a lot of real value, other than the gold, this would prove worthy to the authorities as relics that could be placed in a museum.

Meg had been complaining about a toothache for several days, so Jon decided that he had better get her to the dentist in George Town. Even though the Davenports would have to abandon the project for the day, Ann and Jose still planned to continue diving.

After spending the day in town, Jon and Meg returned to their cabin on *The Discoverer* late that evening. Meg's jaw was still a little numb, and her cavity had a new filling. She poured water in a cup, grabbed some ibuprofen, and joined her husband on the couch of their cabin. As Jon picked up the remote control to their satellite television, the phone rang.

"Hey, Cindy," Meg said. "How in the world are you?"

"Hey, girl. I'm doing fine, now that I've finished up with Professor Strange. How are you? You sound a little funny."

"First of all, I'm doing okay," Meg answered, "except I had to get some work done on a tooth today. My jaw is still a little numb. Secondly, who is Professor Strange?"

"That's not his real name, but let's just say he's not quite normal. You know—the guy I've been working with for the last few weeks. Anyway, I'm all done with him, and I'm giving my full attention to you."

"So, how do you plan to start on our project?"

"I've already started, and I have some news. I found the crown listed on the manifest. While this doesn't say definitively that the wreck is the *San Ambrosio*, it does say it was one of the ships of the *Terre Firma* armada."

"Wow. That's great news, Cindy. I'll share it with Jon. Thanks for all your help."

"You're welcome. When are you guys going to come back to Spain for a visit?"

"I'm not sure," Meg acknowledged. "Maybe it can be soon. Take care of yourself."

"You too, Meg."

Meg hung up and told Jon what Cindy had said about the crown. Though they had assumed this information already, it was nice to have it officially confirmed. Jon yawned and suggested they go to bed.

As Meg climbed down the stairs toward the mess hall the following morning, Ann greeted her with a big smile.

"We found something you might be interested in," Ann blurted out.

"What did you find?" Meg asked.

"Come and see."

The little group went below to the lab, and Ann pointed to the table where two beautiful gold bars glistened in the light. Ann motioned to the tub of the cleansing chemical where Meg could see additional cannon balls, daggers, and another jewel studded sword's hilt.

"We found it inside the reef," Jose offered.

Ann continued, "We decided to blast a little more of the reef out while you were at the dentist yesterday, and we discovered another compartment. It's kind of like the reef grew over the ship leaving small treasure troves. We're going to find the mother lode. I can just feel it."

Jon called the group back to task, and they set about planning their next dive. Jose suggested they go into the reef with the seavac and dig down into the sand. He was thinking the ship had settled into the sand, and the treasure would be further down. Jon agreed with the idea, and the four partners dove together again into the warm waters.

The group worked nonstop for the next four weeks taking small breaks, but to their disappointment, very little treasure was found. Meg was beginning to think that someone must have beaten them to the treasure many years earlier. When they had started this venture, she had no idea that she and Jon would be staying on a boat for such long periods of time.

By the middle of February, the whole area of the wreck had been excavated and numerous collectable items were found for the national museum, but a few gold coins were all they picked up. Meg and Jon even took the submarine back down into the crevice and discovered the crack in the ocean floor to be a fraction over 500 feet deep. Although it gave Meg the creeps to go so deep, she was fascinated with the strange world. They used the claws on the sub to pick up numerous objects from the sea floor, but their experience gained nothing except sightings of strange fish.

The team worked on through March and April as they searched tirelessly over the sea floor and around the reef for more signs of the treasure, but they found nothing else. On the second of May, Jon decided the treasure had either been lost at sea or someone else had gotten to it many years earlier. While he planned to resume the search, he told Meg there was no reason to continue guarding the wreck site. Jon also determined that everyone needed a break and therefore declared to the crew one night at dinner they were going to take a month off.

"Captain Buffington, let's sail to Pirate's Cove in the morning," Jon instructed. "You can take *The Discoverer* back to Miami on Saturday, and anyone who wants to go along may do so. We'll plan to resume our search after we do a little more research. It may be this treasure has petered out, and we'll need to go in search of a new ship."

"I'm sorry to hear that," the captain said "but I'm sure everyone can use a break."

****

Carla bent over with the dustpan in one hand and the broom in the other. She had almost finished cleaning up the kitchen from lunch and looked forward to retiring to her room. She could tell at dinner that The Four, which was the name she had given to Meg, Jon, Jose, and Ann, looked very discouraged. It had been a long few months, and they had evidently not found anything else since the last couple of gold coins.

She heard the door close and looked up to see Captain Buffington.

"Carla, we're going to be heading back to Miami in the morning. Jon has suggested that we take a month off while he does more research."

"Oh, we are? So, does Jon think there's nothing else down there?"

"I think that he believes someone must have discovered the treasure a long time ago. Because it's so shallow, it's possible that the king of Spain had slaves recover the treasure after the ship sank."

"I thought Meg said no one had ever heard of the ship after it sank."

"There's no telling what happened four hundred years ago. All I know is that we are going back to Pirate's Cove for the night and heading to Miami in the morning."

As soon as Captain Buffington was out of sight, Carla hurried to her room to send Luis an e-mail. She told him that Jon was thinking there was no more treasure at this spot, and she didn't know what was going to happen now. She reminded him of the gold that had been taken from the sea floor, but had no idea of its worth. While she didn't know for sure where it was kept, Carla suggested to Luis that Jon might be hiding the gold in a vault at his house. She asked him if she should go back to Miami with the captain or stay on the island, and then she told him she didn't care so much about the treasure as long as they could be together.

Meg and Jon invited the whole crew to eat dinner at the main house, so Carla took a shower and changed clothes so she would at least be refreshed for dinner. When she joined the group at the main house, Judy was serving everyone southern barbeque. Carla was quite excited to have something different for a change, and it was delicious.

Meg sat down beside Carla with a small plate of apple pie. "Carla, why don't you just spend the night up here at the house tonight? I'm sure you would enjoy sleeping in a bed that doesn't move."

"Thanks, Meg. I believe I will take you up on that, but I would like to go back to the ship to get a few things."

Carla wanted to go back to the boat to check her e-mail one more time. She still had not heard from Luis and was not sure what to do next. She thanked Judy for the wonderful meal and followed the crew toward the ship. As she closed the door to the house, she saw The Four sitting at the table and heard Judy say she was going over to prepare the guest house.

CHAPTER THIRTY

Deja Vu

Meg made some coffee, and the group sat down around the kitchen table to talk. Meg heard the door to the mudroom open up and assumed it to be Carla coming back for the night. She was shocked out of her mind when she felt a strong arm suddenly go around her throat, and she was jerked up from her chair. Cold steel pressed against the side of her head. Ann screamed as Jon jumped to his feet and instinctively moved toward the intruder.

"If you take another step," Luis said, "I will shoot this trouble maker and be done with her."

Meg trembled with horror as she felt Luis' grip tighten and her mind raced back to her experience with Luis and Philippe on the boat so many months earlier. While he had been gentle with her then, she had no doubt that this man was a killer. He had full intentions of killing her back at The Fortress, and he had been a part of the attempt to release the virus at the Convention. Meg felt tears flowing down her cheeks as she began to fear for not only her life, but also for the rest of the group as well.

Telling the group to lie down, Luis motioned toward the floor with the gun. As Jon started moving toward the floor, Luis began rubbing Meg's shoulder and throat with his free hand. Jon lunged for Luis, and Luis hit him in the head with the butt of the gun so fast, no one had time to react. As Jon crashed to the floor, Meg cried out pulling against Luis' strong, unmoving arm.

"Any more stupid moves and this girl dies," Luis said as he pulled Meg close against his body. "All I want is payback for all of the trouble you have given me. Now big guy, get the idiot into the chair and wake him up."

Jose turned and stooped to pick Jon up off the floor. Luis slid his hand down to Meg's bare throat, and Meg turned and slapped Luis with all of her strength. Though the slap shocked him, he hit Meg hard with an open hand and knocked her to the floor. Had Jose not been getting Jon into the chair, he could have made a move on Luis, but by the time he turned at the sound, Luis was pulling Meg back up to her feet with the gun pressed against her head. Jon opened his eyes, but appeared to be quite dazed from the blow.

"Now," Luis said through clenched teeth, "you can go to wherever you have the treasure stored and fill up a box with it. I have a vehicle outside you can put it in. I will take this pretty chick with me as a little insurance and leave her somewhere for you to pick up later. If you try anything at all, she's dead."

****

Carla walked up to the house wondering why Luis had not e-mailed her back. She didn't know if she was supposed to go back to Miami or stay in George Town. Didn't he care about her? Had something happened to him? She still wondered about the sabotaged submarine incident, but she had decided there was no way Luis could have done that. He wouldn't try to kill someone, especially someone as nice as the Davenports. Carla had spent the afternoon imagining her new life with Luis.

She was sure she could convince him to give up on this treasure idea, and they could make a nice life together in Miami.

Carla noticed the door to the mudroom was ajar. She thought that was odd because she was sure she had closed it earlier. She supposed anyone could have left it open while she had returned to the ship. She stepped into the house and was shocked to see Luis standing in the kitchen with his arm around Meg's throat. He held a gun to her head. There was blood oozing from her lip, and Luis' hand kept moving from her bare shoulder to her neck and resting on her bare flesh as if he had something very evil on his mind.

Because of Luis' position, he had not yet spotted Carla, and she seemed glued to the spot in horror just outside of his peripheral vision. Carla was livid and shocked. Luis loved her. Why was he holding Meg as if he wanted her? Meg was her friend and wouldn't hurt anyone, and now she was held tightly in the grasp of the man Carla loved.

Meg was bleeding, which meant Luis had hit her. Why was he holding a gun to her head? She had been the one to reach out to Carla and made her feel like she was special. Carla had even felt like she was a part of the family.

As these thoughts raced through her mind, Carla realized that Luis loved no one but himself. Meg and Jon had been her true friends, and Carla had been ready to betray them. In a moment of clarity, she saw Meg's new, heavy iron sitting on the ironing board. She grabbed it and raced into the kitchen. Screaming profanities, she swung it at Luis' head and called him by name. He turned the gun on Carla and pulled the trigger–the explosion of the gun filled the room with an ear deafening sound. At the same time Luis pulled the trigger, the iron hit him in the head with a sickening thud. As he fell to the floor, blood flowed from a severe gash at the top of his forehead.

Carla felt her body flying through the air, and the wind was knocked out of her when she hit the floor. Her chest felt as if it were going to burst. The burning sensation was unbearable, and for some reason, she was unable to move. She opened her eyes to discover that her vision was fuzzy, and it seemed as if the room was spinning. The pain in her chest was beginning to subside as warmth flooded her body.

****

Meg had been thrown to the floor and watched in disbelief as Carla collapsed with blood pouring from an open wound in her chest. It seemed as if everything was happening in slow motion, and Meg felt helpless and unable to move from where she had fallen. She got to her knees and crawled over to Carla. She cradled her head and held her convulsing body. Jon struggled to his feet, grabbed his phone and called for an ambulance. He then knelt down beside Carla putting his arm around Meg.

He pulled Meg close to him and whispered hoarsely, "Are you okay?"

"Yes, I'm fine," Meg said between sobs. "She's dying, Jon. She's dying."

"The ambulance will be here soon. Let's see if we can get the blood to stop."

Jon staggered to the kitchen cabinet to get some towels. Meg looked around at the horrific scene. Blood was everywhere and continued its free flow from Carla's near lifeless body. Meg held Carla's head in her lap and tried to stop the flow of blood with her bare hand.

Jose, who had pinned Luis down after he fell, turned him on his stomach and held the hands of the stunned man behind his back.

Carla coughed as blood trickled from her mouth, and her eyes fluttered open.

"Meg," Carla said, her voice a mere whisper.

"I'm here," Meg managed to say through her flowing tears. "You're going to be okay, Carla."

"Meg…I'm so sorry. You have been…the only true friend…I've ever had. I'm sorry I betrayed you."

"Oh, Carla," Meg cried as she bent over and kissed her forehead. "You saved our lives. You haven't betrayed us."

"Please…" Carla whispered, her voice so low that Meg was having trouble hearing her.

"I'm here Carla. Don't try to talk now. We have an ambulance coming."

"I'm…not going…to make…it," Carla gasped.

"You will, Carla. Just hold on. Help is on the way."

"Thank you…for being my…friend. I…"

Carla's eyes stared up at the ceiling, and the grip she had on Meg's hand slackened. The slow rising of her chest stopped as life slipped from her bleeding body.

"No, Carla," Meg cried. "Please don't go. Don't go."

Kneeling down beside Meg, Jon held her in his arms. He reached over to Carla's neck to feel for a pulse, and when he determined she had passed, he slid his hand over her face to close her eyes. Meg buried her head into Jon's shoulder and sobbed deeply as Jon tried to console her.

The ambulance and two police officers arrived within fifteen minutes, but for Carla, it was too late. Meg gently lay Carla's head down and tenderly wiped the drying blood from her chin. She bent over, kissed her again on the forehead, and eased away so the medical personnel could tend to her body. Meg stood limp, embraced in Jon's arms, and felt numb with grief. She watched in stunned silence as the stretcher was wheeled out of the house.

As the police pulled Luis to his feet, he stumbled with moans of pain and confusion. The officer cuffed him and dragged him outside where he was forced into the police car. A second officer asked the group if they wouldn't mind answering a few questions.

Jon gave the officer a summary of what had happened, and everyone agreed to give more detailed statements in the morning. As soon as the cruiser pulled away from the house, Jon, Meg, Jose, and Ann took the truck to the hospital where they could claim Carla's body and begin making funeral arrangements.

When they arrived back at the house, Captain Buffington was awaiting their arrival on the front porch.

"What happened?" he asked. "Jeremiah told me he saw an ambulance leaving your house."

Being careful to leave off their suspicions of Carla's involvement in the scheme to steal the treasure, Jon shared the events of the night with his team. He told the captain they would be unable to move forward with any funeral plans until the police contacted Carla's family. Even though Jon had planned on sending the captain and crew back to Miami, everyone agreed to wait until they knew the details of Carla's funeral service.

When the officer from the Royal Police Force of the Bahamas showed up the following morning to interview the group, their story about Carla was one of being a hero and not an accomplice. Officer Pedro Sanchez was a short, plump man of Cuban descent. His hair was jet black, and he wore a thin, clipped mustache. He was amiable enough and was quite thorough with his questions.

Luis was wanted in both the Bahamas and the United States for all manner of crimes, so he would be put away for a long, long time. It was possible he might even face the death penalty for a murder in Georgia some years earlier. The officer completed the interview and expressed his condolences to the grief stricken team.

Word came to Jon a day later that Carla was an only child, and her parents were deceased. Though she had family members in Mexico, there seemed to be no way to even know how to contact them. Jon told the officer he would take care of the funeral expenses, and the Davenports drove to the funeral home to plan the service. Because no one was coming from out of town and there would be no need for any type of visitation, the funeral service was planned for the following day.

It all seemed surreal to Meg, and she had a difficult time believing her friend was dead. She had grown to love Carla and knew deep down that Carla loved her. The funeral service was brief as the same pastor who had married her and Jon a few months earlier read from the Bible and offered a prayer for Carla's friends. Meg could not cease thinking about how little she knew Carla, and how Carla willingly gave up her life so Meg could live.

"How do you ever get over the sorrow?" Meg cried as they walked away from the graveside. "She gave her life for me. I'm having a hard time just walking away from here."

"I know, sweetheart," Jon replied. "She loved you. She loved all of us. I don't think you get over it."

"I don't think I want to get over it. She gave me a chance to live again. I'll forever be grateful to her."

Once the group returned to the house, Jon told Captain Buffington to make ready to leave for Miami on the following day. Though Jon made tentative plans to commence their search for the treasure on June tenth, Jon assured the Captain he would stay in touch to firm up their plans. Judy and Meg put together one final meal for the group, and they ate in uncustomary silence. The sorrow Meg felt seemed to be shared by everyone on the team. It was a painful way to end what had been an amazing adventure.

The next morning, *The Discoverer* pulled away from the dock in Pirate's Cove close to 10:00. Jon, Meg, Jose, Ann, and Judy stayed behind at the main house.

The small group of friends spent the afternoon cleaning some of the remaining equipment and storing their things in the small building that had been built down near the docks. The two couples returned to the house bone-weary from the emotional drain they had experienced and from the tiring work of the day. As they walked back to the house, the delectable smell of dinner wafted through the air. It was Judy's special recipe of meat loaf, green beans, and mashed potatoes, and it smelled delicious.

Some of the familiar conversation began to return to the group and even laughter drifted through the dining area from time to time. At one point during the meal, Jose and Ann got everyone's attention and told them they were planning to be married. After the cheers and a toast, Ann said there would be no big wedding but rather a quiet ceremony on the beach when everyone returned from their break.

Before going to bed that night, Jon and Meg sat in their sunken hot tub and talked about what they would do next.

"Maybe we should take a break from the whole treasure hunt and work on our pool," Jon suggested. "A little distraction might be helpful for you right now."

"I suppose," Meg said glumly.

"You always said you wanted a Garden of Eden in the backyard that was complete with a swimming pool. I think we should include a rock waterfall on one end and a sliding board on the other."

"That does sound wonderful," Meg agreed as she warmed to the idea.

Jon continued describing the creative ideas he had considered, and Meg added a few of her own. After soaking for a while, they toweled off, got in bed, and were soon fast asleep.

The following morning at breakfast, Jose informed Jon and Meg that they were going to fly back to Spain to visit with his family and to share their plans to be married. They would leave the following Monday, but they promised to return in two weeks.

"So what will you two love birds do while we are gone?" Ann asked.

"Well, that's a good question," Meg said.

"We've got a few ideas," Jon answered. "I suppose we're going to see what kind of mischief we can get into since you're not going to be around to keep us in line."

"I think I can handle keeping you in line," Judy said with a grin.

"You never know what kind of trouble we'll turn up while you're gone," Jon said, "but we'll make sure we leave a little action for you when you get back."

CHAPTER THIRTY-ONE

Taking a Break

"What will we do with the rest of our break?" Meg asked as they waved goodbye to Jose and Ann at the airport.

"I think the first thing we will do is spend a few days resting and sightseeing. We might even start digging your swimming pool and constructing your little slice of paradise. As far as research goes, we need to get to a major library somewhere and start making a list of all of the galleons known to be lost at sea. We could go back to Seville, if needed. What would you like to do?"

"Well, I'd first like to go back to Conception Island. That's sort of where all of this started. Even though we met at Nassau, I'll always think of Conception Island as the turning point in our relationship."

"I was kind of thinking it was the small bay where we took our first night dive."

"Well, that too," Meg agreed. "Let's go to Conception Island and the bay. Then we can come back and start on the Garden of Eden."

"Sounds like a great plan," Jon agreed. "Since it's not even 9:00 yet, we can be on Conception Island by lunch."

Jon called Judy as he and Meg crawled into the truck, and by the time they returned home, Judy had not only prepared a picnic lunch for them, but had also packed a crate with enough groceries for three days. Jon kissed Judy on the cheek and began the exhausting task of carrying a heavy crate down the stairs to the dock. As he emerged from the galley onto the deck, he looked up and saw Meg coming toward him, and she was wearing her favorite, yellow bikini.

"What about clothes?" Jon asked. "We are going to be gone for a few days."

"We don't need any clothes, do we?"

"I'm going to need more than just my bathing suit, if you don't mind. There could be young women around who might find the sight of me too overwhelming."

Meg snorted and threw him the backpack she was carrying. "I think you'll find all you need in there. We don't need much."

Meg pulled Jon against her body and gave him a long, passionate kiss. She returned to the dock, untied the boat, and jumped aboard. They crawled up to the bridge and turned the bow south.

A little before noon, Jon guided their boat into the bay toward the familiar dock where Meg had once stood wondering if the man she loved was dead or alive. She slipped on her tennis shoes and joined Jon on the bridge.

"Honey, would you ease her up to the dock?" Jon asked. "I'll tie her up as soon as you kill the engine."

Jon jumped over to the dock and tied the rope securely. He then reached out his hand to help Meg climb to the dock.

"Welcome to Santa Maria de la Conception Mrs. Davenport," Jon said.

"Why thank you Dr. Davenport. It's hard to believe all that has happened since we were last here."

Jon and Meg walked down the wooden dock and stepped into the sand. For the first forty-five minutes, they strolled up a sandy trail that ran along the southern side of the island. The trail rose up a bluff where they stopped and looked out over the ocean. The light blue water was as clear as crystal and as slick as glass. Meg could see two dolphins coming in and out of the water down below. She looked to her left and could barely make out the shape of what Lopez and his gang had called The Fortress. Meg felt a shudder run through her body as she remembered the events of that night some nine months earlier.

"Why don't we take our dingy and go up the creek to our cave?" Meg asked. "We could eat lunch in there and check out that part of the island. We didn't get to do much exploring last time we were here."

"Sounds good to me," Jon agreed.

They ambled back to the yacht and pulled out the small, inflatable boat. Jon handed the ice chest down to Meg, locked up the yacht, and climbed down to the little craft. He started the four-horsepower motor, and they eased toward the opening of the familiar creek. Heat permeated the atmosphere, and a small flock of white birds with large wingspans flew overhead. The most distinguishing marks on the birds were the strips of black on the wings and the bright red beaks.

"Those are red-billed tropicbirds," Jon said. "They are printed on the currency of Bermuda."

"Is that so? I thought the flamingo was their state bird."

"Aren't you knowledgeable?" Jon teased. "That's true. I don't know why someone made that decision, but those birds seem to be everywhere around here."

Jon pulled the boat up to the sandy shore of the creek, once the water seemed too shallow to continue moving forward. He picked up the ice chest while Meg grabbed the backpack, and they climbed up the bluff to where the cave was located. This cave brought back some terrifying memories to Meg, but it had become a place of safety and refuge while they endured the hurricane and hid from the pirates. She spread a blanket out on the ground at the cave opening and Jon pulled out a jug of Judy's sweet tea. He took the lid off, poured two glasses, and handed one to Meg.

"I thought the tea was for dinner," Meg said.

"It is, but I feel a toast coming on. To six wonderful months of marriage. I can't imagine being happier."

"Neither can I."

They took a sip of their tea and kissed. Meg knelt down and pulled out Judy's amazing creation of ham and cheese rolls. It was ham, cheese, and lettuce rolled up inside thin pieces of dough. She had packed the rolls along with some chips and homemade chocolate chip cookies. They enjoyed their lunch and drank more tea while sitting together on the blanket at the edge of the cave. They looked out over the island from their elevated position and could see the southern end of a miniature lake surrounded by a lot of low bushes. Meg sat her glass down and laid her head on Jon's shoulder.

"I am so happy," Meg whispered. "Though I will miss Carla, I know she would not want me to spend the rest of my life grieving over her. You have brought joy to my life and more adventure than I knew was even possible. You've made me feel so secure and loved. I love you, Jon."

"I love you, too."

Jon gently lay Meg down on the blanket. His eyes were so dark and deep, Meg felt as if she could fall into them. She reached up and traced the contour of his face with her hand. He kissed her lips and her neck.

An hour later they stood arm in arm at the mouth of their cave surveying the northern side of the island. Meg turned her head and saw that Jon was not looking at the scenery, but rather he was staring at her.

"I am the luckiest man on the earth to have you as my wife."

Meg reached up to kiss him. She was so filled with joy and happiness. They walked together down the path to the spot where the stream opened up into a lake.

As the water of the lake touched their feet, Jon took Meg's hand, and they slipped into the fresh water to take a swim. After swimming the width of the small body of water, Jon playfully splashed water into Meg's face. She retaliated by sending a deluge of water all over Jon's head. After splashing one another for a bit, they fell into one another's arms laughing together in the middle of their perfect paradise on earth.

They returned to the cave, retrieved their belongings, and made their way back to the inflatable. Jon pulled the motor to life, and they slowly putted down the creek toward the ocean. They slid across the top of the placid sea back to the docked yacht. Jon helped Meg aboard and then secured the inflatable. Meg stepped into the shower, and Jon took his mask with plans to get some oysters for dinner.

Twenty minutes later, Jon climbed out of the water with his net bag full of oysters. He stepped into the now empty shower while Meg gathered items needed for a cookout.

Jon found some driftwood on the beach and stacked it all in a pile for a fire. He opened each of the oysters and laid them on the grill that he had rested on the two large rocks on each side of the fire pit. He grilled oysters along with big pieces of grouper filets. After a while, Meg pulled out two large potatoes she had wrapped in tin foil and dropped into the fire earlier.

They enjoyed a wonderful meal while sitting in their lawn chairs on the sandy beach of Conception Island. Before going to sleep that night, Meg left no doubt as to who was the better Rummy player as she beat Jon in four games. Jon decided it was not good for his ego to continue playing cards with his wife. They fell asleep in a contented embrace.

The next morning, Meg dressed in a less provocative black one-piece and slipped on a tee shirt. Jon pulled the anchor and slowly motored out of the bay and headed north for their lagoon. A little more than two hours later, Jon dropped anchor over the reef near where they had shared their first kiss.

"Let's go for a dive," Jon said. "We found our first gold here. You never know, there could be more."

"Maybe we should come back up here with *The Discoverer.*"

"Maybe so. The sailors from the *San Ambrosio* could have started tossing the treasure before tearing apart on the reef further down."

Jon helped Meg into her gear, and the couple fell over the side of the boat into the water. They kicked down the side of the wall and through a school of blue and yellow surgeonfish. While descending, they passed small ledges on which numerous sponges grew that were surrounded with multi-colored fish of all kinds. The reef was an exhilarating place of which Meg knew she would never grow tired. During the dive, Jon netted two lobsters before they swam back to the boat.

He pulled anchor and eased into the small bay they often called "the Lagoon," and they did a repeat experience of their first night many months earlier. The night dive this time, however, was not as frightening for Meg. Jon made a huge bonfire, and Meg brought a lounge chair ashore where they lay together and watched the fire. Meg and Jon slept that night the satisfied sleep of happy lovers.

After eating a breakfast of eggs and bacon on Wednesday morning, they headed back for Pirate's Cove. Over breakfast, they had decided to take the *New Beginnings* to Miami where they would do research in the library at the University of Miami. Once at home, Jon restocked and Meg shared their plans with Judy. Judy informed them that while they were traipsing around the Atlantic, she was going to fly to Knoxville to visit her sister. Meg kissed Judy's cheek, and the couple got up to begin the painful task of carrying their supplies down the steps to the dock.

"When we get back, I'm going to make a driveway down to the docks," Jon said. "I can't keep carrying stuff up and down these steps. I'm getting too old for this."

"I thought I heard your bones cracking this morning," Meg teased.

"Yeah. I bet you just married me as your sugar daddy."

"I don't know about the daddy part, but the sugar part—yeah," Meg said reaching up to kiss him.

CHAPTER THIRTY-TWO

Pool Time

Jon and Meg told Judy goodbye one final time and then took off again in the *New Beginnings* for Miami. The yacht pulled into the Loggerhead Marina where Jon rented a slip.

After three weeks of study at the University of Miami's Richter Library, their list of potentially undiscovered wrecks was quite extensive. Meg pointed out the names of the ships of the *Terre Firma* armada that had made their way onto the list. While they reviewed their research, the four names that continued to pull Jon's attention were *San Roque, Santo Domingo, San Ambrosio,* and *Nuestra Senora de Begona.*

Jon drew a line through the *San Roque.* "We know the story of the *San Roque.* It was lost somewhere around Honduras."

"Of course, there's the *San Ambrosio,*" Meg added as she put a circle around the ship the assumed to be inside the reef out from their home. "I suppose the other two are out there somewhere."

Jon nodded and put check marks beside the names of the two final ships of the armada. They agreed this would require a lot more research of currents, storms, and other conditions in order to determine what happened. It was odd that one ship of the armada sunk near Honduras and the other ships didn't seem to come to its rescue. One more ship made it through the

Straits of Florida and was somehow blown toward the Exuma
Islands.

"*Santo Domingo* and *Nuestra Senora de Begona* have got to be
close by," Jon insisted. "I just don't believe the *San Ambrosio*
was out there by herself."

In route back to their compound off Roker's Point, Jon
and Meg sailed down to Key West to visit the Mel Fisher
Maritime Museum that included displays of artifacts found on
the *Atocha*. Meg was in awe of the pieces of treasure the curator
kept on site. She was entranced by the timeline revealing the
years of struggle this family experienced before finding the
treasure. It made her wonder how long it would take them to
discover their treasure ship.

Jon and Meg played the role of tourists as they visited the
Little White House, strolled by Ernest Hemmingway's home,
and took the ghost tour through the town. Jon's favorite
experience was the visit to the Dry Tortugas National Park,
and he made plans to return to the area to dive some of the
reefs around the islands at some future date.

After being away for four weeks, Jon and Meg arrived back
at their Bahamian home just in time to enjoy the wonderful
dinner Judy prepared in anticipation of their homecoming.
Judy had returned to the island paradise late the night before
and had spent the morning preparing for the Davenport's
arrival.

All day Thursday was spent just lounging around, and Meg
and Judy went into George Town to shop. While Meg was not
feeling well, Judy enjoyed the afternoon as they walked through
the open market.

Jon made plans to put his bobcat to work as he thought
about Meg's Garden of Eden. He told Meg that he was going

to dig out a place for the swimming pool as well as clear out a driveway from the house down to the dock.

"Why don't you just pay someone to do it for you?" Meg wondered.

"I've always wanted to play on a bobcat."

"Suite yourself."

During breakfast on Friday morning, Jon shared his plans to spend the day digging a hole in the backyard. Meg said she needed to make a run into town for a few things but promised to be back soon to help with the project. When she returned, near 11:00 that morning, Jon was well underway with the pool project. She left the truck and walked into the house with a bag from the drugstore under her arm.

Jon had studied a drawing Meg had produced of how she wanted her backyard paradise to look, and as soon as Meg had left for town, he began digging in the sand. As noon approached, not only was Jon dripping with sweat, but he also had a sizable hole dug in the earth. He looked up to see Meg walking out of the house with a tray carrying a glass of iced tea.

"Sweetheart," Jon shouted up from atop the bobcat. "You must be a mind reader. I know I've lost at least a gallon of sweat."

"I don't think I can bring this down there, so you're going to have to climb out of the hole."

When he climbed off the bobcat and up the side of the hole to the firm ground, he saw the glass was indeed full of iced tea, but there was a vase of flowers with a funny object stuck in beside the flowers.

At first, Jon didn't seem to give the flower arrangement much attention, but then the white object in front of the flowers caught his eye. The stem was a flat, white stick, and the end of the stick was made of a purplish strip. He noticed a little pink window on the stick and wondered what in the heck this thing was.

"Thanks, honey," Jon said picking up the glass of tea.

As he started drinking the iced tea, Meg said with a disappointed look on her face, "Aren't you going to notice?"

"Notice what" he said with a look of incredulity on his face.

"The stick. Look at the stick," Meg frowned. "Don't drink the tea."

Jon pulled the white object from the vase and looked at it. He noticed the words printed on the stick beside a window that was filled with two pink stripes: "pregnant" and "not pregnant." After a moment, it dawned on him that he was looking at a home pregnancy test. With further investigation, he grew still with shock.

"You're…you're…pregnant," he said quietly. "You're pregnant!" he screamed out as he dropped his glass on the ground and grabbed Meg. He swung her around as Meg squealed and they both laughed.

"We're pregnant. We're pregnant," Jon screamed out over the bluff.

Without warning, the ground shook, and in their dizziness from spinning, they fell to the ground with Meg landing on top of Jon.

"What was that?" Meg asked with fear in her voice.

"I think it was an earthquake," Jon said as the ground quit shaking.

They lay on the ground looking at one another. Jon pulled Meg toward him even as her body trembled. He kissed her tenderly.

"We're going to have a baby," he said with wonder in his eyes and a tear ran down his cheeks.

"We are, sweetheart," Meg said. "You're going to be a father, and I'm going to be a mother."

"When did you know?"

"I had a suspicion last week, but I didn't think anything about it. I missed taking the pill back when Carla went to the hospital. I meant to get back on it, but then we went to Conception Island, and I forgot to take them with me."

"Do you think we got pregnant on Conception Island? Wouldn't that be something?"

Jon kissed Meg again and helped her up. They looked around at the house to see if there was any damage. Judy was standing on the porch with her hands over her mouth. Jon looked back over the hole and saw that the bobcat was nowhere to be seen.

He and Meg carefully walked to the edge of the pit he had started for the swimming pool and saw the ground had opened up and swallowed the bobcat. While he had dug the hole about eight feet deep and twenty feet across, Jon was now looking down into a dark hole that did not appear to have a bottom. The bobcat was not visible. They were speechless as they stood looking down into the cavernous hole.

"What…What happened?" Meg asked with a quivering voice.

"I don't think it was an earthquake," Jon said. "I must have dug down to a sinkhole. I'll get a rope and see if I can find the bobcat. We'll have to somehow get it out of the hole."

Jon raced into the house and came back with two coils of rope. He tied the two pieces together and then looped one end around a tree. He improvised a figure eight by sliding the rope through two of his belt loops. He tied a third rope around the tree and told Meg to let the rope down as a belay. He created a point of friction by wrapping the rope around the banana tree near the edge of the hole. He ran back into the house and stuck a flashlight in his back pocket.

Jon eased himself down into the hole and discovered it was about forty feet deep. It looked deeper from the top. They could not see the bobcat from above because it had landed on its treads and rolled into a narrow passageway.

"Meg," Jon yelled from down in the pit. "Run down to the boat and get another stretch of rope. Wait, don't run, you might hurt the…baby."

"The what?" Judy said with shock.

Meg smiled at her and said, "The baby. We're pregnant."

Jon heard Judy shout, and he climbed out of the hole to see what had happened. By the time he had reached the upper ground, Meg was hurrying down the stairs and Judy stood on the porch with big tears rolling down her face. She hurried over to Jon and wrapped her arms around him with tears streaming from her eyes.

"We're going to have a baby," she said.

"How about that?" Jon said. "I'm going to be a father."

As Meg rushed back up with another coil of rope, Jon said, "You're not going to believe what I've found."

"What?" Meg raised an eyebrow.

"It's a cave. It's not something made by nature, though. Someone dug it out with shovels. Let's get the rope around you. Judy, would you get us another flashlight?"

Judy wiped her eyes on her apron and hurried back into the house. Within minutes, Jon and Meg were both repelling and sliding down the side of the hole. Meg yelped as her backside dragged against a sharp piece of old coral wedged into the ground.

After a few minutes, their feet found solid ground, and Jon untied the rope from around their waists. They turned on their lights and squeezed by the bobcat that was upright but tilted a bit by the fall.

As they maneuvered through the man-made tunnel, Jon pointed out the shovel marks and what looked like something wedged into the wall to hold a torch. The tunnel smelled musty and damp, but the passageway was plain and unobstructed. Someone had spent months or even years digging this out of the packed earth. Meg couldn't help but be a little nervous about the roof caving in on them.

"Isn't this dangerous?" Meg asked with a tremble in her voice. "I mean, I'm sure this soil has a lot of sand in it. This can't be safe."

Jon replied, "I suppose it could be, but you've got to think this tunnel has been here in tact for a long time. Hopefully it won't pick now to collapse."

Just then, Meg ran straight into a spider web and the strands wrapped around her face. Hoping the spider had not been home, she grunted and wiped her face clean. They rounded a curve in the tunnel that turned toward the sea, and something ahead gleamed in the beam of the flashlight. As they flashed their light around an open cavern, their lights fell on stacks and stacks of gleaming… treasure. Meg gasped as she realized the treasure was not on the bottom of the ocean after all.

They turned to look at one another and said in unison: "*San Roque.*"

AFTERWARDS...

Baby Carla pulled away from Meg's breast and smiled up at her father while he continued to provide a distraction from her dinner. As she cooed and smiled, fresh milk ran down her face onto Meg's shirt, and Meg was getting increasingly irritated with her husband.

"Jon, if you don't stop, you're going to be the one getting up with her at 2:00 in the morning for her next feeding."

"Oh, honey," Jon grinned. "You know I would, but I'd have a hard time nursing her. Sorry."

Meg playfully slapped his arm and said, "Give me a break. Now hush and listen. I want to see the rest of the documentary."

Dr. Gerome Russell's voice came over the picture of the wreckage on the bottom of the ocean:

Though the Davenports thought they had discovered the *San Ambrosio* on the ocean floor, it turned out to be the San Roque. Instead of the treasure being buried in the sea, it was buried in their own backyard by a conscientious Spanish captain about four hundred years ago. This find is being recorded as the most valuable discovery ever found from wrecked Spanish galleons, and experts have estimated the total worth to exceed $600 million. A similar discovery, prior to the *San Roque,* was the *Nuestra Señora de Atocha* valued at

$450 million. Though the Davenport's treasure is now locked safely away, the real battle has just begun. Even though Bahamian law says the treasure uncovered on one's property belongs to the property owner, government officials have already filed an injunction in the courts in an attempt to claim ownership of the treasure. Lawyers are preparing to square off, but most legal experts are in agreement that the Davenports will in all probability be determined to be the full owners of this incredible discovery.

Jon picked up the remote and hit mute as the show stopped for a commercial break.

"Are you sure you want to watch the rest of this?" Jon asked. "We've already seen it once."

"You saw it once," Meg laughed. "I was a little busy giving birth to our precious girl."

"That's true, but you've now seen most of it. The rest of the story is that we will fight the government for the next three years until we at least pay them off to leave us alone. I've been told that if I place $100 million in the right hands now, the injunction would be lifted. It's real tempting just to get it over with."

"It's tempting," Meg agreed as her voice grew in anger and frustration, "but this is the one time we have all the law on our side. Every small person in the world is pulling for us to win. If we cave in to bribery, we will let everyone down who deserves to win in their corner of the world. We're doing fine. I say we fight it until the greedy officials admit their defeat."

Jon said, "Carla, you must excuse your mother's temper. She's been a sailor for far too long, but we're working on reforming her for your benefit."

Meg rolled her eyes as Carla stopped nursing once again to grin up at her daddy. Before Carla could get back to the dinner at hand, Jon leaned over and kissed his wife.

"That's for being the most wonderful mother in the world."

He kissed her again and said, "And that's for being the most beautiful woman in the world."

After one more kiss he said, "And that's for putting up with me. I love you, sweetheart."

Meg smiled and held her hand to Jon's cheek. Carla became more interested in nursing and ignored the two lovers. Meg grabbed the remote and unmuted the sound so she could watch the conclusion of the documentary.

"You know, the problem now is the whole world knows exactly how much treasure we found," Meg moaned as the documentary came to an end.

"That's true," Jon agreed with some thought. "You know…we should show them how to use what we have to help others."

Hoping her baby would fall asleep while nursing, Meg began gently rocking Carla. "What are you thinking, Jon?"

"Why don't we use some of our wealth to help young people get a break? Maybe we can start a school for inner-city kids that will encourage them to do something other than get into drugs."

"What kind of school are you considering?"

"We could build a school in Miami that would offer opportunities for inner-city kids to develop leadership skills and even let the older kids work with us in our salvaging business during the summers."

"I like the sound of that," Meg acknowledged as she lifted little Carla over her shoulder and patted her back.

"Oh, baby," Jon said to Carla as she let out a loud burp. "That was a good one. Let's do another and make Daddy proud."

"If she hangs around you too much, she's going to have the table manners of an ape," Meg jabbed.

Realizing the weight of her slumbering little one in her arms, Meg walked up the stairs into the nursery and lowered Carla into her crib. The full moon outside her window cast an ambient glow across her tiny form and revealed the miniature facial features that were a perfect blend of her parents. Meg stood speechless as she gazed upon the wonder of such a miracle. She tenderly touched Carla's little round face as she thought how blessed they were to have such a perfect baby.

Meg turned and offered her husband a tender smile as he watched lovingly from the doorway. She caressed Carla's miniature fingers as Jon joined her beside the light blue baby bed.

He put his arm around Meg's waist and pulled her close to his side. "You are so amazing," he whispered. "How was I lucky enough to get a wife who is both a beautiful woman and an amazing mother?"

"You say that quite often. You must want something."

Jon lightly touched his beautiful daughter before turning the knob on the mobile that started Pooh, Tigger, Eeyore and Piglet in their monotonous spin over the sleeping head of their daughter. The Brahms Lullaby, which Jon often now hummed without thought, began to play as they tip-toed out through the nursery door.

Thinking back to Jon's hesitations about the nursery theme, Meg looked around at the Winnie the Pooh characters. When Meg had first chosen the colors, Jon was skeptical. She was sure now, however, that even Jon thought the room looked nice. He had hired a local artist to come in to paint Pooh and his buddies all over the room.

When Meg was putting the finishing touches on the room, Jon questioned whether Pooh was a boy bear or a girl bear. "His voice in the cartoon sounds more like a whiney boy, but with a name like Winnie, one has to wonder."

During the "How Should We Decorate the Nursery" phase of the pregnancy, Jon told Meg that if Pooh was supposed to be a boy, they should have named him Butch the Bear or something like that. Jon had concluded that if he had a name like Winnie, he might be a whiner too. Meg was thankful that Jon went along with the Pooh theme, but he insisted that whenever they had a boy, his room would be something masculine like pirates or Georgia Bulldogs.

Meg had changed her mind so many times before landing on the Pooh theme. Jon joked that the square footage of the baby's room was going to get smaller over the next couple of years just from the layers of paint that would be added every time Meg decided to do something different. She knew that he didn't care but just enjoyed teasing her.

They walked into the master suite next door and out onto their balcony that overlooked the quiet bay. The moon was full, casting a white, reflective light across the calm waters of

Pirate's Cove. Jon pulled Meg into his arms, and the two of them stood in a tight embrace for a long time.

"This has all been quite a ride," Jon whispered into Meg's ear.

"You can say that again. It's like a dream or a fairy tale. Like a 'happily ever after' come true!"

"I'm planning on it."

Jon saw the water in the bay ripple as something large must have surfaced and submerged. The ripples were enough to cause both of his smaller boats to rock a bit as the disturbed water passed under their bows.

"What now?" Meg wondered aloud.

"I guess we need to go back to the research table so we can start looking for a new ship wreck."

"It's kind of hard to think about another wreck at the moment," Meg assented. "I haven't even been in the water since Carla came along."

Jon said, "Why don't we go on a short trip? Judy can keep Carla for us."

"I can't leave her right now," Meg protested. "She's just three months old."

"I don't mean an overnight trip. Just a picnic. You can leave enough milk behind for Judy, and we could go do a short dive. You realize that tomorrow is the anniversary of your conception, assuming it happened on Conception Island."

"You know, I think it did," Meg said. "Think about it. Carla was born on Valentine's Day, which was exactly forty weeks after we made our brief excursion to Conception Island."

"If you say so, I believe it," Jon smiled. "So, how about a dive tomorrow? We could go back to Conception Island or Cat

Island if you prefer. There's a great reef to the north of Conception that I've always wanted to dive."

"Isn't that where we found the Southampton?" Meg asked.

"Well, the reef I'm talking about is further out than that. The Southampton was twenty-five feet deep, if I remember right, but this reef is more like forty or so. I read about it once in Skin Diver magazine."

"Well, I guess I could do that. I do want to get back in the water," Meg said wistfully. "Okay. It will be fun."

Upon entering the kitchen the next morning, Jon presented the idea to Judy.

"So, you're going to trust me with the baby after all?" Judy joked.

"Now, Judy," Jon asserted. "You know we have always trusted you with Carla. Just don't be offended when Meg calls you every hour."

Judy nodded with understanding. "Carla will be fine. I'm so glad you two are taking some time away."

"We'll be back before nightfall," Meg promised. "We're just going over to Conception Island for a picnic."

"You take your time. As long as I've got enough milk, stay away as long as you like."

"By the time we leave, I should have plenty in the refrigerator," Meg estimated.

"You two go have a good time," Judy insisted as she picked up the baby from the swing Jon had placed in the kitchen.

Jon and Meg pulled away from the dock in Pirate's Cove by 9:00 the next morning and motored toward Conception Island. The first plan on the agenda was to take their picnic lunch in the dingy up the creek to their cave. Just like a year earlier, they ate lunch in the mouth of the cave overlooking the beautiful pristine island.

"So, are you ready for another baby?" Jon asked as he held Meg against him.

"Not yet," Meg uttered with shock in her voice. "I mean, I do want to have another baby; I just think I need a little more time."

"Let's go for a dive," Jon said pulling Meg to her feet.

Jon noted how fast she was working off the extra weight from her pregnancy. He was amazed that Meg had gotten back into her regular clothes within a little over two months after Carla was born.

After returning to their yacht, Jon pulled out a pad to check the coordinates he had transcribed earlier. He plugged them into his GPS and took the boat out to sea around the northern end of the island. Once over the spot, he lowered the anchor.

"So what do you expect to see down there?" Meg wondered.

"The reef is about forty feet deep, and it's supposed to have numerous fingers, caves, and tunnels. Since it's deeper than the Southampton wreck, we could see some larger fish as well as the normal small reef fish. I'm taking my bang stick, just in case. I'm hoping we can find a lobster or two to take home."

The two of them stepped off the platform on the back of the boat and dropped into the crystal clear water. Feeling as if she was returning to a beloved neighborhood, Meg was exhilarated as she kicked her way down toward the reef. Though the colors were not quite as brilliant because of the depth, it was still incredibly beautiful.

Jon secured the anchor in the sand on the south side of the reef while Meg swam over to inspect the largest brain coral she had ever seen. It was a perfect sphere of coral that resembled what she imagined a brain to look like. Jon joined her, and they glided over the top of the reef.

They swam through a short tunnel and ended up on the deeper side of the reef. Meg suggested they return to this spot by pointing out several tentacles sticking out of small holes in the side of the reef. Meg aimed her body downward to the sand on the deepest side of the reef, which took her to a depth of almost fifty feet. She picked up a conch shell that was in perfect condition and showed it to Jon. He placed it in his net bag attached to his belt and looked at his dive computer.

After a fulfilling dive, Jon stopped at the lobster holes as they swam back toward the boat. The lobster was resting a few feet from the front of its home, and Jon carefully placed his net behind the creature. Before Jon could even pull out his stick, the lobster shot backwards right into his trap. He held the net bag containing the creature out to Meg, and she took hold of the prize. Repeating this process at another hole, Jon found this lobster to be smaller, but it was still big enough for dinner.

Meg had begun her lazy kick up to the surface, when she looked back to make sure Jon was following. He had just pulled the lobster from the reef's ledge, and Meg could see the debris falling that had been knocked loose by the catch. She was about to turn back toward the surface when something shiny caught her eye as it drifted toward the sea floor.

Would you like a
FREE GIFT?

We would like to offer you a free gift as our way of saying thanks for reading the first book of Judah Knight's *Davenport Series*. Judah has written a short story, or novella, about the two main characters in *The Long Way Home*: Jon Davenport and Meg Freeman. This story takes place when they are childhood friends and is mentioned in *The Long Way Home* in Chapter Five. You can request a free copy of this novella, *A Girl Can Always Hope*, by visiting www.Judahknight.com/free-gift. Include your e-mail address, and we will send you the story in a pdf format as our gift. We are respectful of your privacy and will not share your e-mail address with anyone else. We invite you to turn the page of this book for information on books one and three in the Davenport Series. We look forward to hearing from you.

GreenTree Publishers

THE JOURNEY CONTINUES…

Book Three: Finding My Way

Can you really find peace and healing by simply changing your address? Eighteen-year-old Lacy Henderson fled the upheaval of abuse and a broken home in search of a fresh start and renewed hope. Jon and Meg Davenport, her aunt and uncle, invite her to the Bahamas to help out in a special program for troubled boys. Lacy joins the team, along with intern Kerrick Daniels, in hopes of discovering sunken, Spanish gold. Through an adventure of scuba diving and treasure hunting, Lacy finds a lot more than lost treasure. Join the Davenports as they begin a new Bahamian adventure in the third book of Judah Knight's *Davenport Series*.

Did you miss book one of the series?

Book One: *The Long Way Home*

He had a boat. She needed a ride. A simple lift turned into the adventure of a lifetime.

When Meg was stranded in the Bahamas, her life was dramatically changed through an encounter with an old friend that turned into adventure, danger, and discovery.

Meg Freeman and Jon Davenport began a surprising adventure, connected to a 17th century, shipwrecked Spanish galleon. Both Freeman and Davenport had experienced the sorrow of losing a spouse, but they found a renewed friendship as they had an amazing undersea discovery and encountered terrorists along the way. Join this couple's adventure of romance and suspense where the long way home became a ride that would change their lives forever.

The Long Way Home is book one in *The Davenport Series*.

Book Four: Ready to Love Again

The Davenport Series - Book 4

Ready to
Love Again

Judah Knight

She had given up on love until...

Jon and Meg Davenport invited their niece, Lacy Henderson, to join their salvage operation in the Bahamas as a summer intern. While their work focused on hunting for sunken treasure, the real task was to shape the lives of five inner-city boys who were invited to spend the summer on the Davenports' salvage ship. Reeling from past anger and rejection, Lacy begins to warm to the advances of another summer intern, Kerrick Daniels, but love doesn't come easy to an embittered heart.

An undersea accident nearly ended in tragedy, but Kerrick and Lacy struggle to find love in the midst of chaos. While searching for sunken treasure in the Bahamas, Lacy becomes a target of something far more threatening than the normal underwater challenges of treasure seekers. Join the Davenports, Lacy, Kerrick and the whole crew in the continuing undersea adventure where love is challenged and hope sometimes seems like an impossible dream.

Book Five: Love Waits

The Davenport Series - Book 5

Love Waits

Judah Knight

The Dream of a Lifetime…or a nightmare in disguise?

Lacy Henderson and Kerrick Daniels are no longer summer interns at a boys' program in the Bahamas because the summer is over. Their relationship, however, is far from over. Lacy discovered that the gift her aunt gave her, a golden medallion, had a secret message that was part of a clue for hidden, Viking treasure. She put all of the pieces of the crazy summer together and is convinced that she knows the whereabouts of King Harold Bluetooth's treasure trove. All she needs to do is get back to the Bahamas, team up with Kerrick and her aunt and uncle, and make one more dive around Coral Cay, the island of the skull. The only problem is that she's not the only one in search of the treasure.

FROM THE AUTHOR

Thank you for reading my book, *Hope for Tomorrow*. If you enjoyed it, will you please take a moment to leave a review on Amazon? I have truly enjoyed sharing with you the second book of my *Davenport Series* and hope that you will choose to pick up the third in the series: *Finding My Way*. To date I have completed five books in the series, and I'm currently working on book number six. I would enjoy hearing from you and dialoguing with you about future books, or anything else on your mind. You can reach me through my publisher (www.greentreepublishers.com), through the contact page on my website (www.judahknight.com), or through one of the social media links listed below. I also have a free gift I would like share with you. My publisher offers this gift on a previous page in this book. I look forward to hearing from you soon. Thanks again for taking the time to read my book, and I'll see you in the next adventure.

Judah Knight

Follow me on Twitter: http://www.twitter.com/judahknight
Check out my website at http://www.judahknight.com
Have a discussion with me on Goodreads.com:
http://bit.ly/1m5heLe

FINAL CHAPTER – BOOK ONE

Meg walked with determination into the dining room. "Jon, our time in the Bahamas was most enjoyable, but I need to get back home today. I've got to begin putting some plans together to start job hunting."

"Oh…I was hoping you would at least stay the weekend. I mean, I need some help organizing the ammo boxes, and part of it is yours anyway. I've got plenty of space here; you are welcome to stay as long as you want."

"I appreciate the offer, but I need to get home and figure out what's next for me. I do appreciate your hospitality. I told you that none of it is mine because it was on your boat."

"But…" Jon interjected.

Meg ignored Jon's interruption. "I don't mind helping you with it, though, as long as I have time. Maybe I can come back and help you count it later. Could you give me a ride into town, or at least get me to the closest MARTA station?"

"Meg, you know I'm happy to help you any way I can. As a matter of fact, I've got a spare car you can drive. You can return it whenever you would like. Could you come back tomorrow and help count?"

Meg processed in her mind what a millionaire's spare car might be. If she had a spare car, it would probably be an old Ford Escort or something like that. She paused as she tried to decide what kind of statement she would be making to Jon if she accepted his offer. Would driving his spare car say that she was coming back and that there was something romantic going on between them, or would she just be accepting the kind offer of a friend?

Meg replied, "I will think about coming back tomorrow. I'll just have to give you a call."

"Would you two quit talking in code?" Judy interrupted. "What discovery? Ammo boxes? What are you counting?"

"We found something pretty amazing," Jon said to Judy. "I'll have to tell you about it later."

"I suppose if it's your spare car, I could drive it," Meg continued. "My car is at the airport, but I can pick up Ann. She can help me get it back to my house."

"Why don't you ask Ann to come help us do the counting tomorrow?" Jon suggested. "If you want to, the two of you could come back here tonight to spend the night. We could start our project first thing in the morning."

"I guess I'll have to let you know," Meg replied, wondering why this man could not seem to make up his mind about her. One moment he seemed to want to hug her, but in the next, he couldn't stand to touch her.

After breakfast, Jon took Meg out to the garage and handed her a key fob. When Meg peered into the garage through the open door, her mouth dropped as the beautiful red contours of a dream car met her gaze. Inside was a deep red Mercedes-Benz SLS AMG sports car.

"Are you sure you want me to drive this car?" Meg gasped. "I mean…I'm a little nervous to drive it just down your driveway."

"You'll be fine. I would love for you to drive it for as long as you want to keep it. I bought it a few months ago, but I don't ever drive it. I'm kind of partial to my truck."

"Thank you, Jon," Meg said as she laid her hand on his right cheek without thinking of her resolve to end their relationship.

Meg got into the sports car, placed the key in the cup holder, and pressed the starter button. She had never driven a car in which she didn't have to put the key in an ignition switch. Within a few minutes, she was out of the driveway and on the main road leading away from the ranch. She was so confused. It was like Jon was a man who couldn't make up his mind, and the truth was that she couldn't make up her mind either.

Meg resolved to move on with her life and let Jon sort through his own issues. Maybe she would go back on Sunday to help count and organize the gold, but other than that, she would wash her hands of the man. Sure, she had an interesting vacation in the Bahamas, with an incredibly sexy man, but that was just all for fun and memories—nothing more! True, she was now driving his $200,000 sports car down the road toward Atlanta, but it wasn't unusual for a friend to loan a friend a car.

Meg pressed the number two speed dial on her phone and heard Ann say, "Where in the world have you been? What are you thinking? You have called me twice with this mystery talk, and you have not bothered to call me to tell me what in the heck is going on."

"I'm sorry, Ann. It's all so complicated and hard to believe. Let me take you to lunch. I'll tell you everything, and I need some help getting my car home from the airport. Can you help me? I could pick you up now. Then I'll treat you to lunch."

"How can you pick me up if your car is at the airport?" Ann asked in confusion.

"Trust me. I have a car you won't believe. I'll be at your apartment in about thirty minutes."

Meg broke the connection with a smile on her face. Ann was going to freak out when she saw this sleek sports car. She reminded herself that the car was just a loaner from a friend and not even worth getting excited over. True, she had never driven anything like it, and it was pretty amazing. However, she would be returning it to Jon that night or the next morning. Of course, he did say she could drive it for as long as she wanted to, but there was no way she could just keep his car. It's not like they were lovers or anything. It is true they could have been lovers, but now that would never happen.

Meg would never forget Jon's hard body pressed against hers and the electricity that went through her. She could almost feel his hands holding her and his lips against hers. Meg shuddered with the memory, and she slammed on the brakes as she realized the tires on the right side of the car were going off the road. She pulled over to the shoulder and turned off the car. Her body was trembling, and her mind was fuzzy.

What was she doing? Meg laid her head back on the headrest and closed her eyes. This kind of fantasizing had to stop. People didn't dream about kissing their friends, or did they? No! They didn't! Meg knew that if she was ever going to move on with her life, she could not dwell on what had been or on what could have been. Her relationship with Jon was over. Of course, she wondered if it had ever even started.

Meg started the car up again and pulled back onto Canton Road. Within a few minutes, she was driving down the interstate toward Marietta in the direction of Ann's apartment.

"Meg! Where in the world have you been?" Ann said with unmeasured irritation as she ran up to the car.

It was evident she had been watching for Meg from her apartment window and had hurried out as soon as Meg crawled out of the Mercedes. Ann's five-feet, nine-inch willowy body stood erect with her balled up fists placed angrily on her hips. Her long, red, wavy hair looked as if she had just come from the beauty shop.

"What is this? I mean, where did you get this?" Ann continued, before being interrupted by Meg.

"Oh Ann," Meg said as she hugged her friend close. "I have the most incredible story to tell you. Come with me to the airport and let's get some lunch. I'll tell you all about it. You have to be sworn to secrecy, though. There's some of this story that cannot be told to anyone–ever. Do you understand?"

"Good God, Meg. Are you like working for the CIA or something?"

"Nope, but I've had to give an oath to some pretty tough looking guys that I would not talk about my experience. I will tell you what I can tell you, but I can't give details that would compromise my promise."

The two friends drove to the airport, picked up Meg's car, and then drove back around Interstate 285 toward Cobb Parkway. Ann followed Meg into the parking lot of the Chipotle Mexican Grill. Over lunch, Meg told Ann the whole story, leaving out some of the details about the Convention

Center. Meg hinted about the thwarted terrorist attack, but was careful not to reveal too much.

"Meg! That is unbelievable. It's like a movie or something. I want to know about Jon. It sounds to me like you are in love, and from the looks of his car, he's not a bad man to be in love with."

"No, I'm not in love. We're just friends. I've known him most of my life, and I see him sort of like a brother."

"Really? The look on your face when you talk about him does not say *brother*."

"Okay, so I first thought it might be more, but trust me, it's not."

"I knew it. I knew there was more to the story than you were telling me."

"It was a mistake. He's not over losing his wife. We kissed, and that's all."

"You kissed?" Ann nearly shouted, and the people in the surrounding tables stared at them.

"We never should have done it," Meg said quietly, "and we both regret it. I'm moving on with my life."

"Are you sure? For starters, I don't think you want to move on."

"Dang it, Ann. I am moving on."

"I'm sorry, Meg. I didn't mean to make you mad. Okay. You're moving on."

"I'm sorry, Ann. I'm a little touchy about it, and I shouldn't be. Maybe I need to be honest and say I am trying to move on. I nearly had a wreck coming into town today thinking back to that night on his boat."

"Wow. That night must have been some experience."

"I will never forget it, but I have to move on. Let's not talk about it anymore. He has asked me to come back tonight or tomorrow morning to help count the gold coins we found under the floorboard of his boat. He suggested I get you to come along and help. What do you think?"

"Sure. I wouldn't mind spending some time with a gorgeous millionaire counting his gold. Come to think of it, if you're not going after him, I might."

"Oh brother," Meg said with exasperation.

"He's not my brother," Ann said, laughing at her own joke. "I'm just kidding, Meg. I think you're in love but just won't admit it."

"We're not talking about it. Remember?" Meg said.

"Oh yeah. We're not talking about it. I'm happy to help count the old ugly jerk's gold."

Meg rolled her eyes and said, "Do you think you could stay with me tonight? We can go up to Jon's ranch tomorrow morning?"

"Jon's ranch? Okay. That sounds fine. I'll need to run by my apartment on the way."

"No problem. You can follow me to the ranch tomorrow morning in my car, so I will be able to drive home when we're all done."

The two friends left the restaurant and stopped by Ann's apartment long enough for her to pack her overnight bag. Ann begged to drive the Mercedes, so Meg reluctantly took the keys to her old Honda. She had to admit that getting into her worn-out, blue Accord after driving the sports car was more than a little disappointing.

When Meg pulled into her driveway, tears began to fill her eyes. She felt like a total idiot crying over her house, but she couldn't help but be overwhelmed when she thought about all that had happened since she had last been at home.

Meg walked through the door of her utility room and stepped into her kitchen. She stood in silence as she looked around the home she had shared with Steve. She began making a mental list of all of the things she needed to do: turn on the water heater, call her mother to let her know she was back, make plans to pick up her cat, and let the neighbor know she was home. She didn't even seem to be aware that Ann was standing behind her.

"Meg, I've missed you, and I was so worried," Ann said breaking the spell Meg was under.

"I've missed you too," Meg said as she hugged her best friend. "At times, I wondered if I was going to make it back. It's so good to be home."

"I've got to meet your millionaire, and I feel like you're not telling me the whole story."

"I'm telling you everything," Meg lied, "at least everything I'm allowed to tell you."

"I'll decide that for myself when I meet your man."

"He's not my man," Meg insisted.

Ann grinned. "I'm not convinced. I suggest you sort it out tomorrow. What was it Einstein said? 'Learn from yesterday, live for today, hope for tomorrow.'"

"You are incurable," Meg laughed. "If it will shut you up, I'll hope for tomorrow."

CPSIA information can be obtained
at www.ICGtesting.com
Printed in the USA
LVHW022130270521
688690LV00012B/1261